# Shadow's Due

## T. M. Hart

Shadow Series: Book 3

There is shadow under this red rock,
(Come in under the shadow of this red rock),
And I will show you something different from either
Your shadow at morning striding behind you
Or your shadow at evening rising to meet you;
I will show you fear in a handful of dust.


~*T. S. Eliot, The Waste Land*

# PROLOGUE

O NCE UPON A TIME, I stood on a cliff and remembered all I had forgotten.

My Light had been returned to me in the very place where I had lost it. And I had burned.

I had sacrificed it for another. I had hoped I could save him.

I thought I could somehow mend him. Restore him. And he could rise up to become all he should have been.

I had been a foolish child.

He was a monster.

# CHAPTER 1

I 'M SORRY," I WHISPERED. "I'm so sorry." I squeezed my eyes shut. "I didn't mean for any of this."

I was disoriented. Everything was a scrambled mess in my mind. I couldn't understand the sequence of events in my life. It was all too disjointed.

With a flood of memories slamming into me, I felt as if I had never left the cliff above the manor. It felt as though being there had been one continuous act. Yet time had somehow snapped, and all the details altered around me. For me, facing The Contessa and leaving Zagan was the last thing that had happened.

Worse still was the chaos churning inside. There was Light and Dark. Warmth and cold. Enmity and devotion. Want. Need. It all warred within. Clashing and whirling in a sickening frenzy.

I looked into maddened, hate filled eyes . . . and I wailed.

I had done this.

It didn't matter what my intentions had been. He was a monster because of me. I had turned him into the very beast we had all feared.

There was still a rational part of me that knew we had been pawns in a game, one in which we did not know the rules. But I felt a responsibility for the creature Zagan had become, or at least, a need to somehow save him from it.

And I believed I had a chance. He had told me to run. Inundated as he was with violent fury, he had tried to spare me. There must be a way to reach him, to assuage his demons.

If recompense was what he demanded, I would pay the price and give the Darkness its due.

I would give him whatever he needed. If the urgency to stake his claim was driving him—if the bond still somehow compelled him—I would give into it. And if the evil which possessed him clamored for castigation, I would accept that too.

While he held me, shoved against the tree, I hitched my leg around his hip. I would make this as easy as possible for him. I closed my eyes, too broken to see him this way.

His cold, deadened voice was cutting, and he leaned his pelvis into mine. "How easily you give yourself away, bride. Throwing yourself around."

I squeezed my eyes shut tighter, craning my head to the side. I knew he felt a need to punish me. I focused on every pelting raindrop, pouring from the black sky, that stung my skin.

I braced my hands on the trunk behind me, at my lower back. I hitched my leg up higher on him. He leaned his face into mine, and I felt the compulsion to meet his gaze. Rain was running in rivulets down his nose and hollowed cheeks. His eyes were as black as the night sky above, and shadows swirled and swayed across his skin and all around him.

"As if I would want you," he seethed.

"I'm so sor—"

He clamped his hand over my mouth, his anger and wrath redoubling. He did not want my offering of remorse. And I understood that. Instead, shuddering on a breath, I reached for his waistband, feeling cheap and empty as I did. I would swallow my dignity if it meant I could ease him.

I didn't know if it would help. It would probably make everything worse. But I desperately wanted to appease him. To calm him. Maybe . . .

With his hand thrust against my mouth and the dark chaos churning in his eyes, he squeezed my fingers in a vice grip, stopping me.

"You enjoy being fucked by monsters," he hissed. It was an accusation. But I knew it was just as much an affront, an act of self-loathing.

Still his hand was over my mouth, and still I said nothing. I would accept whatever he had to throw at me if it would allay the wrath—the betrayal.

I nodded. Perhaps he was right. In that moment, he was a monster. And I was swollen and slippery. In spite of everything, the need for him—the connection—remained, maybe even more so than before.

But there was another tone to it now. There was a bond of a different ilk. The Darkness coursing through my veins...*wanted*. I began to feel it pump with each beat of my heart, extending to my fingers and toes.

My own wrath. My own vengeance. They were great as well. He was not the only one to have such things.

Had I not suffered? Had I not been wronged? I had my own demons now, and they too thirsted.

In the light of day, in the clarity of it, I would come to realize the extent of the egregious acts executed against me. And while I did not yet comprehend these violations, the Darkness did.

I embraced the wrath and vengeance, reveling in it, drawing on it, thrilled by the power of it. I loved being pushed against the tree trunk. I loved having his hand clamped over my mouth. I wanted him to wedge his cock into me. To force me to widen for him. I wanted him to fill me.

I became desperate for him—my own demons demanding their due, demanding their hunger be satiated. Under his hand, my lips began to curl.

I stared at his black eyes, waiting.

It was almost imperceptible, but there was a shift in him. I could see it. Through the miasma of turbulent emotions, something registered.

He stared at my eyes which I knew had begun to branch with black veins, and he paused. He warred with himself. He wanted to shove into me. He needed to. But somewhere deep inside, there was a part of him buried beneath all the rage and Darkness that did not want this for me. I could feel it. He was disturbed by the Darkness he found in my eyes. It was enough to jar him from his thirst for vengeance.

I shook my head beneath his hand. *No.* He was a monster, maddened beyond reason. He should not have such determination. That part of him was supposed to be broken, lost forever. He should not deny his demons.

And I certainly would not allow him to deny me.

I was anger. I was greed and need. I could feel my eyes become consumed with black. I tried to tilt my hips into him. He hissed and backed away from me, shuddering, becoming cloaked in shadows.

I would not allow him to reject me. He had no right to turn from me. I would have my thirst for recompense met.

I tried to claw at him. To stop him. Refusing to let him forsake me.

But he was gone.

And with him, in the churning shadows that surrounded him . . . went my dark thoughts.

\*\*\*

Shaking and shivering, drenched from the punishing rain and in shock from the flood of elements now coursing through me, I took one stumbling step after the other down the cliff and through the front door of the manor.

Millions of pieces of broken glass littered the ground. They sliced my bare feet as I walked upon them. The front entrance was a gaping hole. And inside the large entry hall the floor was covered with more broken glass and pulverized wood. The rain sprayed through the shattered windows, flooding the cavernous foyer.

The blackness of the hall was interrupted with bouts of sinister red light as bolts of lightning continued to lash the sky—a reminder of the earth's displeasure.

I sat on the floor of the hall with my knees pulled into my chest. Flayed. Raw. Confused. And soaked. My teeth chattering.

I was in shock. And I rocked there on the floor for a long time. Unable to calm the tempest within.

There was too much. It was all too much. It was more than one person should possess . . . It was more than I could bear. I became lost in it all for a small eternity.

I did not see the sun rise. But eventually the rain and lightning were gone, and the black sky shifted to gray.

I rose. I commanded myself to do so. I wrestled the chaos. I battled. And while I could not tame the demons, they were leashed.

Climbing the stairs, I ascended higher and higher. The Dark Manor now proffered a floor of broken glass. And with each step I took, I left behind my sacrifice of blood.

I changed.

I wore my leather pants, my black halter top, my tight leather jacket, and my boots.

From my closet, I pulled out two short fighting swords and strapped them to my back in a specialty sheath so that they crossed in an X.

I didn't braid my hair. I left it loose, now dried in waves, and wild.

I looked at myself in the mirror and laughed. Once upon a time I had worn these clothes and used these weapons to hunt Shadows in the night. I had thought myself so strong, so skilled, so capable. I had considered myself an infallible warrior, facing the darkest of foes.

I laughed now at the child I had been.

I now knew better. I knew of the evil the darkness brings. And I realized there was so much more than I had ever bothered to imagine.

I assessed myself in the mirror without emotion. My skin was paler than it had once been. The waves of long dark hair wild and

14

untamed. My eyelashes were darker with a darker lining. The rosy hue to my lips and cheeks was now a pale pink.

And while my figure was the same toned hourglass shape it had been, my eyes were different.

They had always been violet. But when I had lost my Light, they had turned a more mortal-like blue. Now they were violet once again, but I could see little crystalline flecks of gray...

And sometimes the branching veins of black.

I turned away from the mirror. I was ready to leave. Aside from the swords, the only other items I took were some cash and my unrestricted credit card. I did not search for my discarded cloak, which had carried my phone. Nor did I try to retrieve my dagger of Light. I did not believe either would work any longer. And more importantly, I didn't need them.

I left.

I walked for a long time. I abandoned the manor far behind me. One step and then another. On and on.

I feared neither The Contessa nor the Umbra. They could come. I no longer cared. What more could they take?

And at some point, the gray day transitioned into black night. Still I walked. I considered not stopping. *Ever.*

Maybe if I kept going, I could find the ends of the earth. Maybe I could find comprehension. I could turn around and survey everything before me in a new light. I could understand.

But I did stop eventually. With the lights and noise of the city bustling around the dark, deserted alley...I reached my destination.

# CHAPTER 2

IT IS A FUTILE EXERCISE TO try and disassemble the reasoning of a mad man. But sometimes we do futile things . . .

Zagan had followed me to the ends of the earth, with a rabid determination, only to then renounce me. I had known when he turned away from me up on the cliff, that he was leaving. Where he went, I could not say. But I had not felt his presence anywhere within reach. He had not been at the manor.

I hadn't waited for his return. I knew he was not coming back, at least, not while I was there. I had seen it all in the way he'd looked at me.

He had warned me over and over again. He had feared what he would do to me. And when he'd seen the Darkness in my eyes, he'd known he was right—all his objections validated.

Everything had changed. Nothing had changed. Both were true. And that was why I left. If there was any chance to fix all the damage twisting around me, I needed answers. I needed to return to the Radiant Court.

I would have liked to talk with the Crone. I still didn't know who she was, but it was apparent she perceived much more than her frail and silent demeanor suggested. She had a role to play in all this.

Yet she too, like Zagan, had been gone. I'd known it, without a doubt.

It was clear that I had been the only soul in the broken manor throughout the black and rainy night.

*** 

I banged on the large steel door, pounding my fist without cease, desperately wanting salvation from the foul dumpster parked beside me. With a screech of metal against metal, the door finally began to slide open. I was met with the noise of a blaring television, and neither of the occupants inside seemed happy to see me.

The woman—*gatekeeper?*—stood there in her robe and slippers with her cigarette dangling from her lips. She was grumbling something about bunions and my impertinence. I couldn't quite make it all out with her cockney accent. Her little dog hunched next to her, yapping and snarling at me. Behind them the shabby sitting room was lit with a single lamp, and the old-fashioned television played commercials.

I didn't wait for an invitation. I thrust my payment at her. I expected the same disinterest she had shown before, when I had visited with Elijah.

However, I had no idea how long ago that had been. Time had been ripped apart. I now knew almost everything that had happened, remembered it all as my own experiences, but there was no sequential order. My concept of the passage of time had been upended.

I did not know how much time I had spent locked in Zagan's room after he had returned me to the Dark Manor. It could have been hours…or days. Time had not existed down there, not in the normal sense.

I did not know how long I'd spent shaking and shivering down in the hall after Zagan had left. There was no keeping of time for any of it.

That had been then. This was now.

And now instead of taking the money, the woman eyed me for a moment seeming wary. "Nah," she finally said without explanation and began to slide the door shut.

"Wait!" I insisted, bracing my foot against the metal track. "Is the club still standing? Are there people visiting?"

And with a ferocity I would not have thought possible, her mangy little mutt bit my foot. His supernatural teeth tore through the upper of my boot and impaled my toes. Hopping and cursing, I had to shake him off.

"Ow!" I snapped, pulling my foot back.

The woman didn't seem concerned about her dog's rabid disposition in the slightest. In fact, one of the sloppy curlers, which had been randomly snapped upon her head, was falling dangerously close to the burning cigarette dangling from her lips. It looked like her bright red, frizzy hair was about to catch fire. And I wondered if anything ever alarmed her.

"You want te come in 'ere?" She threw her hand at me. "Like that?"

I looked down at myself, inspecting the black leather jacket, pants, and boots. I didn't see anything wrong with them. I thought perhaps she was disturbed by the sword handles which were visible over my shoulders.

"Nay that, ye twat!" she replied when she saw me eyeing my clothes. She gave her head a nod, staring into my eyes, and her cigarette bobbed against her lips. "Practically dead inside, you are."

I reached up and placed my hand on my cheek, taken aback by her comment.

She began to close the door again. I pulled on my Light, allowing a rush of bright energy to pump through my veins. I stopped the door with my hand and met her eye, wanting her to see some of the sparkle I now held there.

"I'm fine, really," I told her. "I just want to find some of my friends. That's all." I tried to keep my voice as breezy as possible.

She eyed me for a long moment. Then it was as though her ability to hold any interest in me suddenly expired, and she became bored. Exhaling a fed up, "Uh," she allowed the door to open fully. After finally taking the money from me, she passed it on to her little beast who snatched it in his jaws. Without another look my way, the woman returned to her recliner in front of the television, and the dog trotted into the dingy sitting room to bury the bills under his bed.

I didn't wait for any more of an invitation. I slid the door shut behind me and took the long elevator ride down.

\*\*\*

The Den of Iniquity was still standing. In fact, it was bustling as if there had never been a near collapse. Music pumped, bodies swayed, and cocktail waitresses served drinks.

However, the gaping hole all those stories above had not been fixed. And the club now lacked a roof, exposed to the night sky. Several crows circled overhead. Every once in a while, they would

20

perch on the edge of the destroyed structure only to begin gliding again.

I found them unnerving.

I tried to look as innocuous as possible while I passed through the crowd. It wasn't hard to do. The lighting was dim, and the club was packed with immortals. Every race you could think of seemed to be represented by the patrons.

And I didn't know what most of them were. I realized just how sheltered I had been—how tiny my little world had been.

I had spent my entire life within the confines of the Radiant Court. Aside from visits into the surrounding mortal cities, I had never ventured beyond the boundaries of our world. And for the very first time, I realized how jarring that was.

But I hadn't come to gawk at the crowd or socialize. I'd come for specific reasons. The first thing I did was make my way straight to the private room I had seen Elijah enter. The curtains were drawn, and an unattended velvet rope blocked the entry.

I reached past the rope and tried to pull back one of the red velvet curtains. It didn't budge. It was a dead end. The drapes were spelled shut.

I didn't waste any more time there. Instead, I made my way to the main bar that ran through the center of the club. Mick, the bartender I'd encountered before, was nowhere to be seen. But his dried blood was still smeared along the counter top. I wondered why no one had cleaned it up. I was willing to bet it was somehow aiding the stability of the building.

Tending bar tonight was a woman with fiery red hair and creamy skin; I knew because it was all on display. I had seen her during my last visit, and Elijah had referred to her as a snake charmer.

Just as before a large bright green snake slithered around her naked body, somehow being sure to cover her modesty with each shift and sway.

While remaining on the woman, the snake curled its tail around a tumbler and set it down in front of me. "What'll you have?" the woman asked.

I didn't really want a drink, but I ordered one anyway, hoping to blend in. "Jameson. Neat," I told her. I figured I would take my lead from Lilly.

She grabbed a bottle and filled the tumbler. Then the snake seamlessly took the bottle, wrapping its tail around the neck, and set it back down.

When I went to pull out my cash, the snake charmer patted my hand resting on the bar. At her touch, her snake leaned its head my way and flicked my fingers with its forked tongue. "This one's on the house," she told me. "You look like you could use it, hun."

"Thanks," I replied. I was unsure how to take her comment. I was fairly certain it was an insult, but I tried to focus on the fact that she was attempting to do something nice.

Before she could walk away, I asked, "Do you happen to know if there's an oracle here?"

"An oracle?" She shrugged and shook her head. "Sorry, babes."

"What about the—" I stopped myself, realizing I was about to say *Femme Fatales*. I reminded myself that they were pretending to be *Fallen Angels*.

"Any of the Fallen Angels in tonight?"

The snake charmer rolled her eyes and pointed to the other end of the bar.

A handful of leather clad females, just oozing sex appeal, were doing body shots off of some large shirtless males.

"I'll take a tray of—" The bartender looked at me expectantly. I racked my brain, searching for a way to finish my sentence. I finally gave a defeated sigh, slightly embarrassed. "—something dirty."

When the snake charmer and her reptilian friend were done making the shots, I paid with my card, downed my drink, and made my way over to the group of gorgeous women with shot tray in hand.

I stood next to them for a moment, not quite sure how to get their attention. Two huge, shirtless men were lying on the bar in their jeans and boots, with hands folded behind their heads.

Standing on the bar between them, one of the Fatales held a bottle of tequila which she was pouring over the ridges and valleys of their incredibly defined abs. Then the girls who were gathered around would suck the tequila off the males before taking a bite from lime wedges…which were being held in the mouths of more huge men sitting on the barstools.

It seemed like they were competing against each other, one group versus the other, to see who could finish faster.

And on a barstool, next to all the action, was a woman with voluminous blond pigtails just below her ears. She was straddling someone who had his arms wrapped around her, his face at her neck. When I took a step closer, I realized he had his *fangs* embedded in her flesh.

"Ah, Lilly?" I tried.

"Fuck. Off," she moaned.

"Sorry. I'll wait," I told her, taking a step back.

She darted her half-closed eyes in my direction, and they widened. She tapped the vampire's shoulder and tried to pull back from him. He snarled and bit her harder.

23

Lilly whispered something in the vampire's ear. I couldn't hear what it was over the noise of the club, but the vampire's eyes flashed open. He withdrew his fangs from her. Then he picked Lilly up as he stood from the stool and set her down like a delicate flower. I couldn't be sure, but I thought he shook slightly. Before disappearing, he held Lilly's hand up to his mouth for a kiss.

She gave a guilty giggle and jumped off the bar stool to give me a hug. "What are you doing here? I thought we'd never see you again!"

I set the tray down on the bar and shrugged. "You know, *men*," I tried.

She rolled her large hazel eyes. "Uh! Tell me about it," she commiserated. Then she gave me a once over. "You look…different."

"A lot's been going on." I didn't know what else to say.

"Oh, do tell. I want to hear every smutty detail!" she said as her eyes widened with excitement. "But first," she stared at the shots topped with whipped cream, "what do we have here?"

"My thanks for all the help," I told her.

"Ooh!" She clapped her hands together. "Oi! Oi!" she called to the group of Fatales. Then Lilly did a little shimmy, pointing both index fingers at the tray. "Who wants a blow job?"

At her question, the two body shot guys sat up on the bar, accidently knocking over some of the Fatales. Lilly reached across and patted the thigh of the one closest to her. "Maybe later, cowboy."

Then she squinted, peering through the crowd of people. "There were some nymphs asking about you." She pointed towards the dance floor. "I think they went that way. Go! Go! Before they find those hunky shifters."

The huge male gave Lilly a sly smile and loped off, with his buddies following. She turned to me and rolled her eyes. "Werewolves," she huffed.

I gave her a sympathetic nod, even though I had no idea what she meant.

"Lilly!" the Fatale still on the bar snapped. "We weren't done with the contest. You totally ruined it." Her eyes narrowed. "I should punch you in the vag!"

Lilly put her hands on her hips and turned to the bar. "We aren't supposed to be here. We said just one drink and then we would leave. That was two hours ago. We need to get out of here. Now, do you want a blow job first or not?"

"Fine," the Fatale grumbled, before jumping down from the bar.

I placed my hand on Lilly's arm. "Before you go, is Bianca here? I'd like to talk to her."

I had met Bianca on my first visit to the Den of Iniquity, and she had warned me about Elijah. She had claimed he hung out with 'shady characters.' I wanted to find out what she knew.

"Sorry, sweetie. She's not around."

"Where is she? Can I get a hold of her at your place?"

"No. She's trying to get Cammy back."

"What happened to Cammy?"

Lilly waved an unconcerned hand. "Oh, Juan Carlos and his guys broke loose. They all escaped. One of them took Cammy on his way out."

"That sounds awful. Did it turn violent?" I asked, clearly more stunned than Lilly.

She shrugged. "Only a little."

"Wow. I hope Cammy's okay."

"I'm sure she'll be fine. I think the guy that took her kind of had a thing for her."

The Fatales had been holding a group of hunky men captive as a sort of indebted maid service. Apparently, the men had been demi-gods and Juan Carlos was their leader.

I remembered walking into Cammy's room while she was practically naked with one of them. I was willing to bet he had been her abductor.

"Is there any way I can get in touch with Bianca?"

"Maybe," Lilly said with a lack of commitment.

"What about Evelyn?" I tried.

Evelyn was the head of the Fatales. I hadn't remembered her before, but I now realized she had been the contact I'd met after pulsing to England with Killian, Watts, and the Archangels.

I wanted to find out why she had been there. I was certain she could be a source of valuable information.

The Fatales had gathered around Lilly as we were speaking. At my inquiry of their leader, they all exchanged a glance.

"Yeah, uh…She's indisposed at the moment. She has Juan Carlos chained up in the basement." Lilly made the comment sound as if Evelyn was redoing wallpaper.

My eyes rounded. Lilly just looked at me, batting her feathery lashes. "Oh my god," I murmured. "Why?"

"When the guys made a break for it, JC stayed behind to make sure they all got out. So Evelyn got a hold of him and chained him up. But she's kind of stressed now. It's just a matter of time before the demi-gods try to rescue him. You know how things like that go." Lilly finished speaking with an unruffled shrug.

"But, hey! A few of us were just going to run a quick errand and then head back to the house. Why don't you come with us? We'll see if there's been any word from Bianca. And I doubt Evelyn will be free, but we can try."

I hesitated to respond. I was raw. It was taking all my energy just to be there, just to interact and function on a normal level. I had so much inside that I was trying to hold in—to hold back. I didn't know how much longer I could keep it up.

Before I could reply, Lilly seemed to snap to attention. "Wait a minute. What are you even doing here? Isn't," she dropped her voice to a whisper, "*the you know who* after you?"

I felt a pang at her comment, and I tried to shove it aside—push it down and contain it with everything else warring within me. I took a deep breath. "No, not anymore."

"So no dungeons for us tonight?" she laughed.

I sighed. "Honestly, I don't know. I'm not sure who Marax was or why he was after me. But I don't think he was working on behalf of the—" I didn't want to say it. Instead I followed Lilly's lead. "You know."

I didn't think Zagan had sent Marax after me. I believed Marax had been acting under someone else's direction. I had my suspicions, but at this point, it was impossible to say for certain who that could have been. I was finally beginning to realize how dangerous assumptions could be.

"It's probably safer if I don't come with you. I don't want to put any of you in jeopardy again," I told Lilly.

"Oh please," Lilly said tossing one of her platinum pigtails over her shoulder. "That was nothing." She tilted her head towards the other Fatales gathered around her. "You have no idea what we're capable of."

But she was wrong. I did have an idea. I had seen what Lilly could do. And I knew better than to doubt her abilities.

27

"Come on," Lilly quipped. "It'll just be a sec and then you can talk to Evelyn."

She batted those feathery lashes at me again, and I let out a reluctant breath. I wanted answers.

"Goddamnit, Lilly . . . I'm in."

# CHAPTER 3

"Y OU'RE ELBOWING MY TIT!" someone whispered.

"You love it," came a hushed reply.

"I think that's the most action she's had all day."

"That's not cool. You don't elbow a tit," another voice chimed in. "The polite thing to do is give it a squeeze."

"Can you blame me? They're huge. It's more like your ginormous jugs ballooned up against my elbow."

"I think that qualifies as assault."

"Will you all shut up?! We're going to get caught!" Lilly hissed.

"Don't be jealous, Lilly. You have nice tits too."

At that, the Fatales all broke out in muffled laughter, including Lilly.

We were crouched behind a row of bushes in the dark. We had just trespassed onto an estate by scaling the huge wall which surrounded the grounds. And now a sprawling mansion sat before us.

I had no clue what we were doing there.

Lilly eyed the four other Fatales that had come to *run the errand* with her. "If any of you get caught, you're on your own," she warned. Then she surveyed the mansion. "It's that balcony, on the top floor. Over there. The one with the doors open."

She turned to the rest of us and I was reminded that she was more than an overgrown, sexy baby doll. Lilly was legit when she needed to be. "Stay to the shadows. And follow me," she directed.

Before she could take off though, I placed my hand on her arm. "What are we doing here? You said you were picking up a package."

"Yeah," she confirmed. "Kind of. Let's go!"

Lilly darted out from the shrubs and began to make a run for the mansion. I gave an exasperated breath and followed after her and the other Fatales. I knew I shouldn't have agreed to this. I didn't know what the hell was going on, but it couldn't be good. For Light's sake, I just wanted to talk to Evelyn.

And the worst part was that I looked just like them. We were all in leather. All carried packs or weapons of some kind. No one would believe I had been dragged along, that I was just an innocent bystander, somehow mistakenly caught up with these sexified hooligans.

We made it to the mansion and pressed ourselves against the building. We were huddled to the side of the balcony which Lilly had pointed out, and she began throwing rocks up onto the ledge and whisper shouting.

"Gem! Gemma! We're here! Gem!"

After a minute of calling for Gem and some choice expletives from Lilly, Gemma emerged from the open doors, hopping onto the balcony. Her wrists and ankles were bound, and she wore black workout leggings and a matching black sports bra. Her long brown pixie cut was mussed and her delicate features fierce.

31

"Get me the fuck out of here!" she whispered down to Lilly.

"We need the stone," Lilly replied.

"I have it," Gem responded. "You have to take me too."

"We can't, girlfriend. We promised we wouldn't. We need the stone."

"You goddamn, bitches!" Gem spat. "You're seriously going to leave me here?!"

"Gem, we can't bust you out. Bianca swore an oath. Come on. We'll figure something out. We need the stone."

Gem's face fell, and a note of genuine distress seemed to emerge from beneath the vexation. "Please, Lilly. Don't leave me here. I can't do this."

"It's going to be all right," Lilly told her. "We'll figure it out. Just hold him off for a little longer." Lilly jabbed her finger in the air towards Gem. "You are a fucking badass. You can do this."

"Totally!...Yes!...Seriously!" the other Fatales whispered in support.

I could hear the confidence and belief in Lilly's words. And Gem must have also, because she closed her eyes for a moment. A look of pain crossed over her face, but it was for a brief moment only. When she opened her eyes again, she straightened her spine. And while the pain was still there, there was also resolve.

She nodded once and pressed her lips together. "Okay," she murmured.

Then she bent forward and began to shake her chest at us with her hands bound behind her back. After a minute of the cleavage show Lilly quipped, "This is riveting. Really. I can see why Bannan is so crazed when it comes to you. But we need to get out of here!"

"I'm trying," Gem gritted.

From inside the balcony doors, the silhouette of a towering figure appeared, eclipsing the light from the room.

"Oh shit!" Lilly squeaked. "We're fucked."

"Almost," Gem breathed. And then with a final wiggle, a huge red gemstone the size of a plum, popped out of Gem's sports bra and tumbled down from the landing.

Lilly snatched it in her hands before it could hit the ground. And with a final shout she cried, "Remember! You are one badass mother fucker, Gemma Woods!"

Launching out of the crouch she was in, Lilly screamed, "Run!" without looking back. Each and every one of us sprinted across the lawn for the property wall.

But halfway along the manicured grass, two earsplitting screeches tore through the crisp night.

Lilly stopped in her tracks and turned, shouting, "Get ready!" Then she withdrew an oversized axe she'd had slung across her back, standing her ground. Following her lead, the strawberry blonde Fatale, Scarlet, pulled free a rocket launcher from a tubular carrying case, bracing it against her shoulder.

At the same time, the two medium toned blondes, Lucy and Cora, disassembled the backpacks they'd been sporting in an instant. That was when I discovered their utility packs were flamethrowers in disguise. They now pointed the firing shafts up towards the sky. And the fourth Fatale, Millie, brandished a longsword that glinted in the night.

With an irritated huff, I withdrew my two short swords. "You didn't mention we'd be battling," I snapped at Lilly.

"I figured we had a pretty good chance of getting out undetected," she replied.

Back on the balcony, the broad male I had seen during my first visit to the Den of Iniquity—the one who'd kidnapped Gemma—stalked towards her.

*Bannan.*

He wore low slung jeans and nothing else. The power of his muscled frame was in stark contrast to Gem's petite stature.

I could see her try to back away from him, shaking her head, but there was nowhere for her to go. He grabbed Gemma and flung her, bound as she was, over his bare shoulder. Across the expanse of the lawn, I could see the electric teal of his eyes flash, and steam hissed from the balcony where his bare feet met the damp slate flooring.

While I was concerned for Gem, my full attention was driven to the sky above. Because over the top of the mansion was the source of the piercing shrieks. Two huge, winged beasts—one midnight blue, the other silver—tore through the air like missiles. And it was clear we were their target.

I was no expert on the subject, but I was pretty sure a pair of short swords was not the best weapon for battling dragons. I was not prepared for this.

"Plan?" I shouted at Lilly over the sonic caterwauls of the jet-sized beasts.

"We got it covered," she yelled. "Just don't let them get a hold of you. Stay close!"

I was less than thrilled with her reply. The last thing I wanted to do was just stand there. But the dragons were almost upon us, and Lilly bellowed, "Now!"

She launched the axe she held, and it went spinning through the air, head over handle. With incredible precision, the blade lodged into one of the dark dragon's eyes.

At the same time, Scarlet fired the rocket launcher. A small missile tore through the silver dragon's wing and detonated upon contact. A blast lit the sky, and the scales covering the silver dragon's entire body crackled like red embers. The explosion resulted in a gaping hole in the dragon's wing.

At the assault, both dragons let out keening screams accompanied by an inferno of fire. The massive blaze was headed right for us. But Lucy and Cora each pulled the triggers on their flamethrowers.

Instead of meeting fire with fire, though, a concentrated hail-like spray erupted from the nozzles. When the retardant collided with the fire, a thick white wall of ice formed, creating an effective barrier from the flames. It was as though a giant, frozen ocean wave had suddenly appeared upon the lawn.

Both dragons came diving over the wall of frothy ice. The silver dragon was unable to keep himself aloft with most of his wing missing. He collided to the ground with a violent crash, plowing a massive ditch of grass and dirt in his wake, before slamming into the solid retaining wall.

He lay still where he was. Unconscious.

The midnight blue dragon had landed upright on his feet. The axe still buried in his eye. His lid convulsed around the impaled blade, desperately trying to shut, but unable.

The dragon lasered his one good eye upon Lilly. His massive chest billowed with each breath and his expanse of wings were folded tight to his body. A ticking hiss clicked in the back of his throat.

But instead of hellfire, deep, guttural, beast-like words shook the ground at our feet.

"I cannot let you leave with the stone," the dragon said. "I will get you the girl, but you must return the stone."

"We don't want her," Lilly said with disinterest.

More hissed clicks sounded from the dragon. "I will give you one chance to change your mind," he growled.

Lilly pulled down her top, exposing her breasts to the dragon. "Eat tits and die!" she yelled.

I really didn't know what that meant, but the dragon was clearly infuriated by her insolence. With an enraged screech, the dragon unleashed an exhale of fire—the inferno hurtling towards us.

But Lucy and Cora triggered their devices the instant the flames erupted. And this time they ran as they did, circling the dragon. He tried to counteract the wall of ice surrounding him by shifting to get around. The act was in vain, though. The two Fatales had him covered.

When the dragon's great wings unfurled and he began to launch off his haunches, Lucy and Cora took a few swift retreating steps, allowing the spray from their throwers to intertwine over top of the dragon.

With a final screech and a flash of flames licking the night sky, the Fatales trapped the dragon inside a filmy, solid cage of ice.

It was just in time, too, because both throwers sputtered and gave empty clicks, their tanks clearly drained of whatever substance they had been filled with.

"Go! Go!" Lilly directed. "More could be coming. And that barrier won't last long!"

We scrambled over to the estate wall, just about to escape, when the silver dragon rose. His damaged wing hung limp and useless at his side, but the hissing clicks in the back of his throat held the promise of fire.

He began to stagger over to us . . . and we were caught.

I was about to send a pulse of energy towards him, hoping it would be enough to knock him off balance while we leapt over the wall; however, Millie began to slink towards him. I thought she was going to try and use her longsword, but oddly she threw it to the ground. Then she unzipped her jacket and let that fall from her arms as well.

She was now in my way, and I couldn't release a blast of energy without taking her down with it.

Yet the dragon did not attack. Instead he paused where he was, and his electric, elongated eyes seemed transfixed on Millie.

Something rippled through the air around us then, and I could have sworn I smelled gardenias. The night seemed to soften somehow.

"Millie, no!" the Fatales warned in unison.

If Millie heard the admonition, she didn't show it. She continued for the dragon.

She had long coffee colored hair with fringy bangs. And a light breeze stirred the night at that moment, sending her hair flying around her, as if she had commanded the wind. Her large almond shaped eyes were focused solely on the dragon. And having shed her jacket, she stood before him in snug black pants and a skintight black tank. Her clothes highlighted her figure, and I could see how Scarlet's elbow had been the victim in the earlier exchange.

The dragon sat there, snorting and chuffing, its massive chest heaving. Millie walked right up to it, staring at it with a hypnotic gaze. She put her hand under the dragons chin and gave it a stroke.

"Millie, don't! What are you doing?"

"It's too late, Lils. She's lost in the thrall," Lucy murmured.

37

Without taking her eyes off the dragon, Millie said, "Why don't you girls take off. I think I'll catch a ride home later."

"Millie, this isn't okay. You can't do this."

It seemed like it was a difficult task, but Millie tore her gaze away from the dragon to pin Lilly with a stare. With an exaggerated effort, she mouthed the words: *You have the stone. Go!*

Lilly let out a sharp exhale before turning to the rest of us. "Come on," she sighed, her voice full of resignation.

I sheathed my two short swords, having done nothing with them. Lilly, on the other hand, didn't try to retrieve her axe from the imprisoned dragon's eye. Scarlet gave her missile launcher a heft, and Lucy and Cora hoisted their flamethrowers against their shoulders.

And just like that, we climbed the wall and walked away from the dragon pack's estate, wandering the night with a stolen gem…and some military grade weapons.

# CHAPTER 4

~Violet's Playlist: Harder, Deeper, Faster – The Bashful~

MAY I TAKE YOUR WEAPONS, MADAME?"
I looked down at the little man in coattails. The top of his head only met my chin, which caused his eyes to be level with my chest. He didn't bother to look up at me. He simply stared—unimpressed—at my chest, waiting for my reply.

He reminded me of a Shar-Pei dog with the incredible number of wrinkles collected on his face. Two tufts of white hair stuck up from each side of his otherwise bald head, and the thickest pair of black rimmed glasses I'd ever seen, magnified his watery eyes.

"Um. Thanks. But I'll hang on to them," I told him.

Lilly, on the other hand, handed her jacket over right away, just as Scarlet dumped her missile launcher into the old man's arms. Lucy and Cora also deposited their packs onto the growing pile, in addition to their jackets.

The tiny old man, no longer visible beneath the clothes and weapons, began to shuffle away with the mountain of goods precariously teetering in his arms.

"Thanks, Mr. Goose," Lilly called after him.

Some kind of muffled reply came from the little man, but it was impossible to make it out.

"Our new butler," Lilly commented.

I looked around the entrance to the Fatale house. Trendy. Modern. Bizarre. Mess.

Bloody daggers sat on the glass entry table—completely abandoned. Next to them was a pile of papers; the word OVERDUE was stamped in red several times. And on top of the documents, acting as a paperweight, was what appeared to be a Faberge egg with a chewed-up wad of gum stuck to it.

Above, in the entry light fixture, perched a monkey—an honest to god little monkey. The light would sway as the monkey scurried along the fixture to then pause and observe those of us below. He gave an angry screech as we passed by and waved a pair of fluffy pink handcuffs. Then he took a hit from a chocolate syrup bottle, which he clutched possessively against his little chest.

Over in the living room, I could see a tent was set up next to a fully inflated eight-person raft. A portion of the raft was sticking out of a broken window and the rest of it flopped over most of the couch. It also looked like one of the raft paddles was lodged into the wall. And there was absolutely no indication why.

I followed Lilly through the chaotic house, and I had to hand it to the demi-gods. They had at least kept some of the mess at bay. Because the disarray was clearly worse now than when the ripped, half naked men had been tasked with the upkeep.

Instead of going into the backyard tonight, we made our way downstairs to the basement level and entered a huge gym. All manner of workout equipment was stationed throughout the space. And in the corner was a large sparring area with mats. *Harder, Deeper, Faster* by The Bashful blasted over the sound system at a deafening volume.

Two Fatales were running on treadmills, side by side. I had a feeling they were every adolescent male's wet dream as their toned bodies were clothed in tiny booty shorts and sports bras. Their sneakers generated a soft pounding rhythm in time with the music, and each had their hair pulled back in ponytails.

They didn't stop running when we entered, but they did look at Lilly and raised their brows. In response, Lilly pulled the large red gemstone from her pocket and tossed it to one of the Fatales on the treadmill. The Fatale caught the stone and jumped onto the side rails of her machine, looking at what she now held in her hand.

Her workout partner followed suit and jumped onto her rails as well. Then she slammed her palm over the stop button on the treadmill dashboard and reached over to do the same on the other. Scarlet cut the blaring music, and the room became quiet.

"You little minx," the Fatale holding the stone murmured. "You did it." She looked up and her gaze fell on each of the women who had helped with the theft. "Nice work, ladies."

Her eyes narrowed on me for a moment as she scanned our group, but she didn't say anything about my presence. Instead she asked, "Where's Millie?"

Lilly gave a sigh, and her voice was full of regret. "She thralled Scythe so the rest of us could escape with the stone."

"What?" asked the Fatale, seeming shocked at the news. "You're joking, right?"

Lilly just shook her head.

The two Fatales on the treadmills looked stricken. "The dragons are going to be out for blood when she kills him," the one stated. "On top of that, if they figure out what she is . . . they'll kill us all. What was she thinking?!"

"What do we do?" the other Fatale asked.

At first no one answered. But then Lilly took a step forward and threw her shoulders back. "We'll figure it out. It's not our top priority yet, and there's nothing we can do about it tonight. Besides, Millie knows the dragons are an ally of sorts. She won't go for the kill right away. We'll have some time before the compulsion becomes too great for her to fight. For now, Scythe will just be wrapped up in a gorgeous female. If anything, it's going to help us. That's one less dragon after us for the stone."

Exhaling a shaky breath, the other Fatale simply replied, "I hope you're right." Instead of continuing the matter, she asked, "What about Gem?"

"Not good," Lilly responded. "We need to get her out of there."

The Fatale on the treadmill raised her eyebrows. "How?"

Scarlet stepped forward. "Hellion was willing to hand her over in exchange for the stone. Maybe we can work something out with him."

"Well, that was before we trapped him in a block of devil's ice," Lilly countered. "Besides it was the stone he wanted." She retrieved the red gem from the other Fatale's hand and zipped it back in her pocket. "I doubt he'll negotiate for anything else."

"There's always something," Scarlet supplied.

"There's always something," the Fatale on the treadmill echoed.

Lilly gave an unconvinced shrug. "How do we find out what *it* is?"

The Fatale on the treadmill pressed her lips together, clearly uncertain. Then she gestured towards me. "Is she here to pay her debt?"

"No," Lilly replied. "She's here to see Evelyn."

Just then a deep, agonized bellow reverberated through the hall outside.

The Fatale on the treadmill tilted her head, acknowledging the roar. "Evelyn's . . . *busy*."

The women all exchanged a glance, obviously unnerved by whatever was happening, but Lilly pressed on. "Any news from Bianca?" she asked.

The Fatale shook her head. "Nothing. We don't know what happened to her and the others. And we don't know where Cammy is."

Lilly crossed her arms. "First Bannan snags Gem. Then Cammy gets taken. Evelyn has clearly gone insane over Juan Carlos. Now Biannca is missing, and Millie is lost in a thrall. What's going on?" She looked around the room at all the women gathered there. "You know what this means, don't you?"

The next words she spoke made my skin ice over. They made my head spin, and my breath trap where it was in my lungs. I had to grab on to an exercise machine, just to stop myself from stumbling.

From her perfectly pink pouty lips, Lilly murmured, "It's coming closer."

\*\*\*

Evelyn was in the hall as we all exited the gym. She was leaning against the wall—shaking. Her strict braid was disheveled, and long dark strands of her hair were falling around her face.

She looked the way a person does when they're holding back bile. Her skin was drained of color and sweat dotted her forehead. When she began to slide down the wall, the Fatales ran to catch her.

And while I did not know what she was going through. I believed I could understand how she felt.

I was desperately trying not to shake, not to collapse, myself. I had been trying to hold back a tidal wave of power . . . and I knew I was not strong enough. It was only a matter of time before I lost control.

On its own, my Light was something I had a mastery over. It had been a part of me my entire life. And in and of itself, it was something I could control without effort.

But the Darkness I felt running through my veins was different. Unpredictable. Perhaps I could control it. Perhaps not. There was something . . . chaotic about it.

And with the two elements together—clashing and warring—it was more than I could take. I was too confused and disoriented.

It was exhausting trying to hold it all back, trying to keep it caged. I was drained. I wanted to disappear, to be far away from anyone else. If I could just find a deep hole somewhere and fade into nothing . . .

But I couldn't. And I had to accept that. I tried to push it all back, lock it all down. I blinked my eyes, wanting to snap back into this moment.

I focused on the Fatales around me. Lilly and Scarlet were trying to hold Evelyn up and usher her down the basement hall. But Evelyn shook them off, refusing the assistance.

"I'm fine!" she snapped, pushing the loose strands of hair from her face. She began to stagger down the hallway, bracing her hand along the wall as she went. However, instead of making her way to

45

the stairwell, she stopped at a gate. After pushing the call button, a set of elevator doors opened up.

"Get Eva," she commanded to no one in particular. Then she selected a button from the inside panel, and the doors began to slide shut.

And while Evelyn clearly needed her space, I couldn't let her go without speaking to her. "Evelyn, wait," I pleaded, stopping the door from closing.

She picked up her glassy eyes to stare at me. "You!" she whispered.

I shivered as her jade irises began to glow, and her hands began to shake. "Do you know what you've done? You're going to destroy everything," she hissed.

Scarlet turned to Lilly and gave her head an emphatic shake. Lilly put her arm around my shoulders and drew me towards the stairs. At the same time the Fatales huddled around the elevator, blocking Evelyn's view of me. As the elevator doors slid shut, I heard someone say, "We'll have Eva here in just a minute."

Lilly gave me a squeeze. "You know, Evelyn's a little tired right now. Maybe she'll be up for chatting later."

Scarlet marched over to us, and her voice dripped with accusation. "What the hell was that about?"

"I'm sorry," I told her. "Evelyn helped arrange a meeting between some of my people and another faction once before. I just wanted to ask her about it."

"What did she mean, 'You're going to destroy everything?' What have you done?" Scarlet persisted.

"I don't know," I said. "I have no idea what that was about."

Scarlet let out a huff and looked up at the ceiling. "I hate it when shit starts getting serious!"

The Fatale from the treadmill stepped into the middle of the hallway. "All right," she snapped. "Evelyn's ramblings are getting worse. It's time. Let's all meet in the office."

Scarlet gestured to the other end of the hall. "Should we go check on him?"

"Absolutely not," the Fatale replied. "Evelyn will go nuclear if anyone sneaks in there. He's a demi-god. Whatever she's doing to him . . . He'll live."

Then she pointed at me. "Violet, right?"

I nodded.

"Look, I don't mean to be a bitch, but you should probably go. There is some weird shit going on, and we need to figure it all out."

The Fatale didn't wait for a response. She opened the door to the stairwell and everyone but Lilly followed her out of the hallway.

I turned to Lilly. "I'm really sorry about this," I told her. "I shouldn't have come."

Lilly waved a hand in the air. "This has nothing to do with you. This is just the way things have been around here lately. I thought it was worth a shot to check in with Evelyn, but something's wrong." Releasing a sigh, she continued, "I have to go up to the office, but you can stay in my room if you want."

"Thanks, but I'm going to head out," I told her. "Just one thing, though." I took a deep breath. "Lilly, what did you mean when you said, 'It's coming closer?'"

"You know. *The Book of Prophecies*." She used a tone that suggested it was obvious what the *Book of Prophecies* was.

"I'm not familiar with that."

She looked surprised. "Really?"

"Really."

It seemed difficult for Lilly to accept my lack of knowledge. "Maybe you call it something else," she tried. "Everyone knows of it."

Her eyes widened, and I felt like she was trying to help me remember. "You know. The collection of prophecies. There are hundreds . . . probably thousands of them in there, spanning across all the races. Pretty much the fate of the world summed up in one book?"

"No, I've never heard of it," I told her.

Pure shock passed over Lilly's face. "Wow. Okay. Well... that's what it is. Literally a book of prophecies."

"Can I get a copy of it somewhere?" I asked.

Lilly laughed. "No. That's the problem with it. The book is in, like, a million little pieces. The prophecies are scattered through this world and the next. Some fiercely guarded, some lost forever, some buried and forgotten. Some whole. Some not. They're impossible to come by. Some races have pages pertaining to themselves. Some races have pages or parts of pages pertaining to other races. It's all a big contentious mess . . . Are you sure you've never heard of it?"

"I'm sure," I confirmed. "But Lilly, why did you say, 'It's coming closer?' What does that have to do with a torn-up book?"

She scrunched her mouth to the side and then leaned in towards me, dropping her voice to a whisper. "We have one of the prophecies that pertains to us. And with everything that is happening lately . . . it seems like our time is almost up."

I dropped my voice as well. "Is there a reason you chose those particular words?

She shrugged. "No. I was just trying to make the point that we're running out of time and royally screwed if we don't finish up some plans we have." She peered at me. "Is everything okay?"

"Yeah. Totally," I lied.

Looking at the ceiling, Lilly repeated, "Well, I have to go up to the office. Are you sure you don't want to stay? I could have Mr. Goose make some food for you."

"No. Thanks, Lilly. I appreciate—"

Scarlet tore through the stairwell door. "Lilly! The stone! Hellion's here with the others!"

"Fuck me, that was fast," Lilly squeaked. She leaned in and gave me a peck on the cheek. "You'd better get out of here. Take the back exit behind the pool. You're gonna want to avoid the front. Let's meet up at D. I. again soon!"

And she dashed off with Scarlet.

I took a moment, alone in the hall. I hadn't found any of the answers I was hoping for, and I had clearly overstepped my welcome.

With nothing else to do, I made my way to the backyard. It was deserted—a far cry from the raucous party I'd witnessed last time.

Without even being aware of what I was doing, I allowed myself to blend in with the shadows. I somehow let the darkness of night wrap its arms around me. And I let myself out into the alley along the side of the house.

I could hear a commotion, and over the noise was a female's voice—shouting. She was yelling something about 'dicks' and 'bestiality'...*I didn't know.*

Under different circumstances, I would have liked to stay and watch the standoff between the Fatales and the dragons. I had a feeling it would be a lively show. But I had somewhere I needed to go.

Discreet, and slinking through the night, I eventually found my way to a private airport. I chartered a jet. I left London.

49

But I could not fly away from that which consumed me. Because the closer I got to my destination, the more I felt myself shift. And with my agitation, the Darkness began to smother the Light.

# CHAPTER 5

I SAT IN THE CHAIR, nestled in the corner, blending in with the shadows. I had come to be good at that.

It was strange to be in the cabin. I looked around . . . *I hated it.*

I hated how it made me feel. I was torn between a dichotomy of emotions. Being in this place made me face my guilt. I felt the shame and ick of what I had done crawl over my skin like thousands of little bugs.

And yet, I couldn't deny a certain sense of longing. Of connection. Of desire.

I was beginning to see how useless feelings were. It would be better to amputate that section of my psyche. To apply a tourniquet and refuse blood. To allow that part of my mind to atrophy and die.

Then I would no longer need to feel. I could worship at the altar of wrath and justice. And I would never know sorrow and shame again.

I sat in the chair, nestled in the corner, blending in with the shadows. And the firelight flickered. Why was there a fucking fire, when no one was home?

I hated the firelight now. Hated the sun. The accusation of day.

I waited. And at some point in the night, the front door opened.

He didn't sense me. I was just another shadow in the corner. I allowed myself a small indulgence. My lips curled into a smile.

He began to cross through the room. His strides eating up the distance, his big body moving with power.

I was willing to bet he was heading for the shower. The large glass one upstairs. Where we had been together once before.

I decided to reunite with him down here instead. "Hello, Elijah," I called from my seat in the dark.

He stopped. Froze. He didn't turn. Didn't move.

I could feel his senses roam. He was searching for me. For my Light. For some identifying connection. And he found none.

I held it back. Instead I let free the Darkness I possessed. I allowed it to seep through the cabin. And Elijah stiffened.

He turned to me, saying nothing. I laughed. He was such the avenging angel. Gold and bronzed in the firelight. Brown eyes glittering with sparks.

He was too big. Too overwhelming. I hated him for it. For testing me. For making me want to be near him just to feel his size.

I stopped laughing, and Elijah said nothing. He waited for me to move, to speak.

"Nothing to say to me?" I asked.

Still he stood there.

Finally I rose from my seat in the dark. I walked up to Elijah, and I twined my arms around his neck, pressing my body into his. "Have you missed me?" I purred.

I didn't wait for a response. I kneed his groin with the intention of sending his manhood into his throat. Then with the grip I had on the back of his neck, I pulled his head down to slam his face into the same knee.

He pulled free from me with blood trickling from his nose. Hulking. His shoulders rose and fell with his breathing. He swiped at the blood with the back of his hand.

"What do you want?" He finally growled.

I threw the ring I held at him and it bounced off his chest. "I want you to pay," I hissed.

He eyed the sparkling, clear diamond where it had landed on the floor. He knew what it was. He knew I had retrieved it from the dresser upstairs in this very cabin.

Without any warning, he grabbed me and flung me over his shoulder. With just a few swift strides, he threw me down onto the large dining table, my back slamming into the wood.

I was about to roll off the side of it, but he laid his body on top of mine.

He grabbed my leather jacket and ripped it open down the center, before tearing at his own shirt.

"What are you doing?!" I cried.

He narrowed his eyes at me and clenched his teeth. "I fucked you back to reason once before. I can do it again."

I swung my hand at his face, nails extended, and clawed him across the cheek. When his head whipped back, he stared at me with sparking eyes. Our chests expanded and contracted against one another.

Beads of his blood dripped onto my lips, one at a time. One slow drop after another. Staining them red.

Elijah looked at the blood on my mouth and paused for a moment. Then he backed off of me. He stepped away from the dining table and turned.

"How did you do it?" I demanded, sliding off of the table.

"Do what?" he growled, keeping his back to me.

"How did you take him?!" I snapped. "Do you have any idea the life he's led? What kind of terrible things were done to him? How could you do that to an innocent child? He was only eight years old!"

Elijah said nothing.

"How did you do it?" I insisted.

I thought back to that night, the night when Zagan had disappeared from right next to me while I slept.

The windows had been latched from the inside. There was no evidence of an intruder. No one had seen or heard Zagan being taken through the Radiant mansion. It was as if he had just vanished into thin air…

When I spoke next, it was with a quiet realization. "You can pulse. Can't you."

Elijah bunched his shoulders and rolled his head before turning around. He looked at me with the gold specks burning in his eyes— unrepentant. And it was all the confirmation I needed.

"How?" I repeated. "Daphne said you haven't passed on, that you haven't become an Archangel. You shouldn't be able to pulse."

"And the bond," I continued. "The *Vinculum*. Giddeon said he couldn't connect with me because he's passed on. So why were you able to? Which is it? Have you crossed over, or haven't you?"

Still he stared at me, jaw clenched, arms crossed over his broad chest. Silent.

"Enough!" I shouted. "Enough…"

55

I walked up to him, and my voice dropped. "Do you know what you did to me? Do you know what you took from me? Have you any idea how I hated myself? How I blamed myself?

"I was a little girl, Elijah. I was scared. I was left feeling empty and incomplete. I grew up thinking something was wrong with me. My entire life was altered because of that one night."

I paused, waiting, but he said nothing. "The least you can do is give me some answers."

Still he stared at me.

We stood like that for a moment, facing each other in the silence of the cabin with the rain pouring outside. The light from the fire shifted around us, while the shadows crept along the periphery.

When he still said nothing, I swept past Elijah and headed for the door. I had had enough.

But I stopped before I could reach for the door knob because, finally, he spoke. "It was for you," he rumbled. "I did it for you."

With the wrath I felt at his words, I pulled on the Darkness inside. I embraced it. I let it wash over me. And I turned to face him, black veins branching through my irises.

Elijah didn't flinch. Towering in the middle of the cabin, with his feet planted firmly apart and his large arms crossed over his hard chest, he looked down at me. The gold flecks in his eyes blazed.

His shoulders expanded with a slow heavy breath. "I will tell you everything you want to know. But there's a condition."

I glared at him…waiting.

"You have to touch me first."

I took a moment to let his words sink in before responding.

"You're pathetic," I spat. I wanted him to feel the vehemence in my voice—to make him feel ashamed. But he continued to stand firm where he was, unaffected by my disgust.

"Doesn't matter," he countered. "If you want to hear everything, you will have to touch me."

"No."

Elijah's arms remained crossed over his chest. If he was feeling any volatile emotions, he didn't show it. He made it seem as if he was a calm, rational adult dealing with an angry child.

And just for that, I decided to give him what he asked for. If he wanted my touch, he could have it. And I would make him sorry.

Yes, my Light had been returned to me, but I still possessed the Dark. And I would summon every ounce of the cold evil which pumped through my veins before I placed my hands on Elijah. I would make him regret his ransom. I would make his blood freeze.

"Alright, Elijah," I purred his name. "Come here."

He didn't reply. Instead he gave a single shake of his head. And I bit down on my cheek. He was going to make me cross to him.

"Fine," I said. I made the comment breezy, holding all the anger that I had for him inside. I began to take a step towards him.

"No jacket," he qualified.

I paused. I could feel my eye twitch. The hatred for him made my chest tingle. But instead of snarling at him, I gave a slight upturn of my lips.

I began to make my way to him, and as I did, I rolled the cropped jacket from my shoulders, first one side then the other. The tall spiked heels of my boots clicked against the hardwood floor. My hips were encased in tight black leather and I gave an extra swish with each step I took.

I tilted my head to the side, allowing the long waves of my hair to tumble across my back. And I eyed Elijah the entire time.

I pulled back on the Darkness. Instead I released a touch of my Light, allowing a slight glow to my eyes.

Shrugging off my jacket, I tossed it to the floor. My black halter top left much of my skin on display. I gave my head another little tilt, letting my hair brush across my shoulders and arms.

I wanted him to think he was getting exactly what he asked for. I wanted him to think I would be the sweet, passive female he so clearly desired. And then I would pour all the dark, empty evil I possessed into him.

His arms remained crossed at his chest. I raised a hand and let it hover just over his forearm, about to place it on him, but he shifted.

He uncrossed his arms and let them drop to his sides. His shirt was still open down the front. "On my skin," he growled.

At that, I closed my eyes, uncertain if I could do it, uncertain if I could live with myself.

But it was a touch, nothing more. And I wanted answers.

I held my hand over his heart, just a few inches away from his skin. It looked so small and delicate in contrast to his hard chest. I pressed my hand against his warm tanned skin. I was going to make him sorry.

But the spark that flared through my body was too much. I had thought I could freeze him with the Darkness I carried, and instead I burned. The cold malevolence which I had intended on pouring into him recoiled, burying itself away deep inside. And I felt warmth and Light surge between us.

I was naive, underestimating the connection I had with him, the power of it. I thought by embracing the Darkness and taking control of it that I could overpower the forces in place between us.

I should have known better.

I tried to fight the connection, tried to push it away. But I couldn't.

I closed my eyes, dropping my head, and I shuddered. My forehead rested on his chest.

His large hand cupped the back of my head, holding me there.

After a moment though, I tore myself away from him, grappling for control, trying to catch my breath, angry that he could affect me.

I took a deep breath. "Start talking," I demanded.

In what seemed like a subconscious act, Elijah raised his large hand and rubbed his pectoral. The muscles along his torso flexed with the motion.

"I'm taking a shower first," he said as he turned and began to make his way to the hall.

I pulled free one on the knives I had strapped to my thigh. It lodged into the wall, inches from his head, as he passed into the hallway.

"Now, Elijah."

He turned—jaw clenched, eyes flashing with his displeasure—but he didn't argue. He yanked a chair from the dining table and settled into it.

I stood where I was and crossed my arms.

Elijah raised a brow, gesturing to his lap.

"I'd rather not throw up," I told him.

At that he actually grinned.

I said nothing, waiting. He took his time, eyeing me. Finally, when I thought I would have to launch my second knife at him, he took a breath, settling back in his chair even more.

"I have passed on," he confirmed. "I can pulse."

Before he could continue, I asked, "Then why didn't you when we were in the Vestibule, before entering Aleece? When…we were in trouble."

59

"They're protected. No one can pulse in or out of the tunnels or the Vestibules," he said, simply.

"Why does everyone believe you haven't crossed over? Why are you not one of the Angela?" I pressed.

"I did certain things that have altered my power. My energy is not that of the Archangels. It's why I'm not recognized as one. And it's why I can still connect with you."

"Why?" I breathed.

"You think you know what it's like to feel empty and hollow. You think you understand loneliness. Feeling incomplete. Unable to desire. You think you know what it's like to suffer," he accused. "But you have no clue. You've experienced a few years of it...Try a millennium."

I shook my head, trying to piece it all together, trying to understand. "Daphne said it eases when you pass on—"

"I wanted. Is that so terrible?" He leaned forward resting his forearms on the table. "I did not choose this life. It was forced upon me. I wanted what was owed to me." His eyes narrowed on mine. "I wanted you."

"So you destroyed the life of an innocent child?!" I countered.

"He was an abomination!" Elijah thundered, and the fire snapped, licking the air around the hearth. "He was half Shadow! I was saving you. I was doing the entire Radiant race a favor. He would grow to be a monster, annihilating our very people."

His voice dropped and disgust covered his face. "And you would have been forced to be with him. You would have had no choice. I didn't destroy the life of an innocent child. I saved one."

He stood then, shoving the chair back and leaning his fists on the table. "And then you go off and fucking marry him! I should have

60

put an end to him when I could. I should have known that bitch was a liar."

"Who?" I demanded.

"She calls herself The Contessa."

I took a step back. He might as well have shoved me. Wrapping my arms around myself, my voice was a whisper. "What did you do?"

Elijah sat down again, leaning back in the chair and crossing his arms. "She came to me. She told me I could have someone. The next female Prism. She said she could show me how to forestall becoming an Archangel. She told me I could be with you and that I could connect with you.

"In exchange, she wanted the boy. She said he was half Shadow. She said he was the lost heir to the throne.

"She was fearful of him. She said he would be the doom of both our races. She said she could prevent it from happening. She told me she would inhibit his rise to power. And most importantly, she would sever the connection between you.

"I had the chance to save you. I had the chance to one day have you. I took it."

My ribs expanded at the ache I felt. "So you pulsed into the room of a child and took him?"

I eyed the sparkling diamond ring that lay on the floor, the one I had thrown at Elijah. It was the ring that had been left next to me the night Zagan disappeared. Elijah followed my gaze.

"Why?" I asked.

He knew I meant the ring. I couldn't understand why he had left it, what it had to do with any of this.

"I wanted you to know you weren't alone. I wanted you to know there would be someone waiting for you."

61

I was disturbed by his logic. *I had been a child.*

"How did you get it?" I asked, glaring at the stone. "It was in my jewelry box. In my closet…my private space." I had kept it all these years, never removing it from under the padding where I had tucked it away.

He shrugged, not caring about the offense. "I wanted to give it to you again. Give it to you myself. I pulsed in one night and took it back."

I shook my head, disgusted by his lack of remorse. "Was I there?"

He nodded.

And although he didn't speak, I could feel what he held back through our connection.

He had struggled that night. I had been older, and the compulsion to grab me and pulse away with me had been crushing. He had seen me lying there with the sheets pushed aside and my hair spread out across the pillow. And he'd had to stop himself from doing anything other than watch.

"Why—"

He cut me off, well aware of what I was about to ask. "You weren't ready. You were still too young. You needed more time, and I was willing to wait."

I felt violated. And Elijah could see it all over my face. He stood and crossed to me, standing too close and overwhelming me with his size. His eyes sparked and the fire flickered.

"Stop being so fucking ignorant, Violet! I am who you belong with. Don't be a fucking child. You need to grow up. This righteous, holier than thou bullshit you have going on is useless. I did you a fucking favor. I made the right call."

He grabbed onto my arms, and I was drawn to the pull I felt towards him. I didn't shake him off. "Look at yourself. Look at what you're becoming—something dark. Something dead. Do you really want to be a fucking nightwalker?"

He squeezed my arms tighter and pulled me in closer, his voice an angry growl. "You have no idea. The one I made the deal with is appalling. And you are beginning to remind me of her. You're beginning to *smell* like her. And trust me when I tell you, that is a bad thing."

"This," he gave me a shake, "is exactly what I was trying to save you from. This is why you belong with me. You were starting to get better. I can help you. We can still find the Oracle. We can purge this Darkness from you. And I can help restore you."

He leaned forward to put his face into mine, and his eyes blazed. "You. Belong. To. Me."

His lips came slamming down onto mine...And I didn't fight it.

Because for a moment, I believed him. I felt the conviction he felt. The bond between us amplified everything. I felt his energy, bright and hot, and it stirred my own.

I gave into him. I gave into his kiss. I let him crush my body into his. I felt the hard planes of his chest and the strain of his erection. And it felt good. It made me want so much more.

But the guilt that came along with my desire was enough to turn my blood cold. I was disgusted with myself. And I didn't even try to stop Elijah. Instead, I shut myself off.

I stood there and gave nothing back, becoming something...dark and dead.

# CHAPTER 6

~Violet's Playlist: Whore, In This Moment~

ELIJAH PULLED BACK FROM ME. His eyes narrowed, and his jaw ticked. His voice was a low growl.

"Fine," he said as he released me. He didn't back away, though. He stood in my personal space, inundating me with his presence. "You'll see I'm right." He gave a slow shake of his head. "I just hope it isn't too late when you do, princess."

I took a step back, needing to breathe in something other than him. Elijah nodded to the ring on the floor. "How did you remember?"

I scooped up my jacket and put it on. "It's complicated," I snapped.

"Did you get all your memories back?"

"Everything," I told him. It wasn't entirely true. I didn't know what happened between sacrificing my Light for Zagan and waking at Elijah's cabin, but I didn't want him to know that.

When I didn't say more, Elijah shrugged. "So what the hell do you want? Why are you still standing here?"

I could feel my nostrils flare with the agitated breath I took, but I forced my voice to remain level. "You were on the phone the last time I was here. You said you knew *her* pressure points. That you could make *her* beg for mercy. I want to know who you were talking to and who you were talking about."

Elijah began to open his mouth, but I continued. "I want to know everything you know about The Contessa. I want to know who you went to see at the Den of Iniquity. I want to know what happened in the alley outside the Fatale house after I fled. And I want to know what prophecy you and my mother were talking about."

When I was done speaking, I planted my feet apart in a wide stance and crossed my arms over my chest before notching my chin.

Elijah smirked. "Alright," he complied easily enough. Then he rolled his shoulders. "But it's going to cost you."

"You owe me." I ground the words through clenched teeth.

"I don't owe you shit," he replied.

Ice and fire began to flow through my veins. I could feel my skin begin to vibrate. I was losing control, about to erupt in one way or another. I was going to launch myself at Elijah. And I didn't know if I would shove him to the floor to then free him from his jeans and impale myself on him or ram my fist into his chest to rip out his heart.

Instead of either of those, I stalked past him, through the hallway, towards the basement. I yanked open the door and began to descend the stairs, not bothering with the candles that lined the way.

Elijah, however, came lumbering behind me and sent a pulse of energy through the dark space. Flames sprang to life.

"Where the fuck do you think you're going?" he growled.

I crossed to the hidden control panel and punched in a code. The wall length bookshelf slid open to reveal my black Maserati parked behind Elijah's Land Rover Defender.

I didn't turn around to see Elijah's look of shock, but I could feel it. He recovered quickly though. "Violet, you need me. You're fucked without me," he promised.

"Don't worry, Elijah," I called over my shoulder as I crossed to my car. "You'll get your payment." I opened the door without looking back at him. "I'll be at the Radiant Mansion. You know, the place where you kidnapped a child. I suggest you meet me there."

I started the car with a furious roar of the engine. The chorus of *Whore* by In This Moment began to blast through the dark tunnel, and I sped off in a wake of dust.

*** 

I didn't have to wait long to see Elijah. He showed up to the Radiant Court bright and early the next day.

I had spent the night in my quarters, discreetly slipping in, without anyone noticing my return. It was a chance to rest, to wash, and to change. I fought the urge to wear more fighting gear, and instead I selected a gray, floor length wrap dress with short sleeves. The last thing I wanted to do was call unnecessary attention to myself.

Although the delicate belt of the dress was cinched around my waist, the rest of the fabric was flowy, allowing me to carry various concealed weapons. Even the long metal pins securing my hair in a low bun were specifically selected for their potential use as daggers.

I had had a rude awakening. I would not be caught off guard again.

But as I rounded the first story hall in the main wing of the Radiant mansion, I came to an abrupt stop. Walking down the other end, straight towards me, was Elijah.

And the goddamn bastard looked handsome as hell. He was wearing a button up shirt tucked into slacks, and the cut of his clothes did a perfect job complementing his frame. His hair was effortlessly combed off his face. Yet, he also managed to maintain a certain rugged quality about himself with the distressed brown leather boots he wore.

Just as suddenly as I stopped, I began walking again. I bit down on my cheek, and I tilted my chin up into the air. Neither of us spoke as we made our way towards one another.

We ended up in front of the door to my mother's office at the same time. I glared up at Elijah. He gave me a wolf's smile, before gesturing for me to enter first. I narrowed my eyes at him.

After knocking on the door, I heard my mother's stern voice. "You may enter, Elijah."

I pushed the door open. The sunlight was pouring through the floor to ceiling windows, glinting off my mother's long blonde hair as if microscopic little mirrors had been sprinkled through her strands. Her back was turned to us while she rummaged through books on one of the office shelves.

"I do hope—" she stopped mid-sentence as she turned around. "Violet!" Her eyes immediately flashed to Elijah. "You found her."

"No," I corrected right away. "He did not."

My mother began to cross to us. "What happened? Are you unharmed?"

I let out a weary sigh. "I'm fine, mother."

Although she kept her face a calm mask, my mother pulled her shoulders back. I knew her well enough to know it was her equivalent to an emotional outburst.

I gave a nod. "I have my memories back," I confirmed, not wanting to draw things out any longer than necessary.

I swung my head in Elijah's direction. "What's he doing here?"

"Violet," my mother chastised.

"Trust me, mother. We are beyond courtly manners at this point." I shot Elijah my best bitch face.

My mother politely ignored the animosity between us and took each of my hands in her own. She looked at me for a moment before pulling me in for an embrace. I tried to hold back the Darkness, not wanting her to feel that part of me.

When she pulled away, she gave a single nod and I knew that meant the feelings portion of this reunion was over. It was now time for business.

I didn't want to give my mother a chance to put any defenses in place. She was incredibly shrewd and intelligent. She could be diplomatic and evasive while offering warmth and reassurance. I needed to catch her off guard if I wanted to know the truth.

"I found Zagan," I said without emotion. "Did you know he was the heir to the Shadow throne? Did you know Elijah was the one who took him?"

My mother stumbled backwards, catching herself on the edge of the desk. The sunlight pouring in through the windows flickered for

69

a moment, casting a dull gray hue throughout the room, before brightening once again.

After closing her eyes and taking a deep breath, she directed her gaze at me. "That's not possible, Violet." Although she tried for censure, her voice was reedy and thin.

"Did you know," I persisted. "Did you know that he was half Shadow? That he was the heir?"

My mother began to get angry at the defiance. She straightened and fought to find her voice. "That is not possible. He was the Prism. He was not half Shadow. You speak about things which you do not know."

"Ask his abductor," I countered, swinging my head in Elijah's direction.

My mother's eyes flashed to him, and Elijah gave a single nod. Without saying a word, she clutched the desk and began to cross around it before collapsing in the chair. She picked up a glass of water and took a sip. A tremor ran through her hand as she did.

When she placed the glass back on the desk, her eyes were wide open pools of sadness. "You took him?" she asked Elijah.

He nodded again.

"Why?"

"He would one day become a monster. Would you have wanted that for your daughter? For your people?"

"How could you possibly know that? What proof of it could you have had?"

"The Contessa. She told me the command which would reveal the mark. It was there. I saw it for myself. There was no doubt it was him. I did what had to be done."

My mother closed her eyes and shook her head. "It's impossible," she whispered. "An Archangel delivered him to me. He was the

70

male Prism. I accepted responsibility of him. I was charged with keeping him safe."

Elijah's words suddenly sunk in, and my mother's eyes snapped open. She stood from her chair leaning her hands on her desk. "*The Contessa?*" she shot at him. Her words turned deadly. "What did you do with him?"

Meeting her square in the eye, Elijah replied, "I handed him over to her."

Electricity buzzed across my skin. My mother began to shake, her eyes sparking. And the rattle of clinking glass and metal from objects around the room filled the silence.

I became fearful that my mother might actually try to kill Elijah.

But before her anger could take form, a large Archangel appeared in the middle of the room. He was huge with short brown hair and a white ceremonial robe. White light radiated from him, and two wings of light framed his back. He clutched a sword of fire in his hands.

I had seen him on two previous occasions: once here in the parlor when he had appeared to enforce Council rule, and once when he accompanied our small group to England when I originally left to enter into the Shadow Court. All I knew about him was that he was an Archangel and that his name was Cord.

His baritone, bell-like voice rang through the room. And while the words he spoke held power, they were emotionless. "Violet Adriel Archer, for your blatant disregard of Council rule, you have been sentenced to immediate death. Have you any last words?"

My mouth actually hung open at that. It was such an abrupt, absurd declaration, I didn't believe him. "Is this a joke?" I asked, confused.

He gave a single, serious nod. "Your words will be noted in the Council records." Then without any further explanation, he took a step towards me and raised his sword.

"Stop!" my mother commanded. She threw her hand out in his direction, and a pulse of energy rippled through the air. However, Cord stepped through the current, unaffected by it.

"I demand you cease!" she shouted, her words booming through the room. There was a strong compulsion to them, I could feel it in my bones, but still Cord continued.

Elijah stepped in front of me and shoved me back. At the same time, my mother placed her hands together and murmured some words. When she separated her palms, a sword appeared within them. It was long and slender, and it shone with an incredible light.

With incalculable speed, she struck, slicing through Cord's robe and landing a blow along his ribs. The instant my mother pulled the sword back, gold liquid began to seep from the wound.

Cord looked down, shocked at what he saw. It was the first time I had seen emotion splayed across his face. He realized he had no choice but to engage with my mother, and he redirected his focus on blocking the second blow which was already arcing towards him.

The two swords met with a hiss. The fire from Cord's licked the air, while the light from my mother's intensified in an almost blinding display.

"*Mom?*" I asked. I was dumbfounded. I wasn't entirely sure that what I was witnessing was real. Her navy dress floated around her as she spun to avoid a blow, and her sparkling hair flew across her shoulders with her motions.

I had never seen her do anything remotely close to this. She was fighting an Archangel. And holding her ground.

Elijah grabbed me and began to wrap his arms around me. "You have to get out of here," he urged.

I yanked free from him, knowing he was about to pulse out. "No! We have to help her!" I countered.

"She's doing this for you, you idiot! She's giving you a running chance!"

I was about to tell Elijah to pulse to my weapons closet and bring back a sword, but Cord struck at my mother's wrist and the blow made contact. My mother's sword dropped to the ground. Once it hit the floor a bright pulse of light lit the room, and then the sword disappeared.

She was defenseless.

Before any other action could be taken, I felt a flood of Darkness surround me. It was cold and fluid, stretching and coiling around my skin. It hadn't even been a conscious choice on my part. Somehow the Darkness just became. And was.

In a motion faster than I was capable, I was upon the fiery sword. I grabbed the blade in my hands, which were now cloaked in shadows, and I began to pull. The fire under my palms sputtered and hissed. The flames there were consumed by the inky swirls.

Cord was strong. He fought to regain control of his weapon. Some instinctual pull directed me, and I jabbed the open wound on his ribs with my finger. The gold liquid trickling there morphed into black sludge. Cord fell to his knees, gritting his teeth. Somewhere under all the chaos and silent screams that churned through me, I found a respect for his ability to withhold his bellow of pain.

I redoubled my effort on his sword, grabbing it with both hands once again, trying to release more cold and Darkness upon it. It was working. The flames turned black all along the center. I squeezed harder and they spread down to the tip and handle. Finally they began to lick Cord's hand where he grasped the sword.

Still, he did not let go, and black veins began to branch through his hand. This time he did let out a roar of agony through his clenched teeth. And that was the moment when I planted my foot on his chest and pushed him back as hard as I could while pulling free the sword.

Cord tumbled, sprawling on his back. I didn't hesitate. I plunged his sword, which was now consumed by black flames, into his chest. His body instantly spasmed, and his eyes rolled back in his head. I withdrew the sword, and black sludge poured from the wound.

I stood over his body for a moment. I was lost in a cold, dark fog. All I could see were shadows roiling around me. But somewhere I thought I could hear something familiar. It was...*my name*.

I tried to look around, but I couldn't see anything other than Cord's body and all the Darkness. I fought to pull it back, to contain the evil. But it screeched and wailed, unwilling to be caged. Somewhere deep inside, I found Light. I pulled on it battling for a balance between the two. There was a source nearby. Light that was bright and strong. Stronger still because I could connect to it. It enhanced my own.

I pulled on the source and finally my vision cleared. The howls and wails in my head were silenced. And all was quiet.

I looked up to see my mother and Elijah staring at me. And in that instant, I could see the horror and revulsion on their faces. But before they could say anything, three whomps sounded outside my mother's office.

Her eyes flashed in the direction of the sound. "Archangels," she breathed. She had a door in her office which led to a private solarium. She headed straight for it. "This way!"

I hesitated, staring at Cord's body. I was shocked at what I had done. I didn't know if he was dead or alive. I had to do something to help him.

But Elijah grabbed my arm and dragged me after my mother. We crossed into the solarium. Only, as we walked into the bright light shining down from the glass ceiling, we seamlessly transitioned into a small grove. And I knew without a doubt we had left the Radiant Court.

My mother's solarium was gone. Orange trees surrounded us, sunlight dappling through their leaves. We were suddenly immersed in a peaceful afternoon. Bees flew in lazy loops around the orange blossoms and somewhere in the distance I could hear a waterfall.

I looked towards the sound of the falls, and through an opening in the trees, I saw a tower surging up into the blue sky, cleaved straight down the middle. One side alabaster, the other onyx.

*We had entered Aleece.*

# CHAPTER 7

ARE YOU INSANE?! Violet can't be here. We just discovered the council wants her dead." Elijah lunged for me and grabbed my arm.

"Wait!" my mother commanded. She was making small motions in the air all around the little grove.

Elijah ran his hand through his hair, clearly frustrated, but he did not attempt to pulse us out.

After a final symbol, my mother turned, crossing her arms over her midsection. "We have time here. I've closed off the grove. They won't be able to find us."

"How are we even here?" I asked. "I've been in your solarium before, it never acted as a Threshold."

My mother shook her head. "It doesn't matter."

"It would be good to know, mom," I insisted. "What if we need to use it again? What if we need to get back?"

Her lips pinched and then she replied, "Before it was my office, it was your father's. He needed an access point, what with his involvement here. The solarium is accessible to Aleece only by him."

I threw my hands up and glanced around the grove. "He's not here."

My mother cleared her throat. "If we have been together, *maritally*, within a certain window of time, then I am also able to access the Threshold."

It took a moment for her words to sink in. But once they did, I took a step back. "Oh. My. God. That is disgusting!"

"Violet!" my mother snapped. "There are larger issues to discuss! We do not have much time."

I nodded, agreeing with my mother—but also trying to shake that information out of my head.

My mother took a deep breath, and then she almost seemed to grow an inch or two. Her hair shone beneath the beams of light filtering through the orange trees, and her spine was ramrod straight. Her voice rang with authority. "The first thing we need to do is get you somewhere safe, somewhere the Angela cannot reach you, while I sort this out with the Council."

She looked back and forth between us, and I knew she was rapidly selecting and discarding options.

Elijah tightened his hold on me. "I'll take her to my cabin. You can do whatever you've done here. Ward it."

I twisted my arm free. "Absolutely not," I snapped.

"This is temporary," my mother explained. "These spells will not last long. She is the Prism." My mother looked at Elijah and seemed exasperated. "You both are. The power of your energy is massive. You both share the very essence of the Angela. It is so easy for them to find. And I am using the power of my own Light to try and block you. It will not last. It is not an effective spell. You need something darker to hide behind, something that will balance the intensity of your energy."

"What about the tunnels?" I tried. "They can't pulse into them, right?"

"They can still sense you there, and find you," my mother countered.

My mother and Elijah both began speaking.

"There is a—"

"Maybe she can—"

But I cut them both off. "I have a place."

"Absolutely not—"

"No—"

They shot each other an annoyed look. But my mother was the one to persevere.

"Violet, you cannot go back there. You are in grave danger. It is a miracle you survived what you went through."

"I'll be safe there, mom. Killian said it was impossible for Giddeon to get a lock on me when I was there—"

"And look what happened to you!" She flung one hand at me while keeping the other cradled against her midsection, and I knew she wanted to shake some sense into me.

"I did this to myself!" I shot back. "I willingly gave up my Light."

My mother looked at me like I'd grown a second head. "That is not possible."

I took a deep breath. "Look, it would take a long time for me to go into it all, but for some reason that woman who calls herself The Contessa wanted my Light. And she didn't want to kill me for it. She wanted me to release it. Somehow, I did.

"But the Dark Manor is warded against her." At least, there was a chance it still was. "And the Angela won't be able to find me there. Plus, I need to return. Zagan is…unwell. He needs my help."

I turned to Elijah. "Before I go, I need to know what the *tanjear* is." My voice took on an accusatory tone. "I heard you talking on the phone. I know it was about The Contessa. I need to know how to stop her."

"This is idiotic," Elijah snarled. "You are not going to be able to take down The Contessa. You need to get somewhere safe." He turned to my mother and jerked his head in my direction. "Where are you going to put her?"

My mother's eyes narrowed on Elijah. "You know of a way to stop The Contessa?"

Elijah clenched his jaw before rubbing the back of his neck. After a long pause he said, "Not exactly."

"Meaning?!" my mother demanded.

"I know there is a way to stop her. To end her. Something called the *tanjear*. But I don't know what it is."

"What?!" I cried. "I need to know how to fight her! On the phone you said—"

"It was a bluff," Elijah growled.

"Where did you hear about it?" I countered. "Who knows about it?" I didn't care that my voice was saturated with desperation. I needed this information.

"It was something I heard from my parents. When I was a child. And they're dead."

My mother didn't seem to be listening to him. "The Gwarlock," she murmured. And the words sent a chill down my spine.

Elijah must have felt the unease because he shifted closer to me. "What?" he asked.

My mother exhaled again, pressing her arms tighter to her body. "He is the god of death. He is known by many names throughout the world. But those from the beginning of time know him as the Gwarlock. And he, above all, would know how to bring death upon her."

I opened my mouth, about to speak, but my mother stopped me. "Listen!" Her voice was stern, almost amplified. I noticed sweat beading her forehead. "Time is running out," she announced.

"Violet. I have a place you will be safe. A place the Council cannot reach you. However, there is a price for such salvation. And should you choose the asylum I offer, it is possible you might never have the chance to return to this world."

Her forehead creased as she looked at me. "I believe it is the safest option for you at this point. The most secure option. But it is not a choice I can make for you. And although I desire your safety above all else, I believe you should know the full truth of the matter."

She paused then, waiting for my reply, and I did not hesitate in answering her. "I thank you, mother, for the offering. But I feel I must return to the Shadow Court."

"I respect your wishes, daughter. But you cannot possibly travel there safely. The Angela will be upon you before I am able to resolve this issue with the Council."

I glared at Elijah. "Elijah can pulse. He can take me."

Elijah crossed his arms over his chest. "You're out of your goddamn mind. I'm not taking you there."

"Either you can take me, or I will go on my own."

He snarled at me before looking away, and I knew I had procured my ticket back to the Dark Manor.

My mother's lips thinned. It was obvious there were things she wanted to ask—things she wanted to say—that we just didn't have time for.

Instead, she accepted what was. "Very well. The Threshold to depart Aleece is just beyond that hill. You will need to pull back on your Light. Hide it deep inside until you are through. Then you must immediately pulse to the Dark Manor. And stay there until I have this all sorted out. Stay away from The Contessa. Stay away from the Angela. And Violet, please, stay in contact with me."

She abruptly turned to Elijah. "If you wish to learn the truth of this *tanjear*, you will visit the Gwarlock. You should be safe from the Angela. He resides in the Realm of Lost Souls. The Archangels will not be able to locate you through the mist there.

"See to it that Violet reaches her destination safely. Then find a Vestibule and look for a door with a cross that has a loop at the top. It is the ankh. It will take you to the Gwarlock.

"Be forewarned. There will be a steep price to pay for the information he can provide. And take care not to become lost. The mist will snuff out your Light. You must not lose your way. You must not let the hunger devour you."

She closed her eyes for a moment and inhaled before gazing at me one last time. "Go now. It is time."

I stepped up to my mother and hugged her. She only used one arm to embrace me, keeping the other pressed to her stomach. And when I squeezed myself against her, she jerked. Reaching down, I pulled her arm free to inspect it. And I gasped.

"Mom, your arm!" There was a deep gash at her wrist. The wound wasn't bleeding because it seemed to have cauterized. The skin there was severely burned.

She grimaced. "I will be fine."

81

"What was that back there?" I asked her. "I've never seen you do anything like that. I had no idea…"

My mother smiled, and there was something in her face—something that I couldn't pinpoint. "I have lived a very long time, Violet," she said simply. "I have lived my own story, long before yours ever began."

"You never told me . . . "

She placed her hand on my cheek. "It is a story for another time." Then she pushed my hair behind my shoulder and leaned her face into mine. "Go now and take Elijah's help. He is untrustworthy and I will see to it that he atones for his sins, but I believe he will keep you safe above all else."

"I don't need him," I replied, resenting the implication that I did. "I am more capable than you could possibly imagine."

My mother waved a dismissive hand in the air. "The fighting? My dear, I know just how skilled you are."

"But…" I interjected. It was impossible. She couldn't know.

"I am the one who selected General Anderson to train you," my mother said gently. "You are the Prism, Violet. You are a warrior. You are destined to become an Archangel. It is at the core of your being.

"I have always known what you are capable of. What you would one day become." She looked as though she regretted her next words. "All of this is just the beginning for you."

I opened my mouth, and my mother cut me off. "I had my reasons for not telling you. I was charged with your safety. I failed Zagan when he was just a child. I was not going to allow myself to fail you as well. It was for your own protection that I did not tell you. I wanted to do my best to try and provide you with some semblance of a peaceful childhood, before you would have to face your destiny."

My mother gave my hand a squeeze. "You must go now. It has begun."

There was one more thing I had to know before leaving. "Back there. What about? Did I . . . ? Will he . . . ?"

My mother met my eye with conviction. "Cord will be fine. You defended yourself. He will heal. Everything will be sorted out." She took a step back from me. "You have to go now," she insisted. "Pull back on your Light. Think of it as holding your breath. Go to the Vestibule. Leave Aleece now. *Run.*"

And I did as my mother told me.

As I pulled back on my Light, I could feel the atmosphere around us change. The grove no longer felt like a secluded, secret place, and I suddenly felt very exposed. The wards had dropped.

My mother gave a final nod, and her sparkling ocean eyes were damp. I knew she thought there was a good chance it would be the last time she ever saw me. I was determined to prove her wrong.

I turned to head for the Vestibule, and Elijah tried to hold on to me as we ran. I sped up to get in front of him, flinging his hand from my arm.

I cursed the vivid green grass as we ran and the puffy white clouds in the perfectly blue sky. I was in the most tranquil, picturesque setting, and yet I was running for my life. It was just too inane—too incongruous.

Once we reached the stone structure, I pushed on the imposing double doors and we entered the cavernous Vestibule. The doors slid shut behind us, blocking out the sunlight. The small pulsing star high above in the middle of the dome lit the space with a divine light. And I caught my breath at the wonder of the place.

83

There were so many doors to choose from, lining the circular wall. I had never known these Vestibules existed before Elijah had taken me through.

*My mother had kept too much from me.*

Elijah snatched my hand. When I tried to pull it away, he held on tighter, yanking me into him. He glared down at me. "Do you want me to take you to the Dark Manor or not?"

I tried to ignore him. I tried to keep a tight leash on my Light. But I felt a flare at our contact. "Which door?" I demanded.

Elijah pulled me towards one and placed his hand on the wood. At the flare of Light beneath his palm, we crossed through, walking down the narrow hallway and out through the door at the other end.

We entered an empty little one room cabin. And the door through which we had emerged was gone. I recognized the cabin immediately as the one I had fled to with Elijah after the Radiant gala.

I spun towards him. "Take us to the southern Shadow territory," I insisted. "Now."

Elijah grabbed me, staring down at me, and his nostrils flared. I quieted for a moment, and a chill ran down my spine at the next words he spoke.

"Before I take you anywhere, princess...*I'm collecting my payment.*"

# CHAPTER 8

"LET GO OF ME!"

I shoved against Elijah's chest, but it was pointless. He overpowered me—his arms banded around my back.

"What are you doing?! We have to go!" I squirmed against him, trying to find a chance to twist free.

"Quit your yammering. Can't you just be quiet for once? You ruin everything." He rubbed against me, leaning his head down, and I could feel his hot breath on my neck. It sent an ache through me.

I looked up into his sparking eyes. "You're disgusting."

He smiled—a wolf's smile. "I like your dirty talk."

I pushed myself into him, feeling every hard ridge and plane. I grabbed his arms, sinking my nails into his triceps. "Let me go. They're going to find us. I can't..." I took a breath, desperately trying to hold back, to avoid the connection. I couldn't stop the heat that was spreading through my chest. "We have to leave."

He leaned into me. "This is our way out, princess." His voice rumbled in my ear. "You want me to get you out of here? You have to hold on."

I tried to turn away from him, and my nose rubbed the notch at the bottom of his neck. "Fine," I breathed. "Let's go."

I felt his chest expand at the contact and he squeezed me tighter, fighting a shudder. His teeth were against my ear. "It takes a minute."

I rubbed my hips against him, unable to stop myself. "It does not." My words were more of a moan than the firm rebuttal I had intended. "You're doing this on purpose."

I tried to hold on to my self-control. "They're going to come for us."

"I want you to come for me."

I turned my face into his neck again. "Ugh, that is so lame." And it *really* was, but somehow his voice shot straight to my center, and I liked it. I wanted to hear him say it again. My hips pressed into him a second time.

I couldn't take any more. I couldn't hold back the Light. The connection. I was about to explode. I needed to pull on the Dark energy I carried. But before I could, Elijah grabbed my chin and forced me to look at him. "Don't," he growled.

The sparks in his eyes were blazing and I knew he couldn't hold back any longer, himself. "Think about where you want to go," he instructed.

I pictured the alley behind the boarded-up pub, The Screaming Banshee, in the Shadow village. And then Elijah placed his mouth over my own. He kissed me. Taking what he wanted. His energy came crashing through me causing my heart to beat faster and an aching drumming between my thighs.

87

I erupted, unable to hold back any longer, feeling the connection that bound us pulling me closer to him, feeling a hot rush of Light course through me.

And in the instant before we disappeared, I felt a presence. Out of the corner of my eye, I saw an illuminated figure appear.

Giddeon.

In his hands was a fiery sword. His face was grim. I knew why he'd come.

But he did not strike immediately. And in that moment of hesitation, we slipped away. We were gone.

I found myself pressed against a wall in a little dark alley. We had made it to the Shadow village.

Elijah covered me with his big body. He had his hand in my hair, and he was pulling my head to the side as he covered my neck with his mouth. The dark strands came spilling free from the loose bun I'd worn. His other hand was on my hip, squeezing—causing jolts of electricity to charge through me.

He began to gather the hem of my dress, pulling it up my legs. I opened my eyes, leaning my head back against the brick, about to reach my hands beneath his shirt, needing to feel his skin. And then I saw the crescent moon overhead in the night sky.

I felt a pang.

"Stop," I whispered.

Elijah kept gathering the fabric of my dress. "Stop," I repeated.

"We both know you don't mean that," he growled.

I curled my fingers into a fist and launched it at Elijah's handsome face. His head whipped to the side. After a moment, he spat blood. When he finally turned back to me, his eyes blazed.

I gasped for breath. "You did all of that back there on purpose!" I accused. "You could have pulsed us out right away!"

A mixture of rage and incredulity tightened his features. "Of course, I did!" he thundered. "What do you think? That I'm some noble hero? That I want nothing in return?"

He grabbed my shoulders. "How do I make this any clearer to you? You can't really be this dense. You belong with me." He tightened his grip. "It's all right here. What greater proof do you want?" Frustration dripped from his every word. "I can help you, you stupid, beautiful woman!"

I had a book's worth of thoughts to throw back at him. But I knew it wouldn't do any good.

I tried for calm. For reason. "Look. We're here. You got us here. Thank you." I glanced around the alley, grateful we were alone. "There's an inn. Let's just get a room, and we can figure out the next step."

I subtly stepped back from Elijah, out of his reach, and he looked around as well. "An inn? Why aren't we at the Dark Manor?"

"Let's just get inside," I reiterated. "It isn't safe out here. The Angela won't be able to find us in this village. At least, they couldn't when I was here before. But there are other...*things*." As if to underscore my warning, an icy gust of wind funneled through the alley, sending my hair flying around my shoulders, and goose bumps broke out across my arms.

Elijah rubbed his own arm and eyed the thin dress I wore. Then he looked at me and nodded. "Inside," he agreed.

I began to make my way towards the front of the inn, but I stopped after a few feet. I looked around a second time, and then I glanced at our clothes.

We were too conspicuous. We needed anonymity. I didn't want to walk into the lodge and stand out. There were too many unknowns.

89

"Change of plans," I murmured. When we made it out of the alley, I didn't turn for the front door of the inn. Instead I began to cross the cobblestone street, trying to avoid the flickering light from the gas lanterns—staying to the shadows.

"Where the fuck are we going?" Elijah asked, clearly unhappy but keeping his voice low.

I eyed the small trailer up ahead. "We're going to see a witch."

\*\*\*

"You're late." The door to the camper swung open as we approached. Belcalis stood in the entryway tapping her foot. "Come on, I don't got all night."

She turned back to the little dining table just inside, not waiting to see if we were following. The glow of the small chandelier above the tiny eating nook offered the promise of warmth from the biting wind, and I didn't hesitate to enter.

I was surprised Elijah didn't raise any objections either. He walked right into the refurbished trailer, stooping in the tight space.

Belcalis began speaking in her Bronx accent with her back to us, grabbing some items on the dining table. "I have the two cloaks. The sizing should—"

She turned around to face us, and her eyes traveled up Elijah's frame. "Oh my gawd." She gave her hair—which was blond and stick straight today—a pat and rolled her tongue over the front of her top teeth. Then she smoothed her skin tight, bright red suit jacket. Since she didn't wear a shirt under her jacket, the swell of her breasts strained against the lapels, vigorously testing the stability of her top button.

"Seeing you in the future's just not the same as seeing you up close and personal. Umm!" She placed one of her hands on his arm and began stroking it.

I cleared my throat. "Ah, Belcalis? What's going on?"

"Oh, I think something is definitely going on right here," she murmured. "What do you say, handsome? You think you could handle two at once?"

"Belcalis!"

She rolled her eyes and flung her head back in a dramatic gesture before placing a hand on her hip and popping it to the side. "Is she always such a pain in the ass?" she asked Elijah.

"Always," Elijah answered, without pause.

Belcalis gave an audible sigh and turned back to the little table before giving a tsk and mumbling under her breath. "I wouldn't want to have a threesome with her anyway. Probably be complaining the whole time."

Elijah actually laughed out loud.

I gave a huff. "Belcalis, what is this all about?" I pressed.

She turned and handed us each a long black cloak. "Just me saving your tiny butt, is all," she directed at me. Then she held her hand up for Elijah. "Belcalis, Time Mage and general witch practitioner. Enchanté."

At that, Elijah took her hand in his. I drew in a breath, fighting the immediate possession I felt towards him. Elijah clearly picked up on the rush of jealousy, and he looked at me with a satisfied smile.

Belcalis took a key from the table. "Um-kay!" she chirped. "Here's what happened. I was glimpsing around in time—"

She stopped herself and eyed us. "For very important reasons," she added, as if we were about to scold her. "And I saw you would be needing my services tonight. So I got everything all prepared for

91

you. You got your cloaks now, and here's the room key for you," she said, handing Elijah the key she held.

She turned to me. "For you, I have a horse reserved at the stable. I tried to look ahead as far as I could, and it seems like your path is clear. Except, there was some kinda dark tunnel I couldn't see into. So once there, you're on your own."

She popped her hip again, highlighting the skin-tight red pants that matched her suit jacket. "You should know the authorities were here looking for you. And even though I saw you'd be coming back, I didn't tell 'em nothing."

"Hold on," Elijah interjected. "She's not going anywhere without me."

Belcalis pursed her lips and looked at me. "Ohh! You didn't tell 'im?" She saddled back up to Elijah and mumbled under her breath. "You should ditch her tiny ass, anyway."

Then she tried to lean around and eye my butt. "There's not enough to grab onto," she concluded before returning her focus to Elijah. "I'd spend the night with you. The *whole* night."

While she had been flirty with him to an exaggerated degree, Belcalis's voice turned quiet with her next words. "Honestly, baby, she's not for you."

But the moment she had made her point, she resumed her over-the-top advances. Giving her butt a pop, she glanced over her shoulder explaining, "That's something to hold on to."

And she was right (not about the butt thing, that was debatable). But I had planned on leaving Elijah at the inn for a few hours while I went to the Dark Manor on my own. I just hadn't wanted him to know that.

I ignored Belcalis and began putting on the cloak she'd provided. Then I tried to reassure Elijah. "I'm going with you to see the—" I

92

realized I didn't know how much to *trust* Belcalis. For some reason I had an inherent belief in her, but for all I knew, she could be aiding The Contessa.

It had been a mistake to come to her for help. I hadn't thought it through. I amended my comment to Elijah. "I'm coming with you." I pulled the generous hood over my head and gestured at the cloak Elijah held. "We should go."

I turned to Belcalis. "How much do we owe you for all this?"

She pursed her lips and shook her head. "I saw when I was poking around that you are going to do something very important for me." She shrugged one shoulder. "Your debt is settled, girl."

Then she stuck her finger in my face. "But I don't want no authorities poking around my place anymore. Got it? I'm trying to lay low."

I glanced around her camper. "What are you doing here anyway?" I asked.

She gave her hair a fluff, and while the action seemed blasé, there was a pained tone to her voice. "We all got somethin' we're hiding from."

"Are you working for The Contessa?" I asked point blank.

"I don' know who that is. And it don't matter. I work for myself."

I wanted to believe her. I just didn't know if I should.

I gave her a nod. "Thank you."

At that, I opened the camper door and stepped out. Once outside, I turned back to assure Belcalis that I'd stop Maxim and his men from bothering her anymore. But instead I ground my teeth at what I saw.

Elijah gave a twitch as he stepped down from the trailer, and he smiled at Belcalis. She winked and gave her head a toss to the side.

The bitch had just grabbed his ass.

# CHAPTER 9

**Y**OU HAVE NO RIGHT TO TRY AND CONTROL
ME—"
        "Save your self-righteous bullshit, princess. It's
getting old fast."

"What you are doing is inexcusable—"

"Are you really trying to tell me that you thought riding a fucking horse through Shadow territory, while the Council has sent an army of Archangels after you and that evil bitch wants you dead, was a good idea? And I don't know what the fuck you did to your nightwalker friend. You haven't shared if he's still after you, or what the hell is going on."

I loathed him. Because he was right. Because he was being logical and reasonable.

But superseding logic and reason was the need I had to get to the Dark Manor. To see if...

After hearing what Belcalis had to say, though, Elijah was not going to lose sight of me. He knew I was a flight risk.

From the moment we'd left the witch's trailer, he'd kept an iron grip on my hand. I'd tried to yank it free, but he was not budging. The last thing I wanted to do was cause a scene. So, we'd entered the inn with our cowls drawn, hand in unwelcome hand.

A fire roared within the massive stone hearth, illuminating the great hall. Candles also sat on tables and up in the exposed rafters, setting the room aglow. Just as before, loaves of bread and skewers of vegetables baked on racks.

Tonight the packed hall was filled with guests socializing, drinking, and eating. There was even a musician playing a lute, and the conversations and laughter were underscored by a delicate melody.

But I knew the cozy, crowded setting did not guarantee safety. I took in the scene from beneath my hood as I trailed behind Elijah, doing my best to be nothing more than a passing shadow.

Once we'd made our way to the dimly lit second floor, Elijah headed straight for the room on the end, matching the room number on the key he carried, and we entered without a sound.

A fire had already been burning in the small hearth, casting the room in firelight. And the muffled sounds of the merriment below created a continual hum of noise within the simple, medieval looking space.

Elijah had discarded his cloak, tossing it onto the bed. And now he stood with his legs apart and arms crossed, taking up entirely too much space in the little room.

I tossed my hood back and tried to wilt Elijah with my stare. Pouring all the contempt I held for him into the air around me, wanting him to know how egregious I found his actions to be.

He gave an unconcerned shrug at the energy permeating the room. "You know what, princess?" He was purposefully calling me that, trying to antagonize me. "I don't give a fuck if you hate me for the rest of eternity. I'm keeping you alive. In spite of the fact that you're determined to make it the most difficult task any immortal has ever had to undertake."

Not giving him the satisfaction of a retort, I looked around at the wood frame bed, exposed beams, glass lanterns, and stone wall. "It isn't safe here. We shouldn't stay. We need to get to a Vestibule."

Elijah walked up to me. He towered over me, invading my space with his big body. He paused, searching my eyes. He spoke his next words with deliberate slowness. "Sometimes I think you are bat-shit crazy."

"Then leave me the hell alone," I snapped back.

He leaned down and gave me a predatory smile. "I didn't say I didn't like it." He pulled back just a fraction and his face grew serious. "But if the Angela can't find you at the Dark Manor and it's warded against that evil bitch, then that's where I'm taking you. You're not going alone. I'll pulse you there. And I don't know what you're talking about with a Vestibule."

"I'm going with you to see the Gwarlock. I just need to stop at the Dark Manor first," I explained.

"Well at least we agree on something. We're going to the Dark Man—"

"No!"

My protest was too loud for the small dark room. I glanced out the window, feeling exposed. At the same time, I strained to hear if it had interrupted the chattering below.

I took a deep breath, trying to regain my composure. I couldn't allow Elijah there. It would be…I didn't even know. Profane. Insulting. Wrong. It was not a place he could enter. *Ever.*

"What I mean is, you can't. There are wards in place. This is as close as you can get." I didn't know if that was actually true, but it seemed plausible.

Elijah tilted his chin and narrowed his eyes at me. His voice was quiet. "What happened there?"

I took a few steps back until I reached the door, and I felt myself melt against it as I closed my eyes. What could I say to that?

At his words, my time at the manor flashed before my eyes. It all came rushing over me. I couldn't help it. Couldn't stop it. And I fought a tremor.

I tried to shove it all back. Hide it. I did not want Elijah to have any part of it. But at the flood of memories I felt an icy pulse on the skin over my chest. I could feel the mark there—the invisible outline of three crescent moons. And although I did not pull aside my dress to see, I had a strong suspicion that my skin shimmered there.

I grabbed the fabric above my chest, trying to stop the physical response I was having. My eyes flashed open. It was too late.

Elijah inhaled, growing in size, dominating the room with his presence. Energy crackled, and the fire licked the air. I could feel a powerful charge all around me, and I knew slews of lightning were about to erupt in the street outside.

His eyes burned with golden sparks. His jaw was clenched, and his nostrils flared. He came for me then. With two long strides, he covered my body with his own, pressing me against the door.

I refused to look at him. I kept my head turned to the side, eyeing the wall.

Elijah's voice was guttural. "You push me too far, princess. You are sending me to the very limits of my self-control. Despite what you might think. I don't want to take anything from you that you are

99

not willing to give. But this," he took a deep breath and his chest expanded, pressing into me, "this is too much."

Elijah dropped his head so that his nose was in my hair, just at my temple. His words were a chilling growl. "You belong with me. To me. If he touched you, I vow here and now that I will tear him limb from limb for the rest of eternity. I will make him beg for death every second of his immortal life. And I will never grant it. He will know only pain and misery for handling you."

Elijah dropped his head lower so that his lips were at my neck while he spoke. "And I will need to spend years covering you until you can no longer remember any touch other than my own."

I desperately tried to control my breathing, to ignore how enticing Elijah smelled. I tried to brush aside the need I had to place my hands under the hem of his shirt and feel his skin, to run my hands over the hard ridges and planes of his abdomen.

The fire which burned so brightly within him beckoned to me, and before I knew it, I saw a violet glow glimmer across the dark wall where I held my gaze.

"Nothing happened," I whispered.

"Lie."

"He's not what you think. He did not and he will not hurt me. He's not a threat."

"He killed Angela to get to you. He is a monster. And he will hurt you too."

"He's not. At least he wasn't. It's because of me. What happened to him...the things he did...it's because of me. He needs my help. I did something to him. Unleashed something in him."

Elijah's fists slammed against the door at the sides of my head. "If you use your mouth to defend him with even one word more, I will give you something much better to do with your lips."

I should have been outraged at his comment, but a shiver ran down my spine. I was afraid he was going to kiss me again. And I was terrified I'd let him. But a knock sounded at the door and I jumped. I had been too wrapped up in Elijah to notice the presence of another just beyond my back.

Elijah's jaw clenched. "Ignore it," he growled.

I patted the wood behind me, searching for the door handle. When I found it, Elijah swore under his breath, but he took a step back from me. I sensed mild Shadow energy, so I opened the door without much hesitation.

First, though, I gestured to Elijah's eyes. He looked unhappy about it, but he closed them, calming himself. When he opened them again, the blazing sparks were gone. Then he grabbed the cloak he'd tossed on the bed and pulled on the hood.

I also adjusted the cowl of my own cloak, pulling the generous fabric as far over my face as possible. Then I sent a flick of my wrist in the direction of the fire to ease the flames down into glowing embers.

"Begging your pardon, ma'am. I'm making my rounds. Will you be needing any extras this evening?" It was the housekeeper.

"No. Thank you," I replied, attempting to shut the door.

"Should you require anything, I'll be passing through again in a bit." She seemed to project the last part of her sentence into the room, trying to take a look at Elijah.

"Thank you. I promise to let you know," I told her. And at that, I did shut the door.

"She thinks you're in trouble," Elijah said removing his cloak once more.

"I know," I answered. "We'll need to leave soon. We're too conspicuous here."

I pulled out the chair at the small table next to the fire and sat, folding down my hood. With another flick of my wrist, I stoked the fire back to life.

Elijah peered out the window and leaned against the sill. He let out an exhale. "Let me take you to the manor, Violet."

"Like I said, you can't. I need to go on my own—"

"That's not happening."

I fought the urge to argue with him. "So the next best option is for me to go with you to see the Gwarlock."

Elijah turned his head from the window to gaze at me. He looked at me a certain way then. I didn't know if it was pity or genuine concern, but whatever it was, it unsettled me.

Even more alarming was the soft tone his voice took. "Violet, I don't think trying to visit this Grandcock—"

"Gwarlock," I corrected.

"—should be our first priority." He turned to face me fully. "We need to find the Oracle."

He searched my face with a pained expression. And although he didn't say any more on the subject, it was clear he was thinking about what I'd done to Cord.

I was ill. Infected. I needed help in purging the Darkness I carried within.

"I'm getting better at controlling it," I tried.

There was no response from Elijah. He just stared at me with that pitying expression.

"Elijah be reasonable. I can't look for the Oracle right now. I can't go back to the Radiant Court or Aleece. The Archangels will come for me. And while they can't find me here, The Contessa can.

"Something happened, before I lost my...memory. And I think she was hurt or injured or something. But whatever happened to her, I don't think it killed her. She's going to be coming for me again.

"You won't be able to accompany me to the Dark Manor—because of the wards. And you won't let me go on my own. At least if I go with you to see the Gwarlock, Giddeon and his crew won't find me. Also, I think it's less likely The Contessa will come for me in another realm. Plus I'll be with you the entire time. It's the best option."

He was quiet for a long moment, but Elijah finally looked at me. His jaw was tight, yet he gave a single nod.

I let out a sigh, glad to have won this battle, but exhausted at the thought of what was ahead.

I placed my elbows on the table in front of me and laid my head in my hands, rubbing my temples. I took my time in speaking again, knowing I was about to stir the pot even more.

"Before we go, though, I want you to tell me about the prophecy."

He ran his hand through his hair. "Which is it, Violet? Are we in mortal peril here or you want to sit and chat?"

"Both."

He walked to the table and pulled out the other chair, sitting across from me. The firelight cast a warm glow over his masculine features and glinted across the highlights of golden blond throughout his hair. I had to look away.

"What was the prophecy you and my mother spoke of? When we were at her cabin?"

"It's part of a prophecy. It's not in its entirety. But your mother believes it is the key component." Elijah's big shoulders rose as he inhaled, and he gave his neck a slight stretch to the side as if burdened by the topic.

103

"When I returned to Court, after you had left for the House of Shadows, I met with your mother. I told her that I'd come for you. She said she'd been expecting me. She said that I had arrived too late. That you had agreed to an arranged marriage with the Dark Court."

The golden flecks in Elijah's eyes intensified. "I was going to come after you. Before I could leave, though, your mother shared something with me; it was a page from the Book of Prophecies."

I couldn't stop the shiver that ran across my shoulders at his words. *My mother had a page from that book.*

"Roughly translated, the prophecy reads: A Prism will come who is made whole. A Prism who shines more brightly than the others. This will be the one who defeats the Darkness.'"

When he paused, as if done with his explanation, I was confused. "What does that have to do with me?"

Elijah cleared his throat and leaned forward, resting his forearms on his legs. "Do you remember what I told you about the Prisms? How the Shadows have been hunting us? Trying to prevent a pair from uniting? There's more to it..."

Elijah reached up and rubbed the back of his neck. He was obviously hesitant to discuss whatever it was he had to say next. He shifted to the edge of his seat, leaning closer to me, and stared at me. "Violet, there has never been a male and female Prism who have lived long enough to solidify the bond. You and I are the first two—*together.*

"The prophecy is about a Prism who is finally whole. Who has finally connected with his or her other half."

"But—" I began to protest.

104

Elijah held up his hand. "There's more. The bond between the Prisms is supposed to strengthen the energy of the race. Somehow it was the best way the Council could arrange such a reinforcement.

"But with the absence of one or both of the Prisms year after year, millennium after millennium, the energy of the Radiants has weakened. And little by little individuals have faded away. One here, another there. Nothing to take note of. But it has accelerated recently. Individuals are beginning to get sick. And people are starting to notice.

"It's similar to what happened to you. Because their Light—their power—is fading, they are becoming ill. Bits of Darkness somehow creep in and take over their system, debilitating and eventually killing them.

"Your mother believes with you and I finally together, we will be able to stop the spread of this Darkness by reinforcing the fabric through which we are all connected. In solidifying the bond, we will in turn defeat the Darkness, preventing it from spreading and destroying...*everyone.*"

I leaned back in my chair and crossed my arms over my chest. "Elijah, if you are making all this up so that I'll sleep with you..."

Elijah didn't move. Didn't speak. Then he stared at me for too long, searching my eyes. He said nothing for some time. Finally he stood. He went to the bed to collect his cloak, and he walked out the door. All without a sound.

The connection I had to him winked off. And I sank back in my chair.

I had hurt him.

I didn't know how to take that. So I sat there thinking about what to do. I felt bad about the comment I'd made. I would apologize.

But in addition to my concern for Elijah, there was the ache I was battling. I was close. So close. I wanted to return to the Dark Manor. I just didn't think there was any way I could stop Elijah from following me.

I looked around the empty room. I was alone. I had convinced Elijah that I wanted to go with him to the Realm of Lost Souls. And I did. But what if…

I stood and crept to the door, opening it just a sliver. I didn't see Elijah through the crack. I opened the door a little wider. Still no.

Elijah had already pulled back from our connection, but to be cautious I also pulled back on my Light, trying my best to lock it away.

I adjusted the hood of my cloak and slipped out of the room. I headed straight for a set of stairs off in the corner. Just as I rounded the wall, about to descend, I crashed in to someone.

The housekeeper.

"Begging your pardon, ma'am," she spluttered. "I was just—"

"It was my fault," I told her. "I'm sorry." I glanced over my shoulder peering down the hallway.

"Are you in trouble?" she asked. "He's down at the bar requesting food to be brought up for you. I thought I'd come check on you."

I looked back at her. "No," I reassured. "I'm not. Really. But I do need you to do something for me. Please. The man I'm with. When he comes back. Can you convey a message for me? Tell him that I will be back in the morning. And to please wait for me."

I stared at the woman. "It's very important. Can you relay the message?"

She didn't look happy about it, but she nodded. I gestured down the stairs. "Can I get to the stable this way?"

She nodded again, wringing her hands on her apron. "Follow me," she whispered. And we scurried down the stairs—with the sounds of merriment from the great hall echoing through the stairway—like two silent shadows in the night.

# CHAPTER 10

IT WAS DARK. And cold. There was no light.

I was alone. I was exposed.

There was no sound. Crickets did not chirp, bushes did not rustle. The twigs beneath my feet did not crunch.

Even the night wind was still. Not a single leaf fluttered.

All I could hear was my breath. For some reason I could not stop the hectic rise and fall of my chest. Nor could I slow the rapid beating of my heart. It was a drum ushering my every step.

I walked. One foot in front of the other through the darkness. Through the tunnel.

The horse I had ridden refused to enter. Stopping at the entrance and going no farther.

The oak trees stood shoulder to shoulder. Their leaves and branches so tightly bound overhead that not one inch of the night sky above was visible.

The air was colder here. And it crept up from the ground to wrap around my bare legs, under my cloak and dress, freezing my skin with its icy touch.

My breathing grew louder in my ears. My heart rate accelerating. I walked faster. Then faster.

I looked to the sides. Behind me. Faster still. Louder breaths. Racing heart.

Something was coming for me.

I broke out in a run. I had to reach the Dark Manor. I would never forgive myself if I didn't.

I had to know if he was there. If he waited for me. If he needed me.

I was gasping for breath. The sound taking up all the space in my ears. My feet pounded the earth with each hammering beat of my heart. Something was not right.

And then I stopped.

I could feel eyes on me.

I was not alone.

The icy chill, wrapping around my legs, scuttled up my spine. The Darkness within me stirred. *Connection.*

Up ahead was the gate. And standing just in front of it was a cloaked figure.

It started towards me.

It wasn't Zagan. Not his energy. It wasn't the Crone. This figure did not hobble. It ran.

I took a step back. I did. I'm ashamed to admit it, but I did. I felt fear.

If the Umbra breathed into me again...The revulsion. The agony. The violation. I began to suffocate at the thought of them.

And then a viciousness rose up from the core of my being. And I let out a roar.

An incredible crack of lightning struck the ground between us. Without hesitating, I sent a pulse of energy towards the figure and began to run for it, unsheathing the dagger strapped to my ankle.

The figure went hurtling back, slamming into the wrought iron gate before collapsing to the ground. But it immediately climbed to its feet and began running towards me again. I sent another pulse of energy. This time though, the figure held out its hand and it was as though the bright hot Light was simply caught and extinguished. Absorbed into a black hole.

We ran for each other. The wind whipped. The hood of my cloak fell from my head. Leaves were swept from the ground, flying into the air. And the oak trees swayed and shook—sending whispers of the wind through their branches.

We were almost upon each other. I launched the dagger and continued with the motion of my hand, reaching down to my other ankle. I retrieved the second dagger strapped there.

I heard the satisfying thunk of steel meeting muscle. The figure let out a bellow and then shouted something in the Dark Tongue.

I went crashing to the ground, skidding and rolling over the dirt before landing on my back. Invisible bindings covered me. I was unable to move.

I felt the Darkness within become caged. I began to pull on my Light about to obliterate that which bound me. But another harsh command fractured the quiet night. And I was unable to use my Light against the forces restraining me.

Then a shadowy form loomed above. Leaning its hooded face over my own. Anger twisting the features I found there. And two large hands reached down to grab me.

111

Hurt and betrayal stabbed at my own heart, as I looked up into Maxim's eyes.

***

I'd made a run for it. And I'd chosen to believe Belcalis.

And now I was being dragged away by another I had thought I could trust. Maxim had dumped me over his shoulder and taken me through the towering gate, trudging up the drive towards the Dark Manor.

Even from a brief upside-down glimpse, the manor was as imposing and eerie as ever. A layer of fog rolled over the ground while the mansion sat even blacker and emptier than before. The moon was hidden behind inky clouds, casting a dim crimson glow along their edges.

I was jostled and my view became consumed by Maxim's cloak. I wanted to curse at him, but whatever command he had bound me with, also prevented me from speaking. It was similar to what Marax had done after the collapse at the Den of Iniquity.

It was difficult to see anything other than Maxim's back, but eventually he threw me off his shoulder, and I bounced onto something padded. My gaze darted around. I was in my room. He had tossed me onto the bed.

Maxim glanced at the fireplace, and he spoke more harsh words. An inky smoke began to creep from the logs there, and then a velvety, dark fire slithered to life. There was no spark. No ignition, No crackle. Just smooth undulating flames. And while the flames were black at the edges, the core of each one was a bloody red, somehow giving off a small amount of heat and light.

Still Maxim looked at me with such anger, saying nothing. And opening the front of his cloak, he pulled out an actual set of manacles which hung from his belt. Blood saturated the front of his white dress shirt.

The soaked fabric clung to his skin, highlighting the hard expanse of his chest and all the ridges down his abdomen. His entire body was tense. The tendons in his hands strained against his skin as he gripped the shackles.

There was no sympathy across his masculine features. His gray eyes seethed with the dark slash of his brow. Standing there in the shadows, he was so obviously powerful.

For the first time, I realized what was buried so deeply beneath his ridged, proper exterior: immense Darkness.

His energy did not pour off him. He was too honed, too strict for that. There was no frenzied, feral chaos.

Maxim maintained a mastery of control over his power. He commanded that which he possessed. And I could see all this because I now held a certain degree of connection to him—a connection to the Darkness.

But I was testing the very limits of his restraint. It was all there in the bunched muscles and flexed hands. For some reason, he was enraged by me. Yet still, he clung to his control.

I looked at Maxim as he snapped the solid bindings on my wrists while I continued to lay there unable to move or speak. I tried to put all the hurt and betrayal I felt in my eyes. I hoped it was enough to make him die a little somewhere inside.

The manacles were just like the ones Marax had used. They reeked of the same Dark energy.

Without emotion, Maxim unclasped my cloak and pushed it off my shoulders before yanking it out from under me. He removed my shoes next, letting each boot drop to the floor. Then he began a thorough search, hitching up my dress around my hips so that only a scrap of fabric covered the tops of my thighs.

He began removing the weapons I had strapped to my legs with quick, deft motions. There was something about his touch, something I hadn't picked up from him before. It sent a shiver up my spine, but I couldn't quite place it. I didn't understand it.

After he finished stripping me of my weapons, he moved his large hands up to grasp my hips over my dress. Squeezing. Finding nothing there his hands roamed up to my waist. And then my rib cage, the tops of his thumbs brushing against my breasts.

Finally he dipped one hand into the V at the neckline of my dress. I tried to still myself, to quiet my breathing. But I couldn't help the rise of my chest. He stopped when he felt the vial I had there. Removing the poison, he flung the small glass into the fire.

Without a word, Maxim turned and left.

I couldn't move. Couldn't speak. I could do nothing other than scan the room with my eyes.

Everything was exactly as I had left it. The only difference was that the floor was clean, having been cleared of the broken glass and debris, and the windows had been repaired.

I tried my hardest to pull on my Light, to blast away at the energy emanating from the chains. But they simply absorbed the power, draining me of it. I could do nothing.

Besides, Maxim returned, heading straight for me. He picked me up in his arms, offering no explanation, and took me to the dining room in my suite. The same type of silent black fire swayed in the hearth there as well, casting a dim red glow. And after setting me down on one of the chairs, he lifted the lid to the silver tray which was perched on the table.

I don't know what I was expecting, but I was surprised to see that a plate of food now sat in front of me. Maxim uttered something harsh and unintelligible. I felt my neck and jaw relax at the command. I opened my mouth about to go off on him, but no words came out. I still couldn't speak. It was infuriating.

So I did the only thing afforded to me. I snapped my teeth at him.

He ignored me. And picking up the fork at the place setting, he stabbed it into the food before holding it up to my mouth.

I pressed my lips together and glared at him. Why the fuck was he trying to feed me?

His grip on the fork tightened. And while he remained in full control, the rage in his eyes amplified, his irises blackening.

With his free hand he grasped my jaw, placing his thumb and index finger along the joints on each side, just below my ears. Then he squeezed and my jaw slackened. He shoved the fork into my mouth as soon as my lips parted.

I could have fought him on it. I could have tried to spit the food out. But I didn't see the point in that. I was at his mercy. If he wanted the food down my throat, it would get there one way or another.

So I chewed the goddamn stuff and swallowed. Again, he forced me to take a bite. And again I chewed and swallowed. Feeling I had done enough, I shook my head when he raised the fork with a third bite of food.

Maxim's nostrils flared and the handle of the fork bent in his grasp. With his free hand, he grabbed my face and squeezed, bruising my cheeks in his grip and forcing my lips apart. He did not let go as he shoved the fork into my mouth again.

When he released my face, he seared me with his gaze. I knew it was a warning. My last chance. I didn't try to defy him again.

He fed me bite by bite, until the last of the food was gone.

The entire time he sat next to me, leaning into me. And I was consumed by his presence. His air of dignity. The venerable power within. I couldn't understand how I had ever overlooked him.

As I stared at him, he swallowed and set his jaw. Then he picked up the linen napkin on the table and dabbed my lips with it. He had to shift closer still to reach the corner of my mouth, watching my lips as he did.

With another swallow, he closed his eyes. When he opened them again, his gaze met mine. The rage was gone. It had lessened bit by bit while I had cooperated with the meal. And now with his face mere inches from mine, he looked at me with something like curiosity.

I stared into his gray eyes, and my lips parted. The connection to him was so strong. I could feel my eyes narrow ever so slightly, as I stared at him, desperately trying to look into him. To figure him out. To understand what he wanted of me.

He opened his mouth as if to speak…and then closed it, changing his mind. Instead, he clenched his jaw once more, and his features hardened. He stood from his chair, and pinching my chin, he forced my head back to look up at him.

With his other hand, he held out his index finger. I knew it was a warning. He wanted my obedience. My cooperation.

I gave away nothing in my eyes, neither confirmation nor negation. I just stared at him. In spite of my defiance, though, he uttered some guttural words, and I suddenly had movement returned to my body.

My first thought was to launch myself at him and rip out his tongue before he could use any more commands against me. But if I was unsuccessful, I was almost guaranteed that he would paralyze me again, and I would lose any chance I had.

It seemed he was trying to work with me to some degree. I would hold out and hope for more freedom, more information, before making any decisions.

Maxim gave one sharp flick with his finger, indicating that he wanted me to stand. He didn't step back, and he didn't take his eyes off me.

Wanting him to see that I was cooperating, I began to rise from the dining chair, inch by inch, keeping my eyes on him the entire time. Maxim had forced me to stand within his space. I still had to crane my head back to look at him. Mere inches separated us.

It felt as though Maxim was trying to force me into submission, trying to assert his dominance. He was forcing me to stand in his space, making a point of our two positions. He was bigger, taller, more powerful. I was helpless standing small and weak before him.

He took a step back and flicked his chin in the direction of the hallway. He clearly wanted me to walk in front of him down the hall, but I found it odd that he was not talking. I had been fooled by a glamour not too long ago…

"Bedroom," he finally said. And it was Maxim's uptight British voice. There was no denying it was him.

I obeyed. I walked down the hall into the bedroom. The evil black fire still slithered in the fireplace.

"Bed," Maxim commanded.

I walked to the bed and sat down on it, facing him.

"Lie back."

I hesitated, wary of the order. I stared at him, and his eyes narrowed, as if daring me to defy him. I wanted to ask him why he was doing this. I hated that I couldn't. I hated that he had taken my voice.

I leaned back, placing my legs on the bed and resting my shoulders against the pillows. I didn't take my eyes off Maxim.

He stood there in the room for a moment, unmoving. I held my breath. There was a part of me that was afraid he would try to join me in the bed. And I knew if that happened, my opinion of him would never recover.

I would fight him if he did. I would wait until he was close then I would use the manacles as a weapon, shoving my wrists into his throat in an attempt to destroy his larynx, before rolling off the bed.

But when he finally moved, Maxim walked past the bed and into the bathroom. I heard water running, and then he was back, making his way to the corner of the room. After removing his cloak, he sat in the oversized armchair which was angled towards the window.

While I could still see Maxim, my view of his torso was blocked because of the wings on the chair. However, based on the movement of his arms, I knew he was unbuttoning his shirt and using a towel to try and clean up all the blood on his chest.

I had to decide what course of action I would take. I knew it was time to face the fact that Maxim was most likely working for The Contessa. Just like Marax.

And I had been such an idiot to ever believe he cared.

Maxim had been nice to me, paid me a compliment, told me a fun little story—and I'd fallen for it all.

I glanced over at him, trying to decide how I was going to extract myself, when I noticed his chin bob. His dabbing motions began to slow, and his head rolled forward again.

I held my breath, uncertain what was happening to him. Perhaps he was succumbing to his wound. Perhaps my dagger had been more effective than I had initially believed.

But I also thought I could hear something. A rhythm. It was almost like a low growling—just a bit different from white noise— that rose and fell within a few close notes. However, it was so similar to the general ambient sounds of the room itself, that it was difficult to detect.

Instead of attempting to discern the presence of a rhythm, I kept my eyes on Maxim while trying not to move my body or call attention to myself. When his head slumped forward for the third time, he didn't pick it up again. And the arm which held the bloody towel sagged at his side.

I didn't move. Not right away. I didn't want to rouse him. I waited. And watched.

When I was certain he was passed out, I told myself it was time. I was about to sit up, when I heard a noise.

Shuffling. Out in the hallway. Someone was coming.

And I knew exactly who it was.

I whipped up in the bed and flung my feet off the mattress, jumping to the floor. I had to make a snap decision.

She appeared in the doorway. Hunched and cloaked in her brown tattered robe with nothing but blackness beneath the hood.

I waited.

I had doubted her before, and I had suffered the consequences. I would give her the benefit of the doubt this time.

She hobbled right up to me and grabbed a hold of the manacles in her arthritic hands. And that little bat snapped them open as if they were a pair of plastic toy handcuffs.

Air filled my lungs with a sharp inhale. I could instantly feel my power again. Both the Light and the Dark.

"Leave," came the Crone's ancient, distant voice on a strangled whisper.

"Is he here?" I asked.

A single shake of her hood. "Go." She wheezed several times before continuing. "Find him." Another long pause. "Lost. Needs you."

Over at the window, Maxim stirred in his chair.

"Leave," the Crone hissed again. Her cloaked arm rose, and she pointed a gnarled finger at Maxim. "Too strong." She was barely getting the words out. "Cannot hold him."

"How do I find Zagan?" I begged.

She turned and began to limp away towards the hallway. Her final command floated back to me on another strangled whisper. "Now!"

I started after her, but when I was just a few feet from the door, Maxim coughed. I glanced over my shoulder, afraid he would use those Dark commands on me again. I would have to charge him and damage his voice box before he could.

But I froze where I was. I could not move. The room around me was lost in a blur as my eyes focused on Maxim. And a chill crept down my spine. I fought to take a breath as my lungs refused to work.

From where I stood, in front of the bedroom door, I had an unobstructed view of Maxim's torso. And even though the room was cloaked in shadows and darkness, there was no mistaking what was on his chest.

His shirt was open. The blood had been wiped away from his skin. And while there was a raw wound running through the center of it, there was no denying the black mark above his heart.

120

Three crescent moons. Intertwined.

I gasped. And Maxim's eyes began to flutter.

The movement was enough to jar me into action. I couldn't stay a moment longer. He was rousing. I no longer wanted to charge him. Now, more than anything, I wanted to get as far away from him as possible.

I needed the Crone to tell me what to do.

I darted out the door, chasing after the decrepit woman, down the hall and into the anteroom of the suite.

But she wasn't there. The double doors out into the main hallway were open. I passed through, making a sharp turn for the grand stairway.

"Wait! Come back!" I whispered. I ran down each flight of stairs, stumbling into the foyer on the ground floor.

The manor had been righted. All the smashed debris cleared. The chandeliers hung from the ceiling as if they'd never crashed to the floor. Rain did not flood the space. And each and every window was intact. The first floor of the manor was pristine.

Even the two imposing doors at the entrance to the mansion were repaired, attached at their hinges. But they now sat open to the breaking dawn outside.

And I stood in the first rays of light. In the gleaming opulence. Totally alone. Wherever the Crone went, whatever she did, she was gone. I could not feel Zagan's presence either. Maxim and I were the only two souls present. And he was coming for me.

I heard a bellow from high above.

Out the doors and down the front drive, I could see the wrought iron gate was open. It was clear the Crone wanted me to go. And while I needed to face Maxim—to collect my weapons and boots—I owed it to the Crone to follow her instructions. I doubted she would be back to bail me out a second time.

I ran for the gate, for the tree tunnel, as the sky continued to brighten. I made it through without incident. Maxim did not come for me. And I began to suspect it was not his injury which had incapacitated him, but the old bat herself who had done something.

I found the horse I had ridden waiting at the end of the tunnel. I knew the Umbra would not come for me in the light of day. The Crone had freed me, and I had been granted safe passage. I headed back to the Shadow village.

I headed back to Elijah, wanting nothing more than to fulfill the Crone's one demand.

Wanting nothing more than to find Zagan.

# CHAPTER 11

THE LITTLE VILLAGE WAS SILENT in the daylight. Shop doors were closed, and shutters were drawn. Not a single individual roamed the cobblestone street.

I returned the horse to the deserted stables and made my way inside, choosing the back stairway. I didn't need to knock on the door to the room. The moment I stepped up to it, Elijah flung it open and pulled me in.

"Get dressed. Now. We have to go."

Something was not right. I knew he was furious with me. I could feel it. But Elijah wasn't even attempting to lecture me on my absence.

"What's wrong?" I asked.

Elijah picked up a jacket from the bed and threw it at me. "Dressed! Now!" he insisted. He unsheathed a sword to inspect it. "There are some men looking for you."

"Who?"

"Two men in suits. I overheard them speaking with the innkeeper when I went downstairs last night. They were asking about a woman who fits your description."

His voice went down a note with anger. "I came back to the room, but you were gone. The housekeeper passed on your message. I was able to pay her for her silence. For the time being at least."

"Are they here now?" I asked.

"I don't think so. They came room to room and then left. But everyone is on the lookout for you now. If anyone saw you return, they could be on their way here as we speak. We need to move."

"Did they see you?"

Elijah slammed the sword he was holding into its sheath and grabbed the clothing on the bed, shoving it into my arms. "What about this do you not understand? Get fucking dressed."

I huffed and glanced around the room. There was no privacy to be had. I looked at Elijah and pursed my lips.

When he realized what I expected of him, he raised a brow. "You can't be serious," he growled.

I stared at him.

His jaw ticked, but he turned, giving me his back. I tossed the clothes onto the bed. "Did they see you?" I repeated as I removed my dress.

"No. I pulsed out and did my best to collect some things for you." He turned his head to eye the wall at his side, sending home his next point. "Just in case you actually came back."

I put on the leather pants first, which had thigh and calf buckles for weapons. Then I picked up the accompanying black jacket. It also buckled up the front with multiple straps that could hold weaponry. On the back was an intricate cutout made from strips of leather which were attached to the rest of the jacket with rose gold rivets and rings.

The circular cutout, which exposed small sections of my skin underneath, was symbolic of a blazing sun.

I knew because it was *my* jacket. My favorite jacket for going out hunting. It had been an incredibly thoughtful and perfect gift from Killian.

I realized I didn't know what had happened to Kil, where he was or what he was doing. The last I'd seen him was the night he brought me my music player at the Radiant mansion when I hadn't remembered who he was.

I was concerned that he would think I was missing and in danger. I doubted he would have had any contact with my mother the previous night. I didn't want him out looking for me. I made a mental note to try and check in with him when I could.

But rather than worry about Killian, who was a grown adult and could handle his own shit, I tried to focus on what was ahead of me—what was in front of me now. And there on the bed, I also found a pair of my boots, multiple daggers, and my short sword harness with the swords still sheathed in the casing.

I glanced at Elijah's back. "Thank you," I murmured. "For all this." I was grateful to have my own things.

Elijah gave a quick look over his shoulder and then turned once he saw I was buckling the top strap of the jacket. His voice was a quiet rumble as he watched me lace up the boots. "It was all sitting at the front of your closet. It seemed like a good choice. But do you have any idea how to use those things," he said, eyeing the swords.

I raised a brow as I slide the harness on my back and began tucking away the daggers. "I'll manage," I told him.

126

Elijah looked doubtful, however he didn't press the issue. Instead he continued, "I was going to try and get more, but Giddeon showed up."

I paused. "Is he okay?" I looked for injuries on Elijah. "Are you?"

Elijah nodded. "His heart wasn't in it. He raised his sword but gave me time to pulse out of there."

"Could he have followed you?" I asked. I didn't know the mechanics of it all.

Elijah shook his head. "No."

I adjusted the short swords on my back. I was grateful to have those in particular. I had begun my training with Anders back when I was sixteen, and he had been brutal in his constant instruction with the short swords. He had insisted they would be a lifeline for me.

As time had passed, though, I began leaving them behind more and more when I went out hunting with our unit. I found after a certain point, I only really needed my dagger of Light.

However, that had been before, when I was still living in my safe little bubble, unaware of the true monsters which creep through the night. Now I silently thanked Anders for the years of training with the swords.

The final thing I did in preparation was to reach back and braid my hair at the nape of my neck. I knew it would be better to keep my sight unrestricted. Then I bent over and snapped a piece of my boot lace off to tie around my hair ends.

I nodded at Elijah. "Alright. Let's do this."

Elijah wore his own boots, jacket, and leather pants with his longsword strapped to his back. His features were tight as he mumbled, "This is a bad idea."

"What other option is there?" I countered.

Elijah ran a hand through his tousled blond hair. "Why are you even here? Why did you come back? You should have stayed at the manor—"

The screech of tires sounded in the quiet daylight outside. We both darted to the window. Maxim's men, Stefan and Rheneas, were climbing out of their black SUV and heading for the front door of the inn.

"Those are the two from last night," Elijah growled. He grabbed a hold of me and pulled my body into his. Looking down at me, his eyes darted back and forth between mine. I could see he was making some kind of decision.

Finally, he whispered, "We'll try the tunnel from my garage, but be ready. Giddeon and the others could be waiting for us. Hold back on your Light. Don't let them get a read on you. Don't let go of me. We might need to pulse out immediately."

Although I didn't hear footsteps outside the door to the room, a board creaked. I whipped my head in the direction of the noise, but I did not see anyone enter.

Because I was no longer there. In the blink of an eye, we left the little Shadow village, and I found myself in Elijah's basement.

After a quick scan of the room, Elijah dragged me to the keypad while he jabbed in the code to open the shelving unit into the underground tunnel. His look of displeasure did not escape my notice. And I knew, in spite of the tense situation, he was irritated about the fact that I'd used his code the last time I'd been there.

I smiled.

But my self-satisfaction only lasted for a moment. The shelving unit began to slide away, and I stiffened, waiting to see what we'd find on the other side.

The empty, dark path greeted us. I stepped out onto the dirt, letting my senses roam.

Elijah came up beside me and grabbed my hand, giving it a tug. "We have to make a run for it."

I didn't argue with him. We took off through the blackness of the tunnel, not knowing if the Angela sat in wait for us.

As awful as it was to consider, I wasn't scared about encountering an Archangel. I knew from my run-in with Cord that I could handle them. But that didn't mean that I wanted to harm any of them. And I prayed that I would not have to.

Somehow, my prayer was answered.

We were the only ones throughout the entire tunnel. We made it through the Veil of Light and into the Vestibule without encountering a single soul.

I found it strange that the Council had chosen not to post any lookouts down here, but I didn't question it. There was no time to. We needed to find the right door and get through the Threshold. For all I knew, Giddeon or one of his crew could be right behind us.

I searched the circular wall of doors, looking for a looped cross. "Do you see it?" I asked Elijah.

Instead of a response, Elijah closed his eyes and gave his head a shake.

"What's wrong?" I demanded.

"It's nothing I—" He let out a bellow, grabbing his head in his hands.

"Elijah!"

"I'm being summoned," he gritted through clenched teeth. "By the Council. I didn't think they could. With me. With what I've done."

His legs buckled and he went down on his knees, roaring in pain again. I ran over to him, grabbing his arms, trying to keep him upright. And that was when I saw the door behind him.

A shiny black marble door with a gold, looped cross—the ankh.

I tried to help Elijah to his feet. "It's right here," I told him. "We just have to get through the door."

Elijah roared again and his back bowed, his head flinging back. The need to try and soothe him, to help him, pumped through my veins.

I kneeled next to him and placed one of my hands on the exposed column of his neck. I released my Light. The connection I had to him was undeniable. It was suffocating. I had no choice in the matter. I had to save him.

The pulsing star that floated high above amid the center of the domed ceiling sparked in a blinding flare of light. Elijah's head slumped forward as he collapsed into me. My hands found their way onto each side of his face, my fingers brushing into his hair. I rubbed my nose against his cheek as I let out a breath.

I was wrapped up in him, bonded to him. Everything about him consumed me. The connection between us burned, fierce and hot. The heat at my chest made my heart pound. The pulsing between my thighs was instant.

I felt Elijah's entire body stiffen, felt the raw power course through him. And more than anything else, I felt the hunger he had. I could feel how much he needed to be with me. And how he fought it.

I believed what he had said. He was not going to take anything from me that I was not willing to give. And in spite of how much I loathed certain things about him, this knowledge, this deeper understanding, established a new facet for me. I had a certain level of respect for Elijah. It was not in any way absolution for the unforgivable things he'd done. It was just another layer in the complicated feelings I had for him.

Elijah picked his head up and looked at me with those gold specks burning in his eyes. It had worked. He was here with me. Anchored. Connected to me. Nothing and no one could pull him away, including the Council. His connection to me superseded all else.

And despite the want and need pouring from him, despite his body's demand for my own, I again found him true to his word.

Elijah drew me up with him as he stood, inhaling a breath of air as if he had been too long without. His nostrils flared and the muscle in his jaw ticked. Summoning all the strength he possessed, he ushered me towards the black marble door.

"We have to go. Now. They're coming for us. They'll have felt the surge of energy."

As soon as the words had left his mouth, a sonic boom sounded from outside the doors of the Vestibule, and the entire chamber shook. In a flash, Elijah was at the entry doors holding them shut.

He yelled at me over his shoulder. "Go! We can't let them see which door you choose. I'll turn myself over and go to Aleece. I'll find your mother. We will come for you. Find a safe holdout and wait for us!"

Elijah let out a bellow as he gripped the doors, fighting whatever force was trying to open them on the other side. With what sounded like a clap of thunder, a crack formed down the length of one door.

"Go!" Elijah insisted.

I slammed my hand onto the door, over the ankh etched there, and allowed my Light to flow from my palm. The door swung open.

I glanced back at Elijah. Uncertain.

With those gold sparks still blazing in his eyes and his jaw tight from the sheer effort of holding the stone doors in place, he gave me a single nod.

It didn't feel right to leave him. Our bond screamed at me to stay. But that same bond was clearly screaming at Elijah to protect me. And if I stayed a second longer, we'd be facing the Angela.

I didn't know if I could handle more than one.

I also believed Elijah would be better off without me. While I had my issues with him, I didn't want to be the reason he was killed. I also hoped he could find my mother. If anything had gone wrong for her in Aleece, I hoped he could help.

I gave a single nod in return and stepped through the Threshold as another bomb blast sounded, and a pile of shattered stone erupted around Elijah. A plume of dust filled the Vestibule.

The door I stepped through slammed shut behind me before anyone could step into the Vestibule. Elijah had guaranteed safe passage for me.

I only hoped the Angela did not kill him outright.

# CHAPTER 12

I STEPPED ONTO A ROCKY LEDGE. Glancing over my shoulder, I saw that the geological shelf dropped off into gray open air with no other structural features in sight. There was nothing but dusky, infinite sky surrounding the small platform.

And of course, the door from which I'd arrived had disappeared the moment I stepped through it.

Ahead of me was a wall of craggy red rock with a large cave opening. The rock ledge tapered off at the sides of the cave entrance offering no possible alternatives. It was either the drop of infinite space surrounding the ledge or the gaping hole ahead.

A gray mist was creeping out from the floor of the cave opening, only to dissipate into the open air surrounding me.

And I wasn't alone.

Outside the maw of the cave was a bench. And sitting on the bench was a man, muttering to himself. He looked like a harmless, nice old man. A tweed cap covered his gray hair, and wire rimmed glasses were perched on his nose. He wore a baby blue sweater vest and white orthopedic shoes. His hands rested on top of a wood cane which stood propped between his legs.

Harmless.

Not wasting any time, I took a few steps towards him. "Gwarlock," I called.

"Hmm? What? Oh!" It took the old man a moment of looking around before he spied me. "Hello there," he smiled.

"Are you the Gwarlock?" I demanded, not willing to make pleasantries.

"The . . . the . . . what? The who?" the old man asked.

"The Gwarlock. How do I find him?"

The old man looked around some more. "I wouldn't know, pretty lady."

"Who are you?" I asked. "Some kind of gatekeeper?"

"I'm . . . uh . . . " he smacked his lips, scrunching his weathered face, and looked up to the open space above us. Then he gave a chuckle. "Well isn't that just the darndest thing? I've been sitting here so long that I don't rightly know."

I took another few steps towards the man, and as I approached, I noticed an overgrown rat—the size of a small child—next to the old man on the bench. The ugly little creature sat the way a person would, upright with its long tail lying between its legs while its spine rested against the back of the bench. Its crusty little paws were perched on its bloated belly.

I couldn't stand to look at it for long. It was a repulsive being with matted fur, bent tangled whiskers, and two long jagged incisors that were a brownish yellow. It stared at me with black, beady little eyes.

"What are you looking at, bitch?"

135

I took a step back, startled. The disgusting creature had spoken. Not only that but it spoke in a deep voice befitting an aging, overweight mortal who had spent his entire life smoking.

I had no idea what to do, but based on its comment alone, the urge to kill the thing overwhelmed me.

"Now, Filbert," chastised the old man.

"Look at the way she's eyeing me," Filbert replied. "She wants it...And she knows I can give it to her good, too."

A bottle, with a plain brown paper bag crushed around it, sat on the bench. The rat picked up the bottle and took a swig. "Fuck, what I wouldn't give for a smoke."

"Is this the Realm of Lost Souls?" I tried.

"Who gives a fuck," Filbert shot back.

The old man waved a hand in front of Filbert, clearly trying to subdue him. "She's a nice young girl. She doesn't mean any harm, Filbert." The old man's voice dropped, and he leaned towards the rat. "Besides, we so rarely see the living," he whispered.

Straightening back up, the old man turned to me. "I'm afraid we aren't much help," he explained. "Filbert and I have been here ages. Too long to remember what came before, you see."

"Fuck you, old man. I know exactly what I'm doing here," Filbert countered.

The old man simply shrugged at Filbert's comment.

"Do you know how I can get to the Realm of Lost Souls or The Gwarlock—the god of death?" I pressed.

"I don't know what those things are," the man replied. Then he licked his lips and something in his gaze unnerved me. He patted the bench. "Why not sit and rest for a minute. You're young. You have plenty of time."

I eyed the rat and the man. The rat was a vile little thing. That was obvious. But now I realized there was something more beneath the fragile, innocuous appearance of the old man. Something that made my skin crawl.

"Where does this cave go?" I demanded.

"Come," the old man insisted. "Come and sit. It would be the highlight of my day to have such a pretty young lady keep an old man like me company for a minute. Be a dear, won't you?"

The old man leaned forward and held a liver spotted hand out to me. At the same time he used his cane to try and push some debris, which sat under the bench, out of sight. But all he did was draw my attention to the pile.

I instantly tensed.

Bones.

The old man was trying to hide a pile of bones.

When he saw the recognition on my face, he didn't wait for a response from me, and he didn't try to make any excuses. Instead he implored, "Just a little taste? Just a little nibble before you're on your way? Howsabout a couple fingers? You could spare that, couldn't you? For a hungry old man? We so rarely have anyone pass by. Especially someone warm-blooded. Eh, pretty lady?"

"Yeah," agreed the repulsive overgrown rat. "And when you're done with that, you can suck me off." He ran his paws over his furry little creature bits.

"Alright. That's it," I snapped. At the same time I reached back and withdrew both short swords with a swish of steel. I stabbed one through Filbert's tail, where it sat between his legs, lodging the sword into the bench. The rat's fat little feet scrambled in the air, going nowhere. The old man sat shaking next to Filbert as I pressed the other sword into his neck.

I gave them each a hard stare. "Where do I find the god of death?"

"I wouldn't know," the old man stammered. "It's the truth. I've been here so long, I've forgotten how I came to be here. All I know is I found this bench and took a seat a long time ago. The only place to go from here is there." He flicked his eyes in the direction of the cave opening. "I've never entered."

I turned my gaze from the old man to the rat.

"Hey, look sweetheart. Leave me outta this. This is between you and the old man. Alright?"

They were useless. I had no choice but to enter the cave. In a flash I withdrew my swords, flipping them into the crossed holster on my back, purposefully making a show of my skills with the weapons.

"I'm leaving," I told them. "If either of you follow me, I will slit you from groin to neck." I eyed them both one last time, giving extra attention to the rat. "Rat jerky is a favorite of mine."

I turned and headed straight for the cave entrance, hyper aware of the slightest sound of movement or disturbance of air from behind. But neither attempted to come for me.

As I passed through the mouth of the cave and my feet became lost in the gray fog there, Filbert let out a prolonged, disgusting belch—far louder than a rat his size should have been capable of. Although I didn't turn around to look at him, I heard him mutter in his deep and gravelly voice from the bench behind me.

"Welcome to hell, bitch."

\*\*\*

The cave was dark. And while the opening arch was spacious enough, the walls of the cave immediately closed in to form a steep, narrow path which shifted downward. After taking a few steps, I found that if I leaned enough to the sides, my shoulders would brush the rock wall. I was completely enclosed. And that thick gray fog covered the entire pathway.

That's it. That's all there was. For a very long time.

I descended step by step without change, without interruption, for far too long. I walked for hours. Then more. I began to wonder if the path was spelled. If perhaps this was all there was, just an unending path in a dark cave. I began to wonder if I would have to turn back to the entrance. I wondered if I would end up joining the old man and Filbert.

I imagined sitting with them on their bench, the old man trying to take a nibble out of me, and Filbert making crude sexual comments. I would end up killing them both. Then I'd be the one trying to hide a pile of bones as the next being passed by.

I began to imagine a hundred different scenarios upon my return to the cave entrance. All the possibilities. How things might play out. After envisioning letting the old man take a bite out of my shoulder while I fondled Filbert in exchange for a swig from his bottle, I wasn't even repulsed by the idea.

And I realized my mind was slipping.

The slope of the path became steeper. I began to feel crushed by the rock wall on either side of me. I had just enough space to pass through. I didn't think I could continue for much longer.

The repetition, the darkness, the quiet—it was disorienting. I began to long for Filbert and the old man, for the openness of sky all around me. I couldn't breathe down here. The rock walls were going to pulverize me. I would never see the sky again if I didn't turn around right then.

It was time to turn back. I would go insane if I didn't.

Only as the path took a sharp, steep twist, it opened to a bridge. I inhaled as if it were for the first time. I was no longer confined between two unending walls of rock; a vast underground space lay before me. And while it was dark, without question, there was the faintest hint of light that seemed to glow from somewhere in the far distance. The mere freedom of openness jarred me from the dark place my mind had sunk.

But the relief of freedom did not last long.

Before me, in the dark, far below the surface from where I'd begun, lay a pool of still water. And from it, more of that gray mist rose. A narrow, rocky land bridge connected the path I had traveled with the area on the other side of the lake. It was the only way to cross. The path ended here.

And the other side of the lake was…*eerie.*

More gray fog covered the dark ground. Bare trees—black trees—littered the land. And in the stark, leafless branches sat creatures, their eyes reflecting in the darkness. Owls, monkeys, frogs, crows, bats and spiders. Their gazes all directed at me.

I did not want to cross the land bridge. I did not want to walk among those dead trees and sinister beings. But my only other option was to turn around and take the suffocating path back up to the cave entrance. And that was something I could not bring myself to do. I had barely clung to my sanity the first time.

Stopping and waiting wasn't an option either. It could take days or weeks for Elijah to come and find me. And that was only if he and my mother were successful in swaying the Council.

I would continue on. This was not a place I wanted to wait.

If you have ever been somewhere truly dark and unsettling, you know you cannot sit where you are, allowing yourself to fester. You must tear your way through, placing one foot in front of the other.

I was alone, but I was strong. I had made it this far on my own. I knew I was on the right path. There had been no other options, no divergence. All I had to do was keep going.

So, I continued. I stepped onto the bridge. With care and deliberation, I chose my first step. Then again. One foot after the other, across the rocky arch.

As I inched along, the gray mist from the lake began to rise. At first, it was almost imperceptible. But as I reached the halfway point, the fog climbed higher. It began to roil in a fervor, surrounding me. I quickened my pace as a cold sweat broke out across my body, and my heart hammered in my chest.

I was in danger.

I could *feel* hunger below.

Yet the rocky formation was so narrow, one wrong step would send me plummeting into the dark depths of the lake. I had to tread with care.

When I heard the sound of churning water, though, I knew my time was up. And notwithstanding the perilous path, I began to run.

As I sprinted for the other side, something swooped through the air in a blur of motion, and a gigantic tentacle crashed through the bridge in front of me. The narrow strip of rock was pulverized, and the great mass of it went smashing down into the lake.

I didn't stop. I didn't slow. I sped up. And I leapt over the gaping drop before me. I tried to fling myself as far forward a possible.

I made it. My foot landed on the bridge. But I couldn't pause. I had to keep my momentum because the arch was collapsing with each step I took. The moment I would pick up a foot to take another sprinting step, the rock would crumble away beneath it.

After being immersed in unending silence, the catastrophic sounds reverberating all around were disorienting. The churning of the water below was intensified by the hunks of rock crashing into it. The creatures on the other side of the bridge hooted, screeched, screamed, and croaked, as they all jumped and flapped their wings on the bare branches where they perched.

Despite the blaring shrieks and tectonic rumbles resonating all around, I tried to focus on the path. And I was doing it. I was going to make it. I was so close. Except…with my final step, my foot did not meet solid rock.

I had been too slow, and the crumbling bridge had caught up with me. I braced myself for impact with the water, ready to kick myself to the surface.

Instead of being overcome by water, however, my body thudded onto hard ground. The breath was knocked from me as my chest and thighs slammed into the dirt. I had made it to the other side. The end of the bridge had overshot the edge of the lake by a few yards. I had made it past the water's edge.

I immediately began to push myself up from the ground, only to have something cinch around my leg. With incalculable speed, I was dragged back towards the lake. The desire to claw at the ground and try to keep myself in place was overwhelming, but I fought the instinct. Instead I flipped over onto my back as I sped towards the water's edge.

A tentacle was wrapped around my calf. I reached both hands behind my head to withdraw my swords as I bent my knees and flexed in a sit-up. I swung both swords in opposite arcs to slice through the rubbery flesh just below the heel of my boot.

I couldn't believe my luck when I was instantly freed. I had been afraid the tentacles would have some kind of resistance to the sword blades. But the arm had severed with a clean cut. And the injured appendage had retracted into the water without me.

The moment the tentacle was cleaved, I began to scramble back from the lake's edge, knowing better than to wait there. I was about to push myself up from the crab walk I was in, but the speed of whatever this thing was, was incredible. Two more tentacles whipped out from the mist to wrap around my waist and arm.

The instant they made contact, I was pulled towards the water once more. Using my free hand, I sliced through the tentacle to liberate my opposite arm. I had already spread my legs as far apart as I could to slice through the second tentacle around my waist.

This time, I didn't wait to see the outcome of the sword swing. This time, as my blade rived through the tentacle between my spread legs, I jacked them backwards and over my head in a reverse somersault while I was still on the ground.

Rolling to my feet, I darted backwards while keeping my eyes on the water. Two additional tentacles lashed through the air, and I swung each of my swords in unison to severe both limbs before they could reach me. They plunked to the ground with a heavy wet slap.

I retreated farther back, my breathing heavy. And I waited.

The water stilled. The creatures in the trees behind me settled. And the thick fog crept across the lake, covering any gaps where it had been disturbed.

I watched for a long time.

All was quiet. All was still. Whatever had been trying to snack on me, had given up.

I turned to survey the land I was now on. An entire other world sat before me...a black lifeless forest.

The creatures in the bare tree limbs stared at me with unblinking eyes, and the fog, thicker than any I'd ever encountered, covered my feet. Although I could not see the ground, I knew I stood at the beginning of a path. I could see how it weaved through the deadened trees.

I let out a breath. I rolled my neck and threw my shoulders back. I looked around one more time, trying my best to take everything in.

Glancing over my shoulder, I eyed the wall of rock across the lake. The land bridge was completely destroyed.

I couldn't change my mind. There was no chance, now, of returning the way I'd come.

I turned back to the path in front of me. In the dark, far below from where I'd arrived, covered with fog and surrounded by lifeless black trees with hundreds of eyes staring at me...

I followed the path.

# CHAPTER 13

I WENT SLOWLY, carefully placing one foot in front of the other. I was unable to see through the layer of fog if anything lay on the path ahead of me.

But I found the ground to be level and free of debris. The animals stayed to their trees, perched in the black branches. And although they did not approach me, the energy they carried did.

They wished me harm. They wished me ill. There was no Light in these beings. No burning energy. Just Darkness. Malice. Evil.

I imagined if the Umbra enjoyed pets, these creatures would make fitting companions.

I did my best to be soundless as I passed them, to disturb the air around me as little as possible. But when I saw what was in the tree to my right, I jumped back, withdrawing my swords. The high-pitched ring pierced the quiet of the forest.

In the tree hung a limp figure. A noose was tied around its neck from one of the bare branches. The person was lifeless.

But the instant I withdrew my swords, the figure picked up its head. It was a young woman wearing a dress, and all color had been drained from her.

She clutched and clawed at the rope around her neck, desperately fighting to get free. Her pruned lips opened and closed as if trying to speak. Her gaunt, colorless face made her look like a corpse. And her gray lifeless skin hung from her body. She stared at me with black hollowed eyes. But she didn't see me. She looked right through me.

The animals in the trees erupted in violent cries. Screeching, wailing, flapping, and jumping.

I crouched down and launched straight up into the air, slicing through the rope above the girl's head, wanting to help her. Then my feet landed back on the path.

With a clean break, the girl thudded to the ground at the base of the tree. And the second her gray shriveled body hit the forest floor, the animals descended upon her. Covering every inch of her.

There was tearing, breaking, crunching…*slurping*. My stomach heaved at the sounds. Just as fast as the animals had flocked to her, they returned to their branches.

There was a fraction of a second after the creatures fled, when I could see the girl, before the fog rolled in to cover the exposed space on the ground.

I will not share all that remained. But it was gruesome enough to make me retch. I had to turn away, and my eyes watered. I gasped for air before eventually forcing myself to breathe—slow and deep. Still on the path, I picked up my head and turned in a circle, searching for any signs of a threat.

The forest was exactly as it had been. Black. Quiet. Lifeless.

I eyed the area under the trees, realizing what would have happened to me if I had stepped off the path. And I forced myself to take another slow breath.

With no other choice, I began forward once again, certain to stay in the middle of the trail.

I took one shaking step. Then another and another. The gentle grind of dirt and rock under my boots was the only sound. The animals did not chirp or rustle or hum. They were deathly silent. And their eyes followed me.

I didn't notice the next body until I was next to it.

The instant I walked past the limp form hanging from the tree branch, it jerked to life—clawing and clutching at its neck, just as the girl had. A man this time. And he too had a corpse-like appearance.

The animals took up their cacophony of sounds once more, filling my ears with deafening screeches and howls, shaking and pounding the branches they occupied.

He was out of my reach. I would have to leave the path if I wanted to save him. And I didn't know if there was any life left inside this man to save.

There was nothing I could do. The forest creatures would swarm me before I could reach him.

I looked away and marched forward, staring straight ahead. But I did not get more than a few paces past the man before I stopped. Because as I looked ahead through the darkness, I saw hundreds of silhouettes appear ahead of me, slowly coming into focus. All along the path. All hanging from the trees.

It was almost enough to bring me to my knees. The sight alone was almost enough to break me.

*Almost.*

But I still had a fight left in me.

And step by step, I made my way through the horror of the forest.

Each and every time I passed a lifeless hanging figure, it jerked to life just as I approached. And each and every time, the creatures of the forest screamed.

Men. Women. Old. Young. I passed by them all.

I did not dare try to free another, no matter how hard I felt the need to.

Over and over again, until I was certain it would never end, I walked through the Realm of Lost Souls.

I did not stop once. And by the time I began staggering, coming dangerously close to the sides of the path, trying to hold my ears and shut my eyes—I was convinced this would be how it all ended for me. There was no doubt in my mind that the instant my foot left the path and landed on the forest floor, the animals would consume me.

I began to long for it. Just so this could all be over. The more it went on, the more I wanted to fall.

But as I staggered, about to topple off the path, something caught my eye. Something that glimmered in the darkness.

I focused on the golden shimmer and forced myself towards it.

With just a few more steps, the trees fell away.

I had reached the end of the forest.

I had made it through.

*** 

Ahead was an empty valley of fog. There was nothing but the thick mist which covered the ground. And off in the distance, rising

149

from the roiling gray smoke, was a stone pyramid. Atop the pyramid, somehow shining in the darkness of the abyss underground, was the golden ankh.

I had found the Gwarlock.

I descended from the forest, down a steep rocky incline, into the valley below. The fog was waist deep in the vast nothingness, and it was so thick that I could feel it impede each exhausted step I took.

Stairs spanned the entire width at the base of the pyramid. Once I'd made my way through the valley of mist, I had to climb step after step of the seemingly endless structure in order to reach the entry. But finally, I did.

The square opening stretched high above my head, and from it crept the thick gray fog—rolling out from the entry and down the stairs to surround the temple. There was no door or gate, just an opening into the pyramid, with one sloping channel to follow.

Moaning and wailing echoed down the hall as I walked. And I didn't know if I could handle more death and horror. I could barely stay upright as I trudged ahead.

Eventually, the hall opened into a cavernous space. The chamber clearly occupied a good portion of the base of the temple. And a vaulted ceiling soared high above us.

In the center of the chamber, on a massive altar, was a group of women.

After spending a small eternity in the dark, the dim light in the temple was a shock to my eyes. It took a moment before I could properly see.

And when I could make out the scene before me, I blinked a few more times to be certain I was not imagining things.

Standing at the head of the altar, among the women, was a ferocious beast. He had the head of a jackal and the body of a man. He was at least nine feet tall.

From his canine head all the way down his body, his skin appeared hard and smooth. If he stood still, he would look like a polished statue carved from black onyx. And every inch of his bare torso and arms was muscled, more so than I had ever seen on an individual.

Instead of eyes, his sockets were filled with a ghastly light. He wore no shirt, but around his neck hung a large gold cross with a loop at the top. And while a loin cloth was slung around his hips, it did not hinder him from his activities at the padded altar.

Standing at the center of the table, he drove mercilessly into the woman in front of him. She would not have been able to remain in place with the brutal thrusts, but two other women held her shoulders pinned to the altar, while the creature held her hips off the padding to carry out his assault on her.

Her neck was turned so that her head was pressed to the side, and from where I stood, I could see rapture across her face.

She and the other women were all undressed, but all adorned with various pieces which looked as though made from gold metal or thread—bralettes and garters, eye masks and head chains, armbands and delicate collars.

One of the females wearing a lace eye mask stood next to the creature, rubbing and stroking his chest and abdomen. Then she would caress his thighs and cup his sack as he pounded away.

When at last the woman in front of him gave a shattering cry, the beast withdrew from her. The moment her hips were released from his grip, she slumped to the altar in a daze. Then the towering creature clutched the ring from a collar another woman wore and

151

pulled her face towards him. She obediently wrapped her lips around the head of his cock, and he began thrusting into her hungry mouth. Tears sprang from her eyes as he shoved himself as far as he could.

He released his grip on her collar to allow her a chance to breathe. Then the ferocious figure picked up another female by the waist and threw her down in front of him. As she lay on her back, she wrapped her legs around his neck. It took some effort to squeeze his shaft into her, but once he did, he resumed with his merciless pounding, causing her breasts to bounce with each thrust.

The beast clutched her thighs against his chest. His claws dug into her flesh where he held her, and streaks of blood trickled down her skin.

I should have been embarrassed or disturbed or…*something*. I should have wanted to turn away. To stop watching.

But I was mesmerized.

There was something about the way the creature took each woman. There was a primal hunger. He demanded to be satiated. And somehow, every ounce he took from each woman was given back to her. Exponentially.

And the women seemed to worship him. To find a certain kind of nirvana in experiencing him. But this was not a celestial, heavenly kind of nirvana. This was a dark rapture, buried away somewhere deep and secretive, long forgotten within the universe.

When finally the last woman's shattering cry echoed from the walls of the chamber, the beast found his own release. He threw his canine head back and howled. Only this howl was not one you would expect from any animal. This howl was a deep reverberation that went on for far too long, shaking the very stone at my feet.

When the beast eventually snapped his head down and opened his eyes, he looked at the women before him with the crackling light that filled his sockets.

The women said nothing. They simply picked themselves up and bowed to him before exiting through a back opening in the chamber.

The beast crossed to a gold throne in front of the altar and sat, taking hold of a staff there. And just like that, without pause or the need for a personal moment, he gave his command.

"Enter." His voice was so deep and low—so hollow—it was as though he spoke from somewhere far below the ground. And I knew the command was directed at me.

I stepped forward, leaving the hall, and entered the chamber. After witnessing what had just happened, I was not ready to face him. But any hesitation I might have felt was overruled by the power of his instruction. He was not someone to defy.

"Approach the altar."

I obeyed. And the closer I got to the beast, the larger he became.

Unsure how to go about this meeting, I bowed my head once I'd reached a triangular area in the middle of the chamber and waited for him to speak.

His voice boomed through the temple. "Do you come to pay tribute?"

"I do," I replied, keeping my head bowed.

"What have you brought in offering?"

"To be certain it is an offering which pleases you, I have come to ask for that which you request."

"So you bring nothing," he said. He paused and I knew it was not yet an invitation to speak. "You wish to ask a favor as well. Do you not?"

153

"Yes, Gwarlock."

"Most know not to ask favors."

"Yes, Gwarlock."

"But I do not receive many petitioners. Most never make it this far." After another pause, he concluded, "I will hear your request. Raise your head and speak."

I finally looked at him. "Gwarlock, I ask of the *tanjear* and how it relates to one known as The Contessa. I wish to know what it is and how to use it in destroying her."

He didn't take a moment to consider my request or mull over a decision. As soon as I was finished speaking, he gave his reply.

"In return for this information you will provide me with your first-born daughter. She will join my harem."

"Begging your pardon, Gwarlock, but I do not know if I will ever have offspring, let alone a daughter." And I sure as hell wouldn't give her to him.

He stood. His chest expanded and the frenzied light in his eye sockets intensified. I had angered him with my refusal. I was afraid there would be no further discussion. But his canine head turned to the wall on the side of the chamber.

"Then you will be charged with a far greater task." He turned back to me, staring at me with that crackling light. "My wife cut my heart from my chest while I slept one night."

Probably because he was fucking a bed full of women.

"I want it returned to me. It will be a fitting offering for the information you desire."

He gave a nod to the wall on the far side of the chamber before turning and disappearing through a dark archway behind his throne. As he exited, two huge slabs of stone slid towards each other to close off the Threshold. They filled the hall with a prolonged scraping sound before a loud boom echoed through the space as the slabs clapped shut. At the same time, the lights in the temple dimmed. But I was not plunged into total darkness; the walls of the pyramid remained illuminated.

"Begging your pardon, but Gwarlock," I called after him, "how do I find it?" I took a few steps forward feeling panicked. "I don't even know how to leave this realm!"

There was no response.

"Please!" I shouted. I ran over to the slabs and pounded on them. "Gwarlock, I need more instruction!"

My plea echoed all around me. I tried to dig my fingers into the seam, tried to pry the slabs open.

"I will fetch you whatever you desire, just tell me where I am to go." At my last words, my voice broke and dropped to a whisper. I could no longer yell. I could no longer keep my head up. It fell forward.

I gave myself a moment to just be. To just accept what was. Then I had a thought.

Perhaps the Gwarlock's harem would have some information I could use. I would have to find where they went and talk to them.

I glanced around trying to decide if I should wait in the temple or actively seek them out. As I did, my gaze landed on the far wall—the one which had held the Gwarlock's eye.

I squinted at the primitive display, disbelieving what I saw. I crossed to it, just to prove to myself that I couldn't be seeing what I thought was there. It was impossible.

A mural was painted all along the wall. It appeared ancient, having faded in most places. And it was impossible to make out the majority of the depictions. But in the very center was the figure of the Gwarlock. And painted over his chest, where his heart would be, was a blood red gemstone, with hundreds of facets, the size of a plum.

I inhaled and placed my fingertips over the painting, barely making contact. I had seen that gemstone before. *Recently*. It had been the same color. Same shape. And it was highly coveted.

It couldn't be a coincidence. Perhaps the Gwarlock had chosen me for this task because he knew I could retrieve his heart. Perhaps I had been given a very simple task after all.

My own heart, which had begun to blacken and harden, suddenly pumped with a rush of blood and oxygen. There was hope. This was something I could do.

I knew where to find the Gwarlock's heart. I just had to figure out how to get there.

I wasn't going to waste any time. I'd make my way as far back as I could. I had to believe my mother would pull through in her negotiations with the Council. I would wait for Elijah.

I turned to leave the way I'd come, but the moment I did two statues, which flanked the entrance to the hall, shifted. They were figures similar to the Gwarlock, only smaller. Both had the head of a jackal. Both wore a loincloth. And both held a staff. They were highly polished onyx, but other than the unexpected shift in movement, they were nothing more than statues.

They had altered position, though. Now instead of standing at attention, they had each adjusted their staffs so that they barred access to the hallway. Another sharp scratch sounded from the other side of the chamber. Two of the exact same lifeless statues had also shifted, making the opening behind them accessible.

It seemed I was to exit the chamber through a different passage, and I was hopeful it would lead me to some kind of exit from this realm. I did not want to stay a moment longer.

I was fatigued. I could barely walk. I needed to rest. I needed to recharge.

I shuffled towards the awaiting guards. But before making my way down the dark channel, I took one more glance at the faded depiction on the wall. I was certain the Gwarlock's heart was the gemstone Lilly had stolen from the dragons.

Confident it would be easy to retrieve, I left the temple.

As I emerged from the massive pyramid, I found myself facing the darkness and fog once more, and my heart sank at the sight of it. But at least there was no black forest on this side of the temple.

Only as I scanned the darkness, I found something unexpected off in the distance. Amid the bleak setting…was a single tree.

It was a weeping willow. And this tree was unlike the others down here. It was alive—green and lush. The falling branches were thick with thriving leaves. They created a cascading veil that entirely surrounded the tree.

Unbelievably, as I stared at it, some of the leaves parted and a beautiful, delicate hand waved me in.

# CHAPTER 14

WHEN I SWEPT ASIDE the branches of the willow, I felt a small tingle buzz through my fingertips. The energy, the life of the tree, was a desperately needed reminder that I too was still alive.

And I stepped into the enclosure of the leaves, inhaling clean rejuvenating air. Somehow there was a beautiful soft light within. I felt as though I was no longer in the Realm of Lost Souls. I was somewhere peaceful and lovely.

Inside the circle of this willow, it was a sunny afternoon with beams of sunlight piercing through the canopy above. There were small birds sitting in the tree branches, chirping and singing. Little bunnies nibbled the grass, and butterflies floated through the air landing on freshly bloomed flowers.

By the trunk of the tree a stream trickled along, sparkling in the dapples of light and tinkling over the pebbles and rocks of the streambed. And sitting on the grass, beside the clear water, was a woman.

159

She was the most incredible being I'd ever seen.

She had iridescent skin. Depending on how the light hit her and the way she moved or shifted, an array of pastel hues would glimmer across her opal complexion. The effect was present across her entire unclothed body. It was the most aweing feature I have ever seen on an individual. And for that alone, she was breathtaking.

Yet complementing her skin was her lavender hair. It was more with which any one person should be gifted, and the thick strands were loose, flowing past her shoulders and down to her hips. There was so much of it that her naked chest was adequately covered by the lilac waves.

I peered closer at her, unable to believe what I saw next. And I knew my lips parted at the wonder of her.

Upon her eyelashes sat butterflies. The brilliant kaleidoscopic patterns and colors from the wings of the butterflies became an extension of her eyelashes. And each time she blinked, the incredible fan of her lashes swept from her cheekbones to her eyebrows.

She sat with her knees bent, and her arms draped across her shins. She waved me over and waited for me to sit before her.

I felt awkward and grimy in her presence. It felt wrong to soil this place with the current state of my hair and clothing. But I wanted to please her. I wanted to be in this space of life and light and beauty. So, I sat.

When I did, the woman finally spoke. Her voice was soothing—calm and unhurried. At the same time though, it was fresh and alive.

"How went your meeting with my husband?" she asked. The 'ow' in 'how' was very pronounced because as she spoke, a plume of fragile butterflies fluttered from her mouth, dancing and flitting through the air. As a result, her question was not only a question but a delicate burst of color and motion.

She was a being whose words were literally full of beautiful life. Dancing between us. Around us. And then floating away.

I cleared my throat, not wanting to hear my own voice in comparison. "Your husband?" I asked.

"Yes," she answered with more butterflies escaping her lips. "The Gwarlock."

I began opening my mouth to respond, but no words came out. I didn't know what to say to her. The idea that this beautiful being was married to the Gwarlock was too horrific.

She closed her eyes and laughed. Still more butterflies flitted from between her lips, swirling around us. And those which were perched upon her lashes fluttered their wings, before settling as she opened her eyes again.

"You find us to be at odds with each other," she provided. "Is that the way of it?"

I wasn't sure how to answer diplomatically. I took a long breath, searching for the correct response.

Luckily the Gwarlock's wife did not wait for one. "You should know, sweet Violet, that we do not appear to each other as we do to you."

I shook my head not understanding.

"Do not be surprised. It is true of all relationships. All connections. However you may have seen him today, it is what works best for your story. Not mine."

She held up a hand and a black butterfly landed in her palm. "He is my protector." Holding up her other hand, an opal butterfly landed in her opposite palm. "I am his strength."

She brought her open palms together and blew onto them. The two butterflies flew away along with the stream of others from her breath.

"Who are you?" I asked, emboldened by her open disposition.

"To you, I am no one. I am a collection of particles, bound together and spinning through this life. I am mostly empty space. I am nothing."

I tried again. "Do you have a name?"

She smiled and a nebula of butterflies scattered through the air as she answered me; the life within the enclosure of the willow tree seemed to intensify. "I am Entropy."

Something within me stirred at her words. "Are you trapped here? Do you need help?" I asked. "I can try and help you escape this realm."

"I do not wish to leave my husband," she replied.

"But," I glanced at the cascading wall of leaves which surrounded us, shivering at what I knew lay beyond the other side. "All around you is death and horror."

She shook her head with a gentle smile, and her lavender hair swept along her bare shoulders—a subtle array of hues shimmering at the curves of her iridescent skin. "Those are not the dead," she corrected. "Those are the lost. My husband's temple is merely the entry to the Realm of the Dead." She held her hands out. "This is the *in-between*. It is where he and I can be together."

I shook my head, regretting what I was about to say. "You should know he is not faithful to you."

She tilted her head and gazed at me. "Because of the women he keeps? Is that why you believe him to be unfaithful?"

I was surprised by her question. "Well…"

162

"Thank you for your concern, sweet Violet." At her words, the butterflies which had escaped her lips, settled around me. In my hair. On my shoulders, arms, and hands. All across my lap. Before floating away. "But I do not fault him for his consorts. He is death. He pursues that which he can never possess: the highest reaches of life."

"Then why did you cut out his heart while he slept?" I asked.

She laughed and clapped her hands together. "For the randomness of it."

I must have looked shocked, because she giggled before saying, "I told you. I am Entropy. I am uncertainty and disorder. Randomness."

Her eyes glinted and her voice dropped as if sharing a secret with me. "I am the driving force of life within the universe."

She straightened. "The act was a gift to my husband. A random occurrence. Life."

Entropy blinked several times, studying my face. The large butterfly wings atop her lashes fanned her cheeks. "You do not believe me?" she questioned.

She gestured to the streambank next to us. "Pick up a handful of pebbles and toss them into the air. Will they fall in perfect rows and columns? Or will they scatter randomly? In beautiful, unpredictable disorder.

"The particles within you? Do they fly through space in an established pattern? Or are they a frenzy of chaotic motion?

"Do you not see?" She gazed around the enclosure at the leaves and grass, the stream and bunnies. "The randomness. The uncertainty. The disorder. It is balance."

I looked around as well. It was a peaceful setting. It didn't exactly scream unpredictable disorder.

163

Entropy studied me and nodded. "It is always so difficult for your kind to accept the idea that life is not predictable and organized. You all desire control over it."

She sighed. "You all foolishly prefer The Fates to me." She eyed the canopy of the willow tree and squinted, as if searching for something bothersome. "Those loquacious wrens. Constantly chittering about in their nest from the heavens."

At her words, the butterflies all changed color to black and gray, their wings batting through the air in an angry fervor.

"Those three toy with the balance of life. Continually spewing forth their prophecies. Trying to shape the future. The ignorant twits! They know not the danger they inflict upon the universe.

"They do not account for me! There must be balance!

"I took their eyes to stop them. And still they defy me! Look at the mess they have made! What lies before us all now." A storm of dark butterflies covered us with her outrage.

It took a moment before I could see her again as all the butterflies fluttered off. Then she shrugged one shoulder and gave a sheepish look, seeming to realize the extent of her outburst. "I am sorry, sweet Violet. It is so rare that I have anyone to talk to."

She rolled her shoulders forward and hugged her knees tighter. "These are not the concerns of you or your people. These are the battles between the higher powers."

A note of regret tinged her voice. "Now you must go out and face the prophecy set before you by the Fates, knowing it distorts the randomness which life so desperately needs for maintaining balance, knowing it will cause destruction."

She tilted her head and peered at me. "Why was it you? Why did they choose you as the catalyst, I wonder?"

"What do you mean?" I asked, not entirely certain I wanted to hear her answer.

Entropy leaned forward and smiled, her eyes shining; yet, she looked sad. "Sweet Violet, you are the one. You have set in motion all the others. You were the spark that started the fire."

I shook my head at her, not understanding.

She closed her eyes and lifted her chin, appearing to try and visualize something. After a moment, her gaze met mine once more. And this time when she spoke, the butterflies which flew from her lips were different. Some had wings of inky black shadows, and others had wings of tiny, brilliant stars.

"You were made whole," she said simply. "And now there is no stopping the book created by the Fates. You were the catalyst. You were the spark. And now the prophecies will come to pass. It is impossible to stop them."

A cold wind swept through the space within the willow tree. The birds quieted and the bunnies froze. Even the tinkling of the stream became muted.

In a blink, the space within the willow branches transitioned from day to night. Stars glittered in the midnight sky above us as their light reflected in the water beside us. And while there was a beauty to the night, the animals did not stir. All were hidden away.

Entropy looked to the veil of leaves behind me. She appeared concerned and scared, but a beautiful blush stained her opal cheeks and her shoulders rose with a deep breath as if she was also exhilarated.

"Our time here is over," she said.

"What? No. Please finish explaining this to me. And I...I need help. I don't know how to leave this realm" I told her.

She laughed, and I was submerged in another burst of color while gossamer wings whispered around me.

Entropy was standing now, her lavender hair tumbling down her chest and across her thighs. Butterflies sat in her hair and across her iridescent skin which glimmered in the starlight.

"Sweet Violet, you do not leave this place. It is the Realm of Lost Souls. That is what you now are."

"But my mother would not have sent me someplace from which I could not return."

"Did she send you? Or did she send another? One who would have certain abilities you do not possess?"

She took my hand and led me to the curtain of leaves, parting them for me. She smiled and her eyes were alight with mischief. "You see? The randomness of life? Go. Enjoy the uncertainty." She spoke as if she was gifting me something, as though I should thank her. And I couldn't help but think she might be slightly mad.

"Please, I need help," I begged.

"My husband comes. If he finds you here, his anger will be great. He does not trust my safety with visitors. You must leave now, otherwise you forfeit your journey and your path ends here."

She gently pushed me forward, and I walked through the curtain of willow leaves to the surrounding blackness and fog. Some of the butterflies from her words had escaped through the tree leaves with me. As they flitted through the darkness they wilted, turning gray, and crumbled to the ground.

***

I had been dismissed. Again.

And while I felt abandoned and cast aside, I also felt revived from my time within the weeping willow.

I had made it through the black forest once. I could do it again. I would dig down and summon all the strength I possessed. I would focus on each step I took, and I would block out the horror of the forest.

I could do it.

I would follow the path back to the lake. Perhaps I could find a way to cross it. I would make sushi out of whatever lived beneath the water. And I would make my way back to the surface, where I would wait for Elijah.

I walked through the plain of fog, past the Gwarlock's temple, to stand before the black forest once more. I took a deep breath, and I entered the trail.

But just minutes after I had begun walking, I came to a fork in the path. I stopped, staring at the two different directions I could take. I had not come across any deviations on my way in. There had been one path only.

I turned around to try and start again, but I was met with an intersection. And a cold fury swept over me. I bit my lip and felt my nostrils flare as I breathed out an exhalation of rage.

The forest was changing.

I rapidly concocted a plan. I would go back to the willow tree. I would hold Entropy at sword point—there would be some randomness for her. And I would refuse to let her go until either she or the Gwarlock granted me passage from this realm.

But I couldn't find my way back. I had barely entered the forest and already I was lost in the maze of it. Everywhere I went were forks, intersections, and dead ends.

My breathing became shallow and rapid.

167

And still, the dying souls, jerking to life each time I passed them. The screams and screeches of the animals in the trees—louder than I remembered them…

I will not try to describe how long this went on for. Just know that I fought to keep going for as long as I could. Please believe me when I tell you, *I tried*.

But I was not strong enough. And at some point, I knew I had reached the end.

I do not like to share what happened next. It was the weakest point of my life. And I am ashamed…because I gave up.

Ahead in the path, was a dead end. And standing before me was one of those dead, black trees. Like all the others in the forest, malevolent creatures sat in the bare black arms.

But unlike so many of the other trees in the forest, this one was not occupied.

This one was mine. This one was for me. The Gwarlock's wife was right.

I was in the Realm of Lost Souls. I was now one of them.

I stood before it for a long time. Struggling. Fighting. Pleading with the Fates or Entropy or the Gwarlock or God—with whomever it was I should plead to. Until finally, I could stand no more.

And the forest claimed me.

At last, all was quiet.

# CHAPTER 15

SOMETHING WAS HAPPENING. After an interminable silence, something was happening.

I jerked to life. I couldn't breathe. Clawing and scratching at my neck, I tried to free myself. My eyes flashed open, but I could see nothing. I tried to call for help. Animals screeched and screamed.

And then something pierced the darkness. A brilliant flare of Light. An inferno of heat. A snap.

The pressure on my windpipe released, and I was falling.

I was vaguely aware of what would happen next. I had witnessed it once, long ago. It was a hazy memory now. The animals would be upon me.

But at least it would be quick.

Only, as my back hit the ground—nothing happened.

Then a hand reached down to remove the broken rope from my neck. A canteen was placed against my lips, and I spluttered and coughed on the cool water filling my mouth.

I was pulled into a sitting position. I blinked several times, trying to shift my vision into focus.

I was still in the dark forest. Still surrounded by those dead, black trees, only now I sat in a small clearing of smoking, charred earth.

I blinked several more times, trying to understand what was happening. Then I looked up into the face of my savior.

"*Mom?*"

"Give yourself a minute," she directed. "Have more water." She handed me the canteen.

"What are you doing here?" I asked, my voice feeble and hoarse.

"The better question is what are *you* doing here," she snapped.

"You said—" I began.

"I said Elijah should come to this realm. Not. You."

The creatures in the remaining trees began to screech at my mother's angered tone. She reached behind her and drew an arrow. With incredible grace and speed, she launched it from a bow.

As the arrow flew through the dark trees, it ignited. An explosion of fire ripped across the forest, clearing and charring everything in its path, leaving smoldering embers in its wake.

My mother stood eyeing the surrounding forest, daring another creature to make a sound.

I looked up at her not only confused by what had just happened, but also by her appearance. She wore an olive-green dress. But it was not regal and dignified, as were the gowns I had always seen her in.

This dress was worn. It had been through hell and back. It had stories to tell.

The material looked to be some type of soft leather. The tight sleeves were stitched along each arm. And two long slits ran up the

171

front of the slim skirt. I could see how the slits enabled a full range of movement.

Cinched around her torso was a brown leather corset. It was thick, offering a layer of protection to her midsection. And running diagonally across the corset was a strap for the quiver she carried on her back. On her bow arm she wore a long gold cuff from her wrist to just below her elbow.

Probably what was most shocking were her boots. They were tall, rugged, laced all the way up to her knees. And the brown leather was covered in mud.

I had never seen my mother in anything soiled.

Equally as jarring was her hair. Although I had seen her blonde strands worn free before, it was always perfectly brushed. Now it was wild, tumbling down her shoulders.

This was not my mother. This was…*Adriel.* A woman—I realized—I did not know.

She reached a hand out to me. I took it, and she pulled me to my feet.

Adriel looked at my hand and squeezed it tighter. "You met with the Gwarlock?" she asked with disbelief.

"How do you know?" I wheezed, looking down.

"You have entered a pact with him. You are marked by it."

There were no marks on my hand, and I knew it was something she felt rather than saw. But what was visible was the grey corpse-like color of my skin. I shut my eyes, not wanting to see it a moment longer, hoping it would return to normal quickly.

Adriel looked at me with creases at the corners of her eyes. "I don't know why I am surprised," she said. "You are a warrior."

I pulled my hand from hers. I couldn't help but take a step back, and I stared at the ground with shame.

"I…I'm not," I told her. I rubbed the front of my neck. With my voice wavering I confessed, "I gave up. I couldn't make it out of this place."

Adriel grabbed me by the shoulders, forcing her face into mine. "Violet. I hung from these trees three times before I made it out of here on my first visit to this realm."

Her fingers dug into my bones and her voice dropped. "Sometimes, on the very darkest of trails, you cannot walk your path alone."

She closed her eyes for a moment before saying, "Sometimes even the strongest among us, need a guide to take us through the darkness." She dropped her hands from me and took a step back, straightening, seeming to shine in the dark.

"Now come," she said. Then Adriel looked around the black forest like a bitch you would not want to fuck with. "We're leaving."

***

Section by section, swath by swath, Adriel incinerated a path through the trees, igniting the darkness with a vengeful fire, leaving nothing but smoke and ash in her wake.

"How are you doing that?" I asked her.

She withdrew another arrow from her quiver and notched it on her bow. "I send a spark of my energy to the arrow's tip," she answered.

As if that explained anything.

She let the arrow fly and more trees crumbled in a burst of fire as we trampled over the newly barren ground.

I stopped walking as a deep anger washed over me. Not once had I tried to use my Light in this place. I was exhausted and drained. It probably wouldn't have helped, but still...I should have tried.

Adriel paused, noticing I had not followed her. She looked back, calling to me, clearly reading my thoughts. "It's not your fault, Violet. It's the way of this realm. It is very difficult to use your strengths here. You are meant to become worn down and lose your way. You are meant to forget your gifts."

She began walking forward again. "Come," she insisted. "We need to leave."

As I caught up to her, Adriel said, "I know my way through, but if I stay too long, I will inevitably become lost. I will forget my abilities; they will be smothered by the mist, and we will not make it out of this realm. We have to keep moving, straight for our destination. If we dither, the forest will shift around us. And we will find ourselves among the souls who occupy the trees. There will be no hope for us then."

"How do you know your way?" I asked. "Why would you have ever come here before?"

Adriel's lips tightened before she let out an exhale and answered, "It is a long story, Violet. One which we do not have time for now."

I took in the woman walking before me, giving her a once over from head to toe.

I had been given the name Violet Adriel Archer. It was my understanding that inheriting my mother's name was a fitting tradition for our roles at Court. I also knew my mother had not altered her name upon her marriage to my father. It would not have been appropriate etiquette for the title and position she held.

I eyed the bow Adriel carried and the quiver at her back. "So a literal archer." I stated.

174

"Violet, there is no need for the adolescent tone."

I couldn't help that my face scrunched up. "You'll forgive me if I'm a little exasperated."

Instead of an answer, Adriel launched another arrow with an incredible flourish. As we continued on though, she finally made an offering.

"I am very old, Violet." She spoke keeping her eyes forward, taking careful note of our surroundings. "When I was a child, I took to archery. I became quite adept at it. I was able to combine my skills with certain gifts I possess." She gestured to the charred earth we walked over. "And at some point, I became known as *Adriel the Archer*. Over time, it became my surname."

I did not want to discuss what had happened to me in this forest. I wanted to bury the memory—the act of it—away somewhere. Never to be found again. But I wanted one question answered.

My words were barely audible. "How was I not harmed?"

"To a small degree I am able to control the energy I release—even once ignited. I made sure that it did not touch you."

"And what?" I continued. "You just go around doing this for the fun of it?"

She gave a sigh. "Violet, try to understand. To you, I just wanted to be a mother. I wanted you to have a mother." Adriel's perfect posture straightened even more. "But I have lived a life, long before you were ever born."

Marching on, eyes forward, Adriel said, "I have been trying to save Prisms from the beginning."

She took a deep breath, and for the first time, she shared with me who she was.

"I was there when the attack occurred on the very first Prisms," she began. "I tried to help. But I was a small child. There was nothing I could do. I had a thousand years to prepare for the next one. And I made sure I was ready.

"There were many Prisms I have been able to save, staging their deaths and hiding them in a realm of fire. And there have been some I could not reach in time. Those weigh heavily upon me.

"Elijah was one of the few I almost lost. While I eventually arrived to drive off the Shadows, it was not before they attacked his family." Adriel shook her head. "That poor child."

I remembered hearing that Elijah's whereabouts had been unknown until just recently. "Did you take him to the Realm of Fire?" I asked.

"No. I had already taken the girl, the other Prism. She was mature enough to embark upon the journey. When I returned, I was about to falsely announce her death. I knew that was all it would take to keep Elijah safe. I had found it just took one. If the Shadows believed one Prism had been murdered, they would not come for the other.

"Before I could make the announcement, however, I learned of the attack upon Elijah. I was too late to save his family."

Adriel's shoulders began to roll forward ever so slightly, and she became quiet. I was afraid she was recounting those she had not been able to save.

After a moment, I told her, "I'm sorry."

At my words, a slight smile crossed her lips. "When I found out that I was chosen to bear the next Prism, I was determined to keep you safe. And then Zagan was brought to me. I had you both. The two most precious, most important children. The weight of our race on your tiny little shoulders. And your safekeeping, on mine.

"I struggled with the decision to take you both to the Realm of Fire, where I had hidden the others. But even if I had decided it was

176

the best option, I had to wait until you were old enough. It is a treacherous journey, full of peril, not suited for a small child.

"And then I lost Zagan. The greatest disgrace of my existence. I failed that precious boy.

"He had come to me after he was a year old. I knew any number of individuals could have known what he was, and where he was. Still, I thought he would be safest behind my walls...I was wrong.

"I wanted to make certain, should you ever find yourself in danger, you would have a fighting chance. So your lessons began.

"And as you grew, I did not take you to the Realm of Fire because I believed you would be safe. I had not told a soul that you were the Prism. Not you. Not your father. No one. I never spoke of it.

"Besides, with Zagan gone, you could not enact the *Vinculum*. No one would ever know what you were. You would be free.

"Then Elijah returned.

"I had heard the rumors of him. That he had been found. That he had not crossed over.

"I wanted him to stay as far away from you as possible. I knew he would be a target and you would become one too.

"At the same time, you were given a proposal. One that I was certain would be the death of you. I instructed Killian to get you safely out of Court. Then I would take you to the Realm of Fire.

"But you are too stubborn! And too skilled! And in the end, what could I do? Your life is not mine to live. And I had no choice but to stand by as you left to greet your death.

"When Elijah arrived at Court to come for you, you were gone. And after speaking to you, I thought perhaps it was possible that you would be safe from Shadow attack. Perhaps, under the protection of their prince, you would finally be out of their reach.

"I convinced myself our people could wait another thousand years for salvation from the Dark. And I began to believe it had all been for the best. I arranged a ball for everyone to see that you were now the bride of, and more importantly under the protection of, the Dark One himself.

"But when you returned to us...after what happened to you...befalling the Shadow's Kiss. I wanted nothing more than for you to be spared from it. After not wanting Elijah anywhere near you, I wanted him to save you.

"And I thought perhaps you could be the one who finally lives. You could be the one who finally saves our people from the encroaching Darkness. Together, you and Elijah could fulfill the prophecy."

Adriel gave a sigh. "Which is another thing I have yet to tell you of."

I held my hand out in front of her. "Elijah already filled me in," I told her, seeing the toll her confession was taking.

I had noticed that her steps were slowing, her arrows not flying as brightly or as far. And I wanted her to save all her strength to get us the hell out of there.

Then blessedly, with a final pull on her bow, Adriel released her last arrow. Ahead of us, through the smoking wake of destruction, was a solid wall of rock.

Some tension seemed to ease from Adriel's shoulders as we approached, and I had a feeling she had been more fearful of this place then she'd let on.

Walking right up to the wall, she placed her palm on the stone. Then she closed her eyes and  murmured some words. A glow of light escaped her palm, followed by a low rumble, and a door shaped section of the rock crumbled away into dust.

Adriel passed through the entry, and I followed behind her.

We were in a cavernous room with a circular wall. Doors surrounded us, and a small bright star was suspended high above, floating in the domed ceiling.

A Vestibule.

Before I could ask, Adriel said, "I created this portal long ago." She glanced back at the rock wall we had just passed through as it slowly reformed behind us. "After being trapped in the Realm of Lost Souls once, I was determined to have a way out in the future."

She turned to me and took my hands in hers. "It is time. We must travel to the Realm of Fire now. If you follow all my instructions, we will make it there safely. But you must know, one wrong step, and you will be greeted by death."

Adriel's eyes creased at the corners. "And it is near impossible to ever return from the realm. You must accept it as your new home now."

I was startled by the sudden direction things were taking. "What are you talking about?"

Her gaze became desperate. "I have tried time after time, to bring the others back. Each time I have taken a Prism, it was with the hope that I could one day reunite them with their other half. But I have yet to find a way."

She squeezed my hands. "I am an exception, though. I am able to pass back and forth through the realm because of the particular qualities of my power. I am able to walk through the fire without being burned. And I will come to visit you often."

"But," I countered, "if you can take a person into the realm, why can't you also leave with them?"

"Violet," she replied, "the way in is not always the way out." She paused, letting her words sink in. "Now we must go."

"I can't," I told her.

"But Violet," she swallowed and I could tell she regretted what she had to say next. "The Council did not take my petition. They refuse to adjust your sentencing. The order for your execution still stands."

"It doesn't matter," I told her. "There are too many things I have to do. There is a stone that I must bring back for the Gwarlock. And Zagan. I have to find him. And...other things."

I cast my eyes to the side. "I can take care of the Archangels who come after me."

Pulling my hands out of Adriel's grasp I concluded, "Besides, if I can help an entire race of people, then I don't see how I can turn my back on that."

The pain on Adriel's face was too much to take. I could see there were things she wanted to say, but eventually, she simply nodded. "I am proud of you," she said.

"And as that is your choosing, then I offer my aid in finding the Oracle. I fear of what may happen to you if the Darkness continues to reside within you. I fear how it may eat away at you.

"And just as pressing—the Oracle is the only one who can now reverse the Council's ruling to abrogate your death sentence. And in doing so, free Elijah."

"Free Elijah?" I asked.

"Yes," she said, "the Council is holding him prisoner. They will not free him until you are dead. I tried to plead for both of you. The Council would not waver."

I wanted to slump to the floor. The road ahead of me was paved with improbable tasks, and the impossibility of it all was crushing.

But like anything, I couldn't think of it in such an overwhelming way. I had to face one feat at a time. And that was exactly what I would do.

I looked at Adriel. "I need to go to London. How can I get there?"

Standing in the center of the Vestibule, Adriel closed her eyes and held her palms up on each side of her. She recited an incantation I did not understand.

As she spoke, her palms glowed and the small star floating above us, flared to life. Then the doors all around the circular wall began to spin. A wind swirled, whipping our hair as the doors flew by. When Adriel was done speaking, the doors stilled, settling into place.

Walking straight ahead, Adriel placed a hand on the Threshold, opening it with her touch. "This is the one you want. Just remember to hold back on your Light if you wish to remain hidden from the Angela."

She turned back to me. "If you must return to the Realm of Lost Souls, bring a fresh body and some illicit periodicals for Filbert and Horace."

"The rat and the old man?" I asked.

Adriel nodded. "If you are able to find one particular publication entitled—"

She paused, her lips thinning with distaste. "*Butt. Man.*" She pronounced the two syllables of the porn magazine separately and with exaggerated annunciation. "Then all the better. I have come to understand it is a favorite of that nasty little vermin's."

"I'm not bringing them shit," I countered.

Adriel raised her brows. "Profanity is a sign of a lazy mind, Violet," she chastised before continuing.

181

"Filbert and Horace guard a path which travels straight to the Gwarlock's temple. Provide them with these distractions, and you will pass unhindered. You will find the entry just behind their bench."

I looked at Adriel in disbelief. Did she honestly expect me to drag around a body and porn magazines?

However, she didn't take notice and continued with her swift instructions. "Also, take a torch with you. Light it before you enter the subterranean grounds. It will serve as a reminder in the dark. Use it to remember your strengths. Your power." `

Finally, Adriel added, "When it is time to leave, use your Light to locate and open the portal."

As meager as it was, I wanted to try and offer my own assistance. "Elijah and I traveled to London to try and find the Oracle—to a club called the *Den of Inequity*. But we didn't find her. If you're going to look for her, it might be a place to start."

Adriel hugged me. "Thank you, Violet. I must first return to the Radiant Court, and then I will begin my search. I value the information."

I didn't know how to properly say goodbye. I had no idea how to show my appreciation for what Adriel had done for me. And yet at the same time, after learning all I had about her, I felt a great distance between us.

Still, I hugged her back. "Thank you. I would have been back there forever, if you hadn't…"

Adriel pulled back and looked at me. "Use my office at the Radiant Court as a communication base. Check in and leave a message for me when you can. If I don't hear from you after a certain amount of time, I will know you need help. I will come looking for you."

Squeezing my arms, Adriel spoke her final words before we parted ways. "You are not alone in this, daughter. There are those of us who stand behind you, those of us who are prepared to fight with you." She leaned in and touched her forehead to mine. "Remember that."

# CHAPTER 16

~Violet's Playlist: Paradise City, Guns And Roses~

"YOU'VE GOT TO BE KIDDING ME."

I found myself in a dark alley between two tall buildings. I could hear the muffled sounds of a blaring television and a yapping dog. Directly in front of me was an overflowing dumpster which sat next to a wide metal door.

I was outside the entry to the Den of Iniquity.

The Threshold had spit me out here, and I wondered why Elijah and I hadn't used it when we'd first visited the club in search of the Oracle. I shook my head. It didn't matter. I was just glad to know where I was.

I paused for a moment, questioning if there could be any benefit from stopping in at the underground immortal hot spot. Perhaps there was information I could learn about the Fatales before I went to steal from them.

When more yapping sounded from behind the door, I decided against it. Instead, I turned, determined to make my way straight to the Fatale house. But as I began down the dark alley, I caught a glimpse of my hand, and the sight of it made me pause.

There was still a gray tone to my skin. It had improved. It was nowhere near as bad as it had been. But it was still unsettling.

I took a deep breath of cold night air, wanting to cleanse away the tinge of death which I felt covering me. And then I retched. Taking a deep breath had been a mistake. I eyed the side of the entry to D.I.

*That fucking dumpster.*

***

From blocks away, I could hear the music. Once I had reached the Fatales' mansion, I had to fight not to hold my hands up to my ears.

*Paradise City* by Guns N' Roses was blasting through arena grade speakers.

I knew the Fatales liked to party, but this was a little much. Wondering what the hell was going on, I approached the front gate to the property.

I suddenly felt power and heat nearby. My eyes flew to the figure standing by the entry.

He took a step towards me, practically blocking out the street light with his size, and steam rose from the ground where his feet met the pavement. In an instant, his pupils elongated as his irises turned a neon teal.

Then a hiss clicked in the back of his throat, and he questioned me in a gritty voice. While he sounded more human now, I could still recognize his voice as the dragon who had tried to stop us when

186

we stole the gemstone. It was the one who appeared to be their leader...*Hellion*.

"What is your business here?"

Keeping my body still, I barely gave my head a tilt in the direction of the Fatale mansion. "They took something from me. I'm here to get it back."

It was a lie, but I hoped it might earn me some empathy from the dragon.

He gave a humorless chuff. "Leave."

I glanced at the huge speakers. "You're going to call attention to the mortals. You're violating all kinds of agreements."

"The neighbors have been bought off and temporarily relocated. We warded the entire block. Mortals cannot enter, see, or hear this street."

Before he could continue, a third story window from the Fatale house was opened so forcibly that the glass shattered. "Goddamnit!" someone cried.

A head poked through the window. "Last chance, Hellion! Turn the song off, or you will be sorry! We do not want a war with you, but you're about to get one!"

In spite of the distance between us, I could see the Fatale looked...*rough*. There were dark circles under her bloodshot eyes. And her hair was in a top knot which looked like she'd tied up about three nights ago and left that way. The bun was dangerously loose, lopsided, and strands were sticking out all over the place.

I wondered how long the music had been blasting. Just then the song ended, but instead of a new track, *Paradise City* started up again.

They were playing it over and over again.

And that was when I understood the scene before me. The dragons had surrounded the Fatale house. The Fatales were probably trapped inside, unable to leave the mansion. And the dragons were trying to drive them out with Guns N' Roses.

Lilly had mentioned that the mansion was strongly warded. I guessed the dragons were unable to forcibly enter.

Hellion raised his head towards the Fatale at the window. "Give us *The Heart of Darkness* and we will forgive all grievances against you."

My skin prickled at Hellion's words. That had to be what the Gwarlock wanted. Entropy or the Fates or *something* had to be at play here. It had been set up too perfectly.

"Fuck. Off!" called the Fatale.

Stepping behind me, Hellion grabbed each side of my upper arms and held me up in front of him, showing me to the Fatale.

I felt like a fish he'd just caught. "Put me down!" I snapped.

He spoke right over me, ignoring me. "I have your ally. She is about to be executed unless you hand over the stone."

The Fatale squinted at me. "Who the fuck is that? What the fuck do I care? Kill her. Eat her. Do whatever the hell you animals do. Just turn off the goddamn music!" she screamed.

"Ugh!" Hellion gave a deep growl of irritation, tossing me aside. "You're useless."

I landed on my ass next to him. He obviously didn't see me as a threat. I was an annoying little gnat he didn't have time for. I scrambled to my feet, trying my best to hold on to my dignity.

The Fatale narrowed her eyes; I could see a fire ignite there. She dropped her voice, no longer shouting over the music, but we still heard her words. "You leave us no choice."

She backed away from the window, and the entire house went dark.

"They're going to try something," Hellion shouted to the other dragons stationed around the property. "Get ready."

For a few moments, there was nothing—just a dark mansion on a deserted street with *Paradise City* berating the night.

I stood there waiting and waiting, increasingly irritated by the violation to my ears, when an explosion lit the sky. The Fatale house erupted in a blast of flames.

And I began to understand why the Fatales had been so successful in their attempts against the dragons. It seemed Hellion...*was a big softie.*

As the blast of heat and debris missiled towards us, he grabbed me and cradled me into his body, turning his back to the burst, acting as my own personal shield.

When we turned around, the Fatale mansion was no more, and in its place was now an inferno. Backlit by the flames and running in all directions were Fatales.

And somehow, the speakers were not harmed by the explosion. Somehow, *Paradise City* continued to blare through the chaos of the night.

It figured the Fatales would have their own personal soundtrack as they filled the street with pandemonium and destruction. I really had to stop getting involved with them.

It was obvious what they were doing. They had initiated the blast and were making a run for it. They had split up in different directions, leaving their fate to chance, hoping whoever carried the stone would run free.

Hellion shifted, and I was suddenly standing under an enormous dragon. He bellowed some deep command and launched into the air. All around the burning rubble, I could see five other dragons take to the sky.

189

They were going to try and weed out the Fatale with the stone. And like the dragons, I had to try and find it. I took a chance.

I ran for the alley on the side of the house. Leaping and sprinting over burning materials, I made it to the park behind the mansion. I scanned the greenway. All the while, music blared, dragons screeched, smoke billowed, and the fire threatened to ravage the entire block.

And then I found what I was looking for—two platinum blonde pigtails. I accelerated through the park, heading straight for Lilly.

Catching up to her, though, I became momentarily distracted. Just ahead of Lilly was a particularly tall and toned Fatale. I kept my eye on her for a moment longer than I should because I couldn't be certain of what I saw.

Through the hazy smoke, it appeared as though Mr. Goose—the Fatales wrinkly, tiny, old butler—was strapped to her back as she ran.

It had to be. I could hear his little involuntary whoops of surprise as he was jostled about.

I forced myself to ignore the bizarre sight. I only had a small window of opportunity. I had to focus on what was important. And so, I shifted my attention to Lilly.

Catching up to her, I shouted, "Lilly, give me the stone. I'm not one of you. They won't think I have it." I began keeping pace alongside her.

Lilly gave me a startled glance. Then she returned her focus to the front, pumping her arms and running faster. "Uh, not a good time, Violet."

"Come on! Don't be stupid. You can use me! I can help!"

"Violet! Fuck off! Can you not see that I am in the most dire situation of my life right now?! I don't have time to chat!"

There was no time to try for an easy way. Too much was at stake. I felt terrible for what I was about to do. "I'm sorry," I told her, "I really am."

Then I tackled her.

We went rolling over the grass. I tried to get on top of her but she dodged away, jacking up to her feet. She looked confused.

I swung a kick for her face. She dodged again.

"What are you doing?!" she screeched. She launched a punch for my face.

I tilted my head just enough to the side to miss the blow. But as I did, I saw a giant figure swooping down from above.

Lilly saw the dragon at the same time. "Run, you stupid cow!" she screamed at me.

I did. We both did. But it was too late. We were each swept up. Talons lassoed around our torsos as the dragon plucked us from the ground.

Lilly screamed at me from the dragon's other claw. "See what you did! Now we're fucked! What were you thinking?!"

She reached down and pulled off her shoe, then she threw it at me. Because my arms were caged by the dragon, the Louboutin ankle boot beaned me right in the face. All the while she swore at me, cursing me with genital warts, hemorrhoids, and granny panties for the rest of my immortal life.

I ignored the slew of verbal attacks and focused on escaping the dragon's hold. Before he could take us any higher, I pulled from deep down inside on all the Light I could find. I tried to send a pulse of it into the claw that was wrapped around me, hoping I could force the talons open.

But nothing happened. It was a measly little blip of energy that pulsed into the dragon's foot, going unnoticed. And it was all I had.

191

In attempting to access my Light, though, I felt a stirring. Then with a rush, I found a wealth of cold Darkness flooding my system. There for the taking. Wanting to be freed.

And incredible power came with it.

I accepted what was offered and unleashed it into the dragon. Black veins began to branch through the dragon's claw, giving off inky shadows as they wrapped farther up its leg.

I felt the dragon jerk, and we started careening to the side. It wasn't enough, though. He wasn't letting go.

I drew upon the Darkness even more, becoming saturated in it myself. And the shadows all around me began to silently wail and screech.

The dragon convulsed violently, opening his claws before crashing to the ground. Lilly and I went tumbling over the grass. I tried to right myself as fast as possible. When I glanced over, she was doing the same. She shot me a terrified look as she tried to run off.

I went after her, tackling her once more. She tried to fight me. But I was too powerful. Sitting on top of her, I ripped off the section of her jacket where I'd seen her store the stone once before. I tore away the material, to reveal the ruby red gem inside, and I shoved it into my own pocket.

Lilly looked up at me with fear and anger. "You fucking bitch! You'll pay for this!" Then her gaze darted over my shoulder and she blocked her face with her hands. Knowing from her reaction that a blow was coming, I rolled to the side.

Giddeon had arrived.

I hissed and slitted my eyes at him. In my state, I couldn't see the weariness that covered him. I didn't notice the somber bleakness in his eyes. I just saw an enemy.

And while his sword was raised, he didn't strike. I took the opportunity and lunged for it, grabbing the fiery weapon with both hands. Then I did to Giddeon exactly what I had done to Cord.

The Darkness traveled down the sword, turning it black. G gritted his teeth and tried to wrestle the sword away from me. But I held tight.

Although I was immersed in the Darkness—in the shadows—it didn't escape my attention that Lilly was lurking behind me. I knew she was looking for a way to retrieve the stone.

With my grasp still firmly on G's sword, I launched my foot directly behind me, striking Lilly in the stomach. She went flying back.

But then she somehow clamped down on my leg, in a way that was close to tearing straight through it. I couldn't imagine how she was doing it. I chanced a glance back and realized one of the dragons had grabbed a hold of me with his razor-sharp teeth.

I couldn't be certain, but it looked a lot like Hellion.

The dragon gave a vicious yank, and both my feet left the ground. I refused to let go of Giddeon's sword, though. And Giddeon held fast, digging in where he was.

I was trapped between a dragon and an Archangel while they played tug of war with me. Then out of nowhere, a hand shot up into the waist of my jacket. Lilly had wedged herself in the middle of us all and was fishing around my clothes for the stone.

The Darkness was just about to reach Giddeon's hand and I knew once it began to travel through him, he'd weaken substantially. Then I would release an eclipse of Darkness over the others, obliterating any Light in their hearts. Just one moment more and I would deal with them all.

But before any of that could happen, I noticed ice begin to scuttle across the grass as the ground froze. The temperature of the air all around us plunged. And I heard unhurried footsteps—slow and steady.

*Thump...Thump...Thump...*

A faint high-pitched sound that was barely audible, pierced my ears. It was the tinny sound of honed steel being dragged across frost.

In spite of the Dark ardor I was immersed in, I suddenly became very afraid.

Not for myself...*But for everyone around me.*

# CHAPTER 17

Violet's Playlist:
Arsonist's Lullaby, Hozier
Down on You Knees, Flora Cash

THE SHADOWS CAME FIRST.

Slipping in and around us, there in the park, inky black swaths of cold malevolence filtered through. They held ghostly wails and screams that had been long forgotten. The wind whipped and black clouds churned through the night sky.

I let go of Giddeon's sword and went flying back. My body snapped through the air with the force of the dragon's bite. But I didn't stay suspended above the ground for long. With a chuff of hot air through his nostrils, the beast spat me out.

When I landed on the frozen ground, I didn't look up at the dragon. Instead, I lifted my head to glance forward. And that was when I saw him.

Amid the miasma of shadows was Zagan.

He was too lethal. He walked too slowly. Step by unhurried step. And while *Paradise City* continued to assail the night, Hozier's *Arsonist's Lullaby* would have been much more fitting.

He wore black pants and a black shirt that was open down the front. His dark windblown hair was swept back from the sharp angles of his face. And all across his exposed skin, inky glyphs shifted—appearing and then disappearing.

He walked straight for me, dragging his sword behind him, the way a madman would.

All around him, those dark shadows spread and climbed. It was probably impossible for others to see him. But I could. I could see straight through the shadows now, straight through to the man inside.

The Darkness I had unleashed began to coil around me, and I felt a thrilling rush of coldness. Of anticipation. A hunger. Clouding my mind with want and need.

*But I was not mad. I was not a monster.*

I dug down to a place very far and deep inside, and I pulled. I was strong. I was my own master. I would decide what I was capable of.

And I caged the Darkness.

I blinked my eyes. My rib cage expanded with a rush of air. And my head cleared.

I looked at Zagan then. I saw him when no one else could. And I saw the death he would bring. Every single being in the park was in danger.

He had come for me once before like this. And he hadn't just plucked me away. Only after he'd painted the ground with blood and gore had he swept me up.

I had to do something. I had to stop him.

I snapped my eyes towards Giddeon. "Leave!" I shouted.

He tore his gaze from Zagan to meet mine. And I knew he was confused. I could see his hesitation. He didn't know if he should try and fight the Dark One, try to get to me, or just pulse out of there.

"Go!" I insisted. "You're no good to the Council if you're dead! He won't hurt me! You can come for me later, asshole!"

Thank the Light, Giddeon was not an idiot. After another fraction of uncertainty, he disappeared.

I attempted to stand up, to make my way to Zagan, to try and get through to him. But my leg gave out from under me. While it was still attached, it was useless. The dragon had crushed bone and severed tendon with his bite. I would need time for it to heal.

I turned over my shoulder to look up at the thing. I was certain it was Hellion now. "Go," I told him. "You'll be killed."

The dragon growled at me, stepping over me, preparing to meet Zagan head on. And I was willing to bet the stupid animal thought he was protecting me and the stone all at once.

"You don't know what you're doing!" I yelled up at the dragon, pushing myself to my hands and one knee. "He's here for me. He wants me. Go now. Or you'll die!"

I could have been mistaken, but it sounded like the dragon chuckled.

I tried to reach into my jacket for the stone, willing to offer it up to the dragon just so he and all the others would leave. I would find it again.

But my hand came away empty.

Either Lilly had snatched it from me, or it had flown out from my jacket when I'd been snapped through the air. Regardless, the stone didn't matter just then. What mattered was getting Zagan out of there.

I glanced across the greenway. Lilly and the other Fatales were running, trying to make their way out of the park, dodging the dragons circling above them. They were trying their best to use their weapons on the beasts whenever they could. I didn't know if they fled because they had the stone or because of Zagan's arrival, but I was glad they were leaving.

I dragged myself forward, to the side of the dragon. And I tried to plead with Zagan. I would have tried to send a pulse of my Light at him, but I had nothing to give. I searched in vain for a spark somewhere amid all the Darkness engulfing him, hoping to find a thread to pull on—but there was nothing.

"Zagan, I know you can hear me. I need your help. I need to leave this place right now. Please, take me away from here. It has to be now."

There was no recognition from him. The shadows swirling around him increased their frenzied dance, swirling higher and higher, screeching and wailing. And then they reached Hellion.

The dragon stiffened and let out a surprised roar. Then a blast of fire shot from his mouth. But the light and heat were gobbled up by the shadows. The dragon roared again in anger. Then he snapped his head forward about to cleave right through Zagan's midsection with his razor-sharp teeth.

In a move too fast for me to follow, Zagan shifted a few inches. He must have twisted his wrist at the same time because his sword arced across the dragon's neck.

Zagan continued to stare at me, not even flinching when the spray of blood coated him. And then it all began. The slicing of tendons and arteries.

I screamed at him to stop. I kept trying to wobble my way over to him. But he wasn't staying still. He was methodically pacing around the dragon. Slashing here and there. Ripping the beast apart.

The dragon fought viciously, not faltering or giving up once. His brute strength just wasn't a match for Zagan's dark madness. The dragon began to stumble, before falling to the ground.

"You better lie still and let me handle this," I gritted through my teeth, not looking at the dragon but knowing he could hear me. "Otherwise this is the end for you."

Then I did the only thing I could. I did what I had to do. I grabbed a blade from one of the straps on my pants, and I launched it at Zagan. It lodged straight into his gut.

He froze—it felt like everything around me did. And very slowly, he looked down at his abdomen. Then his head rose. And his black eyes looked into mine.

It was not the first time I had knifed him. And we both knew it. I had stabbed him once before when I'd been running from him…When I'd chosen Elijah over him.

I wanted him to become consumed with that same betrayal now. I needed him to. Because otherwise, he would finish off this dragon.

While he remained absolutely still, I could feel him. And from deep inside, an icy rage filled him. The blood pumping through my veins threatened to freeze from merely being in its presence. And I felt a need to unleash my own Darkness. To air my own grievances and satisfy my own rage.

*But I was not mad. I was not a monster.*

I maintained control. I knew if he saw me consumed by Darkness, he would not come near me, believing he had tainted me.

Instead of reaching for Dark power, I very clearly grabbed another knife, and I raised my arm inch by inch. I was slow and deliberate in my action. I paused for a long moment with the dagger raised above my head—every ounce of intention written all over my face.

I stared at Zagan, unblinking, and I threw the second blade.

He could have avoided the strike. He could have moved out of the way with ease. Instead he absorbed the blow, and the knife lodged in his shoulder.

A bolt of red lightning cracked, scorching the ground between us. A gust of wind whipped through the night stirring up the smoke and ash from the fire.

I didn't take my eyes off of Zagan. But I knew at any moment another dragon could come. We had to leave now.

I didn't want to hurt him anymore. I didn't want to drive him deeper over the edge. I didn't even know if I could throw another blade into him. I would not show it, but each strike tore at me.

On my hands and one knee, I bent my elbows, sitting on my one good leg while the other lay useless behind me. I let my arms, head, and shoulders sag forward to rest on the frozen ground.

Laying my forehead on the grass, I took a deep breath, praying for more strength, asking for the will and the ability to stop him, to get through to him.

The high-pitched, barely audible, tinny sound of sharpened steel being dragged across ice vibrated in my ear. And I heard one slow, unhurried footstep followed by another.

I didn't have the strength to pick up my head. Instead, I turned it to the side.

I watched—step by unhurried step—as he came for me.

The rest was all too familiar.

***

With an unhinged rage in his eyes, Zagan grabbed me, squeezing too hard, silently swearing his revenge.

Then I became nothing more than smoke. And we were gone.

But a moment later I slammed back into my body and was instantly tossed onto a bed. Pain shot through my injured leg, yet I scrambled into a sitting position, needing to know what was happening, needing to hold on to some semblance of control.

We were in the master chamber at the Dark Manor. Where, for some reason, he always brought me.

A vortex of Darkness whirled around Zagan. He threw his head back and let out a roar shredding the shirt he wore to scraps. And then the damage began.

He threw the floor to ceiling wall length bookcase to the floor, shattering wood, shaking the room and sending the chandeliers overhead clattering with the destruction.

He would have done more. He would have trashed the entire room, but I yelled at him.

"Stop!" I slid off the bed, standing on my one good leg, and I withdrew my short swords from above my shoulders with the swish of steel pinging through the room. "Or I swear to the Light, I will stop you."

Zagan turned from where he was, his entire chest heaving, his nostrils flaring, and the sides of his jaw ticked. He stared at me. Without looking away, he reached up and grabbed the dagger still lodged in his abdomen. He yanked it out before letting it clatter to the floor.

And still with his gaze locked on mine, he reached up and pulled out the second blade from his shoulder. This one he palmed, holding his hand out towards me and squeezing. Dark blood began to pour from his fist. It shook from his rage. And then he opened his fingers. The crumpled steel dropped to the floor, covered in his blood.

His bloody hand remained outstretched in front of him. His fingers bent and straining with tension. His grasp aimed at me. He wanted to hurt me. To punish me. His eyes narrowed on me—the black veins branching and shifting through his irises. He took one jerking step in my direction.

Then he threw his head back and bellowed, fisting his hands at his sides with tendons and muscles straining under his skin, before disappearing in a swirl of shadows.

The chandeliers swayed and clanged above me.

I sank to the ground, dropping my swords to my sides. Unraveling. He was gone again.

But as I sat there, I felt something far below. I reached my hands out, stretching them over the dusty floor board in front of me.

What I felt made me pull myself up onto my one good leg. Hopping. Clutching. Tripping. Falling. I made my way out of the chamber, down the unending staircase, through the first level hall, and I descended into the forgotten wing of the manor.

Into the despair.

***

I pushed open the old rotting door to Zagan's room—a dark decrepit hole in the ground with nothing but a bed…and my lips parted.

I found him sitting on the floor in the corner. His knees were bent into his chest. His head was cradled in the crook of his arms, his hands were clutched tightly to the back of his skull, pulling it down into his body. He was trying to physically hold himself together, to squeeze everything back in. Only he was too big.

The muscles down his back kept him from pressing too closely to the wall. His shoulders were too wide to fold in. His chest too hard to cushion against his legs. And the sinewy cords and tendons running up his arms were too large to tuck into his torso.

Every inch of his body was rigid and tense. My muscles ached just looking at him.

I tried to drag myself into the room, but his body jerked at my presence. So instead, I stopped where I was. I didn't move. Didn't breathe.

When I was finally certain that he was not about to wisp away, I began to lower myself to the floor. I tried not to disrupt the air around me. I tried to be nothing more than another shadow in the room.

I sat there in the doorway, unmoving, watching, as Zagan fought for control. Eventually I scooted an inch closer to him. Then another. And another.

After what must have been half an hour, I finally made my way to him. I began to lift my hand, letting it hover just above his shoulder for a good minute. Then I placed my palm on his skin, and I swallowed a cry.

The shirt he'd shredded had absorbed most of the dragon's blood, but the black marks that formed and disappeared over his skin were still present. And they were so cold, they burned.

Zagan's big body had jerked at my touch, but then he seemed to ease ever so slightly.

Over the course of a small eternity, I eventually placed my other hand on his opposite shoulder. Then a long while later, I rested my head against his arms. And I tried to help squeeze him back together.

In the park I had tried to direct a spark of Light towards him, and I'd been incapable. But here, touching him, being next to him, I felt something. Deep down at the very wellspring of my power, there was a glimmer of Light.

I tried to focus on it. I tried to draw on it. There was not much, but it was something.

I had felt the Darkness too.

Ever since Zagan had arrived, I had felt a Dark need—a pull. But I had kept the Darkness locked away. Mastering it. Even now, being pressed against Zagan. I felt the beast inside rattle its cage, wanting to be freed. And I kept the bars slammed shut.

I would not surround Zagan with more Darkness.

I rubbed my face against him. I stroked his hair. I whispered things to him. I pressed every inch of myself into him. Not allowing anything between us. No space. No Darkness. No shadows.

But the heat. The want. The need. It all came washing over me. I shifted where I sat, pressing my chest into his side, feeling an aching throb begin to drum between my thighs.

The way he smelled, the massive frame of his shoulders, how I could barely wrap my arms around him—it all excited me. The strength and power of his body next to mine consumed me.

That I was the one person in the entire world who was next to him just then...

And I knew I was the only person in the world he would allow next to him just then.

And I was ashamed with myself. Ashamed that I wanted someone who was so hurt and broken. Someone who was tortured. Zagan needed my help. Not my lust.

I had thought I could help him. I had thought I could help hold him together. But all I was doing now was igniting my own desire.

I had to pull back from him. I knew I had to. I just needed to put a little space between us. I needed to breathe air that was not filled with him. I needed to feel something around me other than his big body. I needed to dampen the connection I had to him.

I would ease a foot away from him. I'd be present for him without expecting anything in return. Only the moment that I began to pull back, one of his sinewy arms snaked around me. Then the other. And his head buried in my neck.

My breath sawed out from my lungs and my chest expanded against his. The pull. The connection. The desire to be consumed by him, poured out of me. And at being crushed against him, I felt sparks of Light flare somewhere deep inside.

He rubbed his face against my neck and his breath fanned across my skin. I grabbed his shoulders pulling myself closer to him.

His hands came up between our bodies, and he yanked the buckles on my jacket apart before sliding it down my arms. I rolled my head back trying to straighten my posture so the material could slip away.

And then his lips were on my collarbone and neck. I laced my fingers through his hair. He covered the skin on my back with his hands. And the bare skin of my chest pressed into his.

The icy chill to his skin was gone and the black markings were fading. The pain from my leg had dulled. I felt nothing but him and the pounding throb at my core.

His lips trailed my neck to my jaw, and I rolled my head to the side. He grabbed my waist and shifted my body onto his so I could straddle his lap. And while I gave a sharp inhale at my injured leg being dragged along, it was nothing I was willing to interrupt the moment for. If anything, being this close to him was helping.

But Zagan pulled back from me. He looked at me, my unclothed chest, my leg—as if waking from a daze. And for just a moment, there was a relaxed peace on his face. For a fleeting moment, he had been wrapped up in me and just me and nothing else. No rage. No shadows. No Darkness.

Then as he stared at the wound on my leg, his nostrils flared and his jaw ticked. That maddened glint returned to his eyes.

I grabbed his face with both my hands, forcing him to look at me. "I'm fine. It's nothing," I pleaded. "Just being with you is making it better."

He narrowed his eyes at me and more black veins began to branch through his irises. "Zagan please," I whispered. "Please stay with me."

His jaw was set so tightly that his cheeks hollowed and his big body began to vibrate. I could feel him fighting for control.

I searched his eyes wishing I could find a way to help him. With his face still in my hands, I leaned into him, and I placed my lips against his. "Please." I tried to breathe the word into him, wanting to be the thing which consumed him. Wanting him to choose me over the Darkness. Which I knew wasn't fair. I knew given the choice, this cold evil was not what he'd choose.

He shook harder and his skin chilled. I kissed him again, with more pressure this time. I was already straddling him. With my one good leg bent under me, I pressed my hips into his.

I pleaded with my lips and with my body for him to stay with me.

A jolt of electricity radiated from my core with the pressure of being pushed against him. And with that I felt more sparks of Light inside. I gathered every bit of bright energy I possessed in that moment and I tried to cover him with it.

I refused to let him leave. I kissed him harder, running my hands to the nape of his neck. Against his lips I demanded, "Kiss me back, damnit!"

And with a final shudder rippling through his powerful body...*he did*.

# CHAPTER 18

**B**RIGHT ENERGY ERUPTED in my veins, and I felt it flare between us.

I was crushed against him. He held one hand on my back and the other at the top of my spine, then his hands were on my shoulders trailing down my arms before one brushed over my neck.

He couldn't stop touching me. I grounded him. I was something he could hold on to.

And while I was awash in the desperate need and hunger he possessed, it did not cripple me. I was stronger than I'd been before. I could meet the aching desire he had and give him whatever he needed. Because my own had grown to be just as great.

His lap was hard and bruising. And I pressed myself against him. I hated that there were clothes in the way. But breaking free from him to undress was not an option.

While he kissed me, Zagan's hands slid up to each side of my jaw. He pulled away from me, and with my eyes closed I rolled my head back, exposing my neck to him. Only he didn't lean down to move his lips over me.

My lashes fluttered open and I looked at him. A single streak of ice blue ran through the black in his irises. He took a shuddering breath, and his chest billowed. His grip on my jaw tightened.

I could see he was fighting for control again. Only this time, it was not his demons he was trying to tame. This time, it was lust.

His voice was strained. "Don't ask me to do this to you."

I searched his eyes, confused. "I haven't asked you for anything," I panted.

His hands moved to my shoulders and he held me back. His eyes traveled from my face, down my neck, and over my chest before returning to my eyes. His hands shook where they clutched me "I can't control myself," he said through gritted teeth. "You need to leave."

*And. I. Fucking. Snapped.*

My chest was rising and falling, and between breathes I cursed at Zagan. "You fucking idiot. This is helping me." I stared at the blue streak running through the black in his eye. "And you!"

I felt like every cell in my body was vibrating with pent up need. I was a powder keg on the verge of exploding with no release in sight. And Zagan was making me so angry. There was no goddamn need to torture me—or himself—like this.

I dropped my head into my hands. Through clenched teeth, my voice became unhinged. "Why do you keep fighting this?!"

If only he would accept it. He was so convinced that he would ruin me. That he did not deserve me, that he was fighting the very thing which could free him.

I was enraged that we were in his barren room. Because I was the one who was about to jack up some furniture. And what the hell was I going to do in here? Flip over his mattress? It would probably be an improvement.

I knew my rage would set off Zagan's own. I hadn't been able stop it. It had redlined beyond my control.

There was no hope for us. There probably never would be.

But something strange happened. Something I hadn't expected.

While Zagan's voice was aggravated, it was not maddened. "You are hurt and filthy," he tried to reason.

I snapped my head up to wilt him with my stare. "Did you just call me *filthy*?"

His eyes creased at the corners and he looked at me with frustration. "You are." He raised his hand trying to swipe at my face with his finger and I smacked it away. "You have ash," he continued, "and my blood all over you." His gaze darted around my body at the evidence.

"You just made a big mistake, Zagan Black," I informed him. "You think you're the only one who can fuck a place up? I'm about to school you on how to properly go ballistic."

I scooted off his lap and yanked my jacket on. Pulling myself up, I tried to hop out of his room—with as much dignity as one can hop out of a room with—particularly after being rejected and deemed *filthy*.

I began the long trek to my quarters. Without warning though, I was snatched into the air, and Zagan was striding towards the stairs before I could even respond.

"What are you doing?" I screeched. He had picked me up and was carrying me against his chest. I had grabbed on to his neck in reflex.

"I don't know," he seethed. "In spite of the fact that you are an asinine woman, I feel I must help you." He spoke the words as if disgusted with himself.

"You'd better be careful. You're about to get *filthy*."

"It was a comment on your current state, not your overall disposition. You clearly do not have enough sense to differentiate between such facets of conversation. And seeing as you are witless, you do not realize that you should lock yourself somewhere far away from me. I have not had long bouts of clarity lately. It just so happens that a *witless, asinine* temptress seduced me into some inexplicable connection with her before tearing it away, flooding me with warring powers beyond my control, and then choosing another over me. Not to mention she readily impales me with knives. Therefore, it is only a matter of time before I lose any semblance of sanity once more. And for this reason I tell you: It is not safe for you to be near me!"

"None of that was my fault!" I couldn't control the high pitch my voice had taken. I fired off bullet point responses. "I did not seduce you. I tried to help you. I did not choose another over you—I didn't know who you were! And as far as the knives go…well the reasons vary from instance to instance. Some of the times I haven't even been successful. So…" I realized I had become lost in my argument.

We reached the main staircase in the foyer and Zagan glared down at me. "Will you be cawing the entire five flights? If so, I will increase my pace."

I pressed my lips together in a thin line and tried to jump out of his arms. He shoved me against his chest harder. We stared at each other.

A second streak of crystal blue had broken through his left eye. For that reason alone, I was willing to cave. And so I huffed, settling

213

in his arms, and looked away. We didn't say another word to each other.

Zagan carried me up the stairs with ease, slicing through the dark and empty manor with that lethal precision he possessed. When we reached the fifth floor, however, he did not take me to my quarters. Instead he carried me to the opposite wing, and we entered the master chamber.

He walked over to the old tub which sat in front of one of the fireplaces, and he set me down in front of it. His voice was a low rumble in the dark. "Lean back."

Between my teeth I replied. "I want to go to my room."

Two fires sprang to life—one in the hearth by the overturned bookcase and another in front of the tub. The fires roared and crackled, their light and heat spreading through the cavernous space, casting the shadows to the sides.

"This is where I choose to aid you," he said. "Now lean back."

He towered over me, waiting for me to comply. His dark hair was swept off his forehead. I could now see a streak of blue in his right eye in addition to the lines breaking through in his left. Stripes of soot ran over the perfect angles of his face. Somehow, they highlighted his strong features, making him even more attractive.

The hard planes and ridges of his shoulders, chest, and abdomen stood in stark relief against the firelight. I felt a twinge of guilt at the dried blood there, but the knife wounds had closed and looked as though they would heal quickly. Most of the inky glyphs had faded. The one mark which remained solid black and prominent was the symbol of the three crescent moons intertwined over his heart.

My gaze traveled lower. The ridges from his abdomen disappeared into the waistband of his pants. And he wore no shoes.

I looked back up at him. "Why don't you ever wear clothes?" My voice was quiet.

After a pause, he uttered two simple words. "They hurt."

His reply wasn't at all what I had been expecting. Silenced, I leaned against the lip of the tub. Then Zagan knelt in front of me and began to remove my boots.

"You don't have to do this," I told him.

He didn't respond.

After he had slipped each foot free, he grabbed the hem of my pant leg. His dark head was bowed in front of me; the muscles on his shoulders flexed with his deft movements.

With a controlled motion, he tore the pants up the side of my leg from ankle to waist. He left the waistband intact, which I could easily snap apart. However, the fabric above my knee was clotted to my wound.

When Zagan saw this, he slipped one hand between the pants and the top of my thigh, attempting to hold my leg in place as he peeled the material away.

At his touch, my head fell back, and my chest bowed forward. He looked up at me and instantly withdrew his hand, his brows slashing in anger at himself, a reminder of the monster that he was.

I grabbed his wrist. "It feels good," I told him. "It's helping," I reassured.

He didn't look convinced, but I drew his hand towards my thigh again. He prevented me from placing it back on my skin, and I thought it was becoming too much. I figured he had reached his limit and was going to leave.

I freed his wrist from my grasp. "It's okay. I can take it from here," I said.

215

But then he slid his hand against my thigh once more. He continued to peel away the material, and I could feel my bones begin to knit and mend beneath his touch.

Once the fabric was freed from my damaged skin, I found my leg was able to support a little weight and pressure, although the wound was still an open mess.

Zagan stood and leaned into me. His arm snaked around my side. I drew in a breath at the closeness. When water began to pour from the tub faucet behind me, I realized what he was doing.

Zagan straightened, easing his body away from mine, and he had that pained look on his face. Without another word, he turned and left the room.

I looked around at the cobwebbed chandeliers, the crumbling hearths, the dark shadows that covered most of the chamber, and now the massive bookshelf that was scattered across the floor. I sighed. I would have much rather been in my own room.

I glanced over my shoulder at the tub filling with water. Steam was rising in the chilled air. At least the water was hot. But there was no soap or shampoo. No washcloth. No towels. No music player. And the tub was dusty.

I didn't leave, however. I figured I could rinse off the grime here and then take a proper bath in my room.

In hindsight, though, I think it's obvious that was not the real reason I stayed. The real reason I stayed…was because I hoped Zagan would come back.

So I tore the last few threads at my waist band and let the pants fall to the floor. Then I shrugged off my jacket.

I eased myself into the steamy water taking care not to put much pressure on my leg. The water stung the open wound and I inhaled a hiss of air through my teeth.

In spite of the pain, I sank into the deep tub until I was submerged. I turned the water off, and I immediately began to scrub my hands over myself. After wiping the blood and soot from my chest, hands, and face, I untied my hair from its braid and slipped my head under the water.

I did my best to scour myself clean. And although I lacked the essential bathing amenities, it was still a significant start. I even drained the sullied water and refilled the tub once more.

After I was certain I'd done all I could, I dipped my head under the water one last time. Then I stretched my neck and tried to massage my nape.

When I felt eyes on me, I paused, unsure what to do. I could feel him somewhere in the shadows. And I could feel his fascination as he watched me.

But I stilled, because I knew there were other things stirring and warring within him, threatening to escape. He was trying to gather himself. He needed to keep himself together. And I didn't want to drive him away. So, I waited and sat in the water closing my eyes. And I remained still.

Finally, he made his way over to me. I opened my eyes to watch him.

Zagan had cleaned up. The blood from the knife wounds was washed away, as were the traces of soot from the fire. His hair was wet and it looked like he had run his hand through to push it off his face. He wore a fresh pair of black pants and nothing else. And in his hands, he carried some fabric.

He stopped several yards away from me. "This is all I have," he said. He tossed the black fabric onto the closest bureau. It appeared to be a shirt.

I looked up at him. "I have a closet full of clothes in my room," I said. "You could have grabbed something from there." It wasn't a complaint, just a fact. Had he forgotten that I lived here?

"That is your space." he told me.

I opened my mouth, but I didn't say anything. I wasn't sure how to respond to that. Staring at the faucet in front of me, I finally settled on, "Thank you."

But he had already left the room.

I didn't take long. I slipped out of the bath and limped for the bureau. I tried not to put much weight on my mending leg.

Since there were no towels, I waited a moment letting some of the water dry from my skin. I also tried to run my fingers through my hair to free the excess moisture.

Along with the shirt Zagan had brought, there was an extra piece of fabric which looked like it had been carefully ripped from a garment. Realizing what it was intended for, I wrapped the black band around my thigh, tucking in the ends. Then I drew the shirt over my arms.

It was massive. I had to roll the sleeves several times before I buttoned the front. I didn't have anything to wear under it, but that wouldn't be a problem. The bottom of the shirt almost fell to my knees.

I had never worn someone else's clothes before—a male's clothes. I ran my hands over the fabric. And in spite of everything I'd been through, I suddenly felt very vulnerable and exposed. I didn't know if I could face Zagan like this.

But I wasn't a coward. So, I notched my chin and limped my way to the door to open it.

Yet, the hallway was dark and empty. I didn't know why, but for some reason, I'd thought he'd be waiting there for me.

Shaking my head at myself, feeling utterly stupid, I dragged myself down the hall to the opposite wing.

I found the doors to my suite were open, and there were fires burning within. As I ushered my way through the entry, I felt an incredible sense of relief that I hadn't expected.

However, I could see a fire burning in the dining room fireplace as well, and I shuddered for a moment. I couldn't help but think of the last time I'd been in there—when Maxim had insisted on feeding me.

I pushed the thought away. I would deal with Maxim later.

I was surprised to see food laid out in the dining room. As I hobbled closer, though, I could see none of it was prepared. It looked as if an armful of items had been collected from the kitchen and then dumped on the table.

There was a head of broccoli and cauliflower, raw green beans, and a basket full of uncooked potatoes. Farther down were apples, some jarred fruits and a loaf of bread. There were no plates or utensils.

A jug of water sat at the very end of the table with a single empty glass to accompany it. I filled the glass three times and finished it off with each pour.

Then I grabbed a couple apples and the loaf of bread. I returned to the sitting room to settle onto the settee. Curling my good leg up, I left my injured leg to rest off the front.

I ate. And it was the most delicious food I'd ever eaten. I had gone a very long time without. I sighed at each bite.

When I had finished both apples and half the bread, I looked up, realizing I was not alone.

Zagan stood in the hallway. He hadn't entered. And I could feel how he struggled.

I figured if he was going to be tense and angry, I'd try cool and breezy. After it was clear he was not going to come in, I called over to him. "So, what's up? Are you going to snap back to crazy or what?"

He didn't reply at first, and for a moment I didn't think he was going to, but then his deep voice floated through the room. "Perhaps."

"Okay," I said. "But while I have you here…Those people at the park? That group of women and the dragon pack? They're cool. Okay? So if you come across them again, try not to go all psycho on them. Got it?"

There was no response.

"I mean," I continued, "I should probably stop hanging out with the Femme Fatales. Oh shit," I mumbled. "That was supposed to be a secret. Well just don't tell anyone. They're pretending to be Fallen Angels." I held out my finger and shook it in Zagan's direction. "But I'll tell you what they really are. They're a bunch of leather clad, sexified hooligans, if you ask me."

Zagan spoke through his teeth in reply. "Eat. More."

I noticed he was now just inside the door. I ripped off another piece of the bread. "Don't you worry, tiger. I'm not done yet."

After finishing the bite I'd taken I said, "You know those overgrown barbie dolls suckered me into stealing from a dragon with them? Oh! But that's not even the worst of it. You would not believe their house! You'd think a pack of posh alcoholic hyenas lived in that place."

I shook my head before popping my chin up. My eyes widened at the memory that surfaced. "There are literally monkeys swinging from the chandeliers."

I let my shoulder sink back into the settee. "I actually kind of became friends with one of them." I picked at the bread I held and my voice dropped. "But I ended up stabbing her in the back."

I wasn't expecting a response, yet it seemed Zagan had something to say on the matter. "It is one of the hazards of spending time with you."

I looked up and he rubbed his shoulder where I'd thrown one of the knives. My lips twitched but then I narrowed my eyes at him. "It was a figurative stabbing," I clarified.

"Those are the most painful kind," he countered.

I sighed and looked at my lap, feeling guilty for not just what I'd done to Lilly, but for a lot of things.

Zagan took a step back. "I have upset you."

I glanced up at him. "No. I just regret what I did. That's all. I feel bad about it."

Zagan took another retreating step. He was going to slip away.

"I'm still hungry," I blurted. "I think I'm going to have one more apple." I glanced at the dining room. Then I gave a melodramatic sigh. "But I don't know, they're so far away. Maybe not."

I held my breath and waited. Zagan and I stared at each other. He was assessing me. I arched a brow.

Finally, he took a step forward, and made his way to the dining room. He kept his eye on me the entire time.

I watched him move through the room and I wished he would do it more. He was always standing so still. And it was a shame. Because he moved with latent power, his body working in precision. I doubted he had ever made an awkward motion in his life.

He returned and held out the apple, looking at it as if it were some odd creature in his hand. "Should I have cut it for you?" he asked.

I took it from his hand, careful not to touch him. "No, this is perfect," I told him, taking a bite. By the time I looked up, he had already retreated to the other side of the room.

"Will you just sit?" I couldn't keep the exasperation from my voice.

"I don't like sitting," he replied.

What I did next was manipulative and selfish, I know. But really, I was just trying to get Zagan to relax. So if you ask me, I was helping him.

The bond between us was clearly driving him to ensure I was cared for. I knew the impulse. I had experienced it myself. And for whatever reason, he did not have the Crone to pass me off to.

I sucked some air through my teeth and winced, grabbing my leg just above the wound.

I could feel Zagan tense. "You're in pain," he stated.

"It's just hard for me to try and relax with you lurking around the room. I'd feel more at ease if you were to sit. And it will be easier for me to get my mind off the pain if I have someone to talk to."

"Had I known you wanted to babble incessantly, I'd have left you in that park," he muttered.

"What's that?" I asked in an exaggerated volume.

With a highly irritated exhale, Zagan crossed to one of the wingback chairs across from me. And sat.

I smiled at him. "Now. Isn't that better?" I asked.

He glared at me.

And in the quiet room with the fire crackling and the empty manor all around us, we sat together.

# CHAPTER 19

~Violet's Playlist: Meet Me In The Woods, Lord Huron~

Y OU KNOW WE NEED to talk about things. You know that, right?"

Zagan didn't reply. But I could tell by his expression that he disagreed.

I took a deep breath, not having the faintest clue where to begin. There were too many things. Too many players. Too many threads.

I would have to start with the most important.

"Is the manor still warded from The Contessa?" I asked.

Zagan gave a single nod.

"There's someone else. Someone who works for her. He was the one who brought me here and...I don't know. He was a liaison of sorts." I became flustered talking about Maxim. I wouldn't admit it to myself, but I was hurt. I felt betrayed. And that made me feel hot with embarrassment. *I had been so gullible.*

"Apparently he's the Master-at-Arms for the shadow court," I said. "His name is Maxim Steel." I watched Zagan's face for any recognition. When there was none, I continued. "He tried to—"

I started over. "I came back to the Dark Manor." My voice lowered and I leaned forward, wanting Zagan to believe me. "To see you." I paused hoping my words would sink in.

"Maxim was here. I don't know if he was waiting for me or if it was a coincidence. He used some commands in the Dark Tongue that paralyzed me. And he had spelled chains which I couldn't break. The Crone came, though. Somehow, she was able to free me, and she gave me a chance to escape. But as far as I know, Maxim could come back at any time."

As I spoke, the blue that was beginning to streak through Zagan's eyes disappeared. His chest began to pump with each breath, and his fingers dug into the beautiful upholstery of my wingback.

"Hey!" I clapped my hands in his direction. "Chill!"

He didn't.

"If you're going to ruin my furniture, you can leave, bonehead," I told him.

His fingers dug deeper into the fabric. I wobbled to my feet. "I like that chair and you're ruining it!" I cried.

His eyes shut. His body tensed—the muscles in his arms straining against his skin—and he froze that way. Over the course of a long minute he relaxed his grip, breath by breath, until his fingers finally lay flat on the armrests.

He opened his eyes to look at me. They were cold and black and there was a certain vow there. Zagan's voice sent chills down my spine. "He will not touch you again."

I bit my lip and nodded before averting my gaze to the floor. "Well he comes in and out of here freely, so..."

225

"You need not worry."

I drew in a deep breath, tilting my head back to look up at the ceiling, not wanting to continue. I was probably about to set him off over and over again. But I had to lay it all out there. "He's not the only one. There was someone else named Marax. He came for me when I was…running from you."

I sped up my words, wanting to get it all out before Zagan snapped again. "He used the same commands and the same type of chains. I have no idea if he might come here as well. I think both he and Maxim are working for The Contessa or the Shadow Court or…I don't know exactly."

I chanced a glance at Zagan. He wasn't tearing up more of my chair. He wasn't whipping himself into a chaotic frenzy. He was now leaning forward with his forearms resting on his knees.

He was still tense. The muscles down his neck, chest, and abdomen were rigid. But determination saturated every inch of him. It seemed as though he had come to a certain realization, and with that, a certain clarity.

"No one will touch you here," he repeated.

I looked at him, at the wide line of his shoulders, the way his perfectly honed body dominated the chair. I saw all the coiled power ready at a moment's notice.

I believed him.

"You will leave," Zagan said. And I experienced a moment of incredulity. Would he ever stop saying that? It seemed as if we were getting somewhere, making progress, and now he was going to play this card again?

I had left once before and it had not ended well for either of us. Frustration began to tighten my features. I was about to launch into a tirade of grievances against him.

Then he continued. "Until you do, you will be safe here."

I calmed, composing myself. It was a start.

We sat in silence for a few moments.

The calm, the quiet, the fire—*the security of knowing I was safe*—it all began to get to me.

I blinked, and my eyes were slow to open. My head settled against my shoulder and the settee. "Do you know what The Contessa wants with me? With us?" I asked.

"No," he replied.

"I found a way to stop her. I mean, if I can return a stone to the god of death, I'll know a way to stop her." I sagged into the cushions even more and my voice slowed—the emotional and physical exhaustion of that experience washing over me.

"But I lost the stone tonight. I had it and then it was gone. It's going to be impossible to find again. I should be out there looking for it right now."

My eyes had closed. I opened them to look at Zagan. "Have you heard of the *Heart of Darkness*?"

He shook his head. And my eyes closed again. I struggled with what I'd say next, knowing we needed to discuss things but only finding blank spots in my mind.

My thoughts began to drift and then wink off one by one. I would speak again. I would. I just needed a moment. Then another. And another...

After I began to slip into sleep, I felt two strong arms cradle me. I forced my eyelids open.

Blinking up at Zagan, I told him, "I can..." But I didn't bother finishing my sentence. My head tilted against his chest and my eyes closed.

Before I knew it, I was in my bed with the duvet pulled over me. It was the nicest thing I'd experienced in a very long time. But just before I let myself drift away for good, I looked up at Zagan.

He didn't say anything. And he certainly didn't smile. But the tension on his face eased a degree. I saw his hand rise ever so slightly before it paused in midair and returned to his side.

And then I could fight it no longer. My eyes shut…and stayed that way.

*** 

Sunlight poured through the floor to ceiling windows, flooding my room. I buried myself deeper into the blanket and sighed. It felt incredible. And I soaked in the rays as they restored me.

I rolled over, intending to go back to sleep. But then I sat up, pushing the hair out of my face. I looked around the room— remembering how I had gotten there.

I found that I was alone.

Yet for the first time, in a long time, I was hopeful. There were people after me. Too many to count. But I wasn't being pushed away by the one person I needed the most. And the excitement that instilled in me was unlike anything I'd felt before.

I hopped out of bed, finding that my leg was much better, and I queued up my music player. Lord Huron's *Meet Me in the Woods* flitted through the bright and airy room. I couldn't help a self-satisfied smile at my indulgent choice. But if you ask me, I had earned the right to be a little melodramatic.

While the lyrics were dark, the music was light and uplifting. And it was what I needed. In a way it helped me own all that had happened, instead of letting all that had happened own me.

228

I washed up, deliriously happy to have all my bathroom amenities. And I dressed in a pair of leggings and a long-sleeved tee. I left my hair loose in waves down my back, my feet bare, and my rosy skin nice and moisturized. I even took a moment to swipe some bubble gum pink polish on my toes.

I couldn't help but catch my reflection in the mirror as I left the bathroom, though. My eyes were violet and bright, but there was no denying the small gray crystal specks that were scattered around my irises...

There were more of them now.

I shifted my gaze to the dark fringe of lashes that heavily lined each eye. I told myself they were what stood out—that they overshadowed the gray. I convinced myself the gray wasn't even noticeable. And I turned from the mirror to exit my quarters.

As I passed by the dining room, I saw a plate of bagels had been left there as well as a fresh pitcher of water. I helped myself to the water, and grabbed a couple bagels to take with me. Then I headed straight to work.

\*\*\*

"Fuck me, this place is a disaster." Even in the heavily darkened space, there was no denying the mess.

Across the upturned bookshelf and over the mountain of scattered tomes, I made my way to one of the chamber windows. Just as in my wing, they were enormous, spanning from the floor to the ceiling.

I took a hold of the brocade drapery, and I felt a thick layer of dust squish through my fingers. I struggled with the heavy fabric. It seemed as though the rings had rusted to the rod, and I thought I might have to try and yank the whole thing down. But I finally jostled the curtain loose and was able to slide it to the side.

I managed to part enough of the drapery for a wide beam of sunlight to pour into the long-forgotten master chamber of the Dark Manor.

Dust motes drifted through the swath of light, and a section of mirror sparkled from the other side of the room. I looked at how the beam of light cut through the darkness and I couldn't help but wonder when the last time light had been allowed into this space.

I worked relentlessly on each window, throughout the chamber, until the entire space was flooded with light. I collected my discarded short swords and clothing from the night before, and returned them to my quarters. I brought my music player and speakers back to the master chamber with me. Then I got to work, trying to stack up all the discarded books in an attempt to make space around the overturned bookshelf.

What I needed to do was go after the stone. I knew that. I should have gone after it the previous night, but there had been a lot going on.

And I would. I would. I just needed to...see if there was any important information here first. That night with the Crone there had been a text burning which I knew was special. So I stacked books.

Some were in the Dark Tongue, some I could read, some had pictures lending clues to the subject matter, and others were filled with only words. I tried to organize them as best I could.

I was flipping through one particular tome on beetle potions when I glanced at the open doorway.

There was no one there, though. I was alone.

230

I continued with my organizing for some time. Every once and a while I would look around—at the door, in the corner of the room, somewhere behind me—but there was no one.

I felt like an idiot. What had I been expecting? That we would hang out, flipping through books together while we listened to my indie folk playlist?

I focused on the task at hand and tried to force myself to stop hoping that Zagan would appear.

By the time the sun had set, I'd made very little progress. There were simply too many books. I'd organized a little section of those which had spilled out from one corner of the bookcase, and that was it.

I left my little piles, left the mountain of toppled books, and I returned to my suite. I helped myself to more water and bagels. I intended to go down to the kitchen to look for something more substantive, but I was filthy from all the dust. So first I cleaned up, changed into fresh clothes, and tidied around my room a bit.

I ended up making my bed, only to lie down in it. It was soft and clean and inviting, and it had felt so good to be in it earlier that day. The room was fully dark now and the fire crackled in the oversized hearth across from me.

I believed that Zagan would not allow anyone to enter the manor. And I still wore the ring which protected me from any spells through my dreams. To round things out, I had placed a dagger under my pillow.

I actually felt at ease.

I let myself snuggle in. My head sank into the pillow. The fire hummed.

And while my dreams were safe from someone else's influence, no dark warrior, or ring, or dagger, could protect me from all that now lived inside me.

I had slept a deep dreamless sleep the night before—peaceful and uninterrupted. This night, I would not be so lucky.

***

*It was dark. So dark. And cold. So cold. All around me was black. And bare.*

*And I didn't know where to go. I kept turning and spinning, trying to find my way. I began to run, but the path was changing. And all around me were the screams and screeches.*

*And I knew it would never end.*

*I began to hyperventilate. I tried to stay calm. I tried to figure out what to do. But a scream was rising. I could feel it begin in the pit of my stomach and as it rose, I had no choice but to let it out.*

*Once I did, I couldn't stop.*

***

My eyes flashed open. In an instant, I was no longer lost, I was in my bed at the Dark Manor.

And Maxim was standing over me.

I grabbed the dagger I'd placed under my pillow and brought it towards his neck as I sat up, knowing I couldn't give him the chance to speak.

But he was too fast. He straightened and leaned to the side. Instead of piercing his throat, I'd gotten him in the side of his upper arm.

"Stop stabbing me, woman!" he bellowed.

The fire which had died down now flared to life in a burst of heat. Zagan grabbed the knife and yanked it from his arm, throwing it to the floor.

"You are no longer permitted to carry knives!" he shouted.

My eyes darted around the room, making sure no one else was there. "I thought you were Maxim!" I cried, trying to control my shaking. "You were just standing there—lurking over me! Who does that?! What did you expect me to do?!"

Zagan pushed a hand through his hair. "I sensed your unease. I came to check on you. Then you began screaming. I didn't know if you were being harmed in some way."

Zagan kicked the knife on the floor. "I am now convinced it was a ruse to lure me in and fillet me." He turned towards the bedroom door, about to leave without another word.

"Wait!" I called. He stopped and turned around. "I...I..."

I couldn't be alone. Not just then. I couldn't let him leave.

"What if it was a premonition?" I tried. "Maybe I thought you were Maxim because I'm somehow sensing him or his intentions?"

Zagan did not look concerned. "No one will touch you here."

In spite of the fear, I couldn't help but look down and mumble, "Don't I know it." Then I shook my head at Zagan and chastised him. "Dude. You can't set me up like that."

He looked confused...and perhaps a bit irritated. He started to leave again. And all I could see was that dead black forest creeping in around me. He couldn't leave me alone with that. I wouldn't be able to take it.

"Uh...Ohh! Oww! Ow, ow, ouch!" I sounded absolutely ridiculous, even to myself, but I was desperate.

Zagan turned back again, this time his hands fisted at his sides, which caused the muscles all up his arms and across his chest to bunch and flex. Of course he was only wearing black pants, and the V of muscles that stretched down his hips popped against his skin.

"Violet." My name was a growl on his lips and it sent a shiver straight down my spine. He had been trying to get out as fast as he could. I was now testing his control.

"It's my leg," I told him, grabbing my thigh under the duvet. "I'm in a lot of pain. I don't think I can sleep like this."

I watched him, waiting to see if he'd care. I half expected him to dash out of there for good. But he took a step towards me. "I don't know what to do for that. The Crone is not here. You will have to assimilate."

"If you stay, it will help with the pain," I told him.

The muscle under his eye twitched. "Just assimilate," he repeated.

"What the hell does that mean?! Why don't you assimilate and just sit down!" I countered. When he didn't make a move to sit, I added, "Look, you can even smash the furniture if you want. Just stay here for a few minutes."

After staring at each other, Zagan finally made his way to the chair by the window. Based on the way he'd looked at me, he wasn't too happy about it.

"Not there," I told him. "Sorry but Maxim sat there. It's too creepy."

Zagan's jaw ticked. He looked at the floor as his next option.

"That's too far away," I said. I looked at the bed. "Can't you just sit here? It doesn't have to be this big deal. I'll stay all the way over on the other side. See?" I wiggled my way to the far edge.

"No," he snapped.

My head fell forward and I looked at my hands. I refused to let my voice waver when I spoke, at least I tried my hardest. "I just...I went somewhere. I was alone for a long time while I was gone. A very long time. And it was very dark. I don't..." It was too difficult to speak the words and my voice dropped. "I don't want to be alone right now."

When I finally looked up at Zagan, he was staring at the bed as if something impossible had been requested of him.

"You don't have to stay long," I added.

With an unconvinced shake of his head, he made his way over to the bed. He looked down at the mattress as if it were covered with maggots. "There are things in the way."

I glanced at the things. "It's just a pillow and blanket," I told him. I pulled the duvet over, clearing it from that side of the bed.

"And the other," Zagan said, nodding at the pillow.

I picked up the pillow and tossed it to the bottom of the bed. Then I waited.

Zagan continued to stare at the mattress with his lips thinned and his jaw clenched. After a long minute, he finally sat on the very edge with his back to me.

"No, not like that. You have to sit with your back against the wall. Like this," I showed him, leaning back.

"Violet." Another growl. A warning.

"Ok, fine," I said. I shivered. Even in the long tee and leggings that I wore, I couldn't escape the cold from my dream. I curled down into the bed and pulled the duvet tight around me, and I stared at Zagan's back.

He would never know how grateful I was in that moment.

Because having him there was a solid reminder that I was not in that dark place. I was not wandering, lost forever.

I was not alone. And that was enough. That was everything.

I saw Zagan's spine stiffen. And then with an irritated breath, he swung his legs up onto the bed and sat with his back against the wall, crossing his arms over his chest.

I didn't shift closer to him, and I didn't say thank you. I stayed exactly where I was and remained silent.

Instead I stared at Zagan's feet. They were actually really nice feet. After a moment, though, he crossed his legs with an intentional rustle. And I knew he had felt my eyes on him.

"Sorry," I murmured.

Zagan's voice was strained. "Why haven't you gone back to sleep? Do it, now."

I couldn't help but laugh. "Okay. Sure. No problem," I told him.

He looked down at me, clueless as to why I found him funny. Yet I could also feel a sense of fascination from him. As he stared at me, his nostrils flared and his jaw hardened.

I stopped laughing. I could feel my thighs tighten and my chest rise. I couldn't stop my shoulder from rubbing against my chin.

Zagan's eyes were locked on every subtle shift. "Stop. That," he insisted.

I closed my eyes and rubbed my head against my pillow, feeling my hair spill across it. "Okay. Sure. No problem," I repeated. Only this time my words were slow and thick.

Zagan tore his gaze away from me, squeezing his arms across his chest and staring straight ahead. "No talking!" He commanded.

I laughed again, which only irritated Zagan more. "I think I would rather you return to stabbing me," he growled.

I laughed harder.

"Why are you laughing?! These are not humorous comments."

I didn't answer him.

And he was true to his word, he did not speak any more.

While I was tempted to speak—and there were certainly things I wanted to say—I was genuinely grateful that he had stayed. The energy in the room had shifted from something dark and terrible to something light and comforting. And for that, I gave him the silence he needed.

At some point, I even fell back asleep. And this time I was not haunted by where I'd been...because I had been comforted by where I was.

# CHAPTER 20

I WASTED ANOTHER DAY.

I did. And I knew I did. But here's the thing: sometimes you need a break.

I could see the danger in it though. I could see how melting into the darkness and shadows of this forgotten place could be alluring. Because then I wouldn't have to face all that was out there.

After spending the day combing through books, I had washed up, visited the kitchen, and returned to my bedroom. Now I fidgeted and paced in the firelight, the sun having set long ago. I was tired, but I didn't want to sleep. I couldn't bear the thought of dreaming. So I tried to find something else to do.

I thought about my mother, Killian, Elijah, and then I shoved all those thoughts down, not wanting to face any of it just yet. I sat on the bed only to instantly stand again. *I needed something to do.*

Making my way through the hall, I moved out to the sitting room and began to look over the books on the shelves there. But just as I began pursuing the volumes, my hand paused on the spine of one. I held my breath and closed my eyes, cocking my head to the side. I couldn't be certain, but I thought I heard something.

Music.

It was a haunting underscore that floated just below the surface of the empty manor. I could picture the notes drifting from deep below, up through the cobwebbed darkness of each floor, until they barely existed anymore, with no way of knowing if they had ever been real.

I opened my eyes and glanced over at the coffee table, spying the journal I'd set there. It was black and leather-bound, with flourishing, powerful script penned meticulously across the yellowed pages.

I didn't know why I'd brought it in with me. It had been one of the books I'd looked through that day. And for some reason, I had found it intriguing, although I had no idea what was written inside since the words were in the Dark Tongue.

Picking up the journal, I flipped through the pages again. I needed to find out what was written there, didn't I? That was something I could do. I needed to know if it was important.

It could be important. I could swear there was a certain energy to it. And I wouldn't know unless I asked.

I looked at the doors to my suite. They were wide open. I had left them that way all day.

Straining again to hear the music, I allowed myself to pass through the manor and follow each melancholy note. If Zagan wasn't going to find me, then I'd go and find him.

\*\*\*

He didn't stop playing when I entered. And I stood and watched his back flex and bend with each slight motion. Wrapping my arms around my chest, I tried not to judge him for choosing this room.

There were other rooms in the manor which held pianos. Rooms that were not so black and rotted. Rooms that were not so cold and dark. So filled with shadows. But I knew I couldn't—I shouldn't—try and convince him to be anywhere but here.

I looked over at the few glowing embers in the fireplace, wanting to at least stoke them brighter. But I didn't.

And whereas I could barely withstand the notes he played once before—barely withstand freezing forever from them—tonight, I was not so broken by them.

I realized I could understand them. Not wholly. Not completely. But there were now a few scattered dips and swells that resonated with me. Because I now knew certain tones and notes that I had never known before.

I sat on the dirt floor with my back against the freezing wall. And I listened.

When he was done playing, he spoke without turning to me. In a level voice he said, "You shouldn't be here."

I stood. "I found something I need help with," I told him. "It's a journal in the Dark Tongue. I was hoping you could tell me what it says."

Zagan stood as well and crossed to me. He looked down at me and spoke with long pauses. "I do not want you to be down here." He searched my eyes. "Do you understand that?" he asked.

I pursed my lips and nodded. Because I did understand. I knew very well what he thought about this wing. Why he remained here. And why he did not want me visiting.

I looked down at the journal. "I just thought maybe you could help with this."

He passed by me. "No," he said as he walked out the door.

I followed behind him. "You don't have to do anything with it," I told his back. "Just tell me what it says."

I could feel the Darkness of the hallway pressing in on me, and I fought the urge to hiss at it over my shoulder. Instead, I picked up my pace to stay on Zagan's heels. He was already climbing up the stone stairway which led to the main foyer, and I basically had to run to keep up with his swift strides as he sliced through the dark.

"Your leg is better," he said without looking back.

"Yeah, so I was right," I replied. I hadn't meant it to come out so petulant, but I was becoming annoyed that he was forcing me to chase after him.

An irritated breath was all I received in reply.

I stopped walking. We had reached the foyer and I called, "So are you going to help me with this or what?"

Zagan's voice came drifting back to me as he disappeared into the darkness ahead. "I can't."

"Ugh!" I yelled after him. Then I began jogging to catch up to him again. I found him at the base of the main stairway and started following him up. "Why?" I insisted. "It's not that big of a deal."

He stopped and turned to look at me. "Because I can barely read, Violet." He stared at me for a moment, letting the words sink in. "I can't help you."

He continued up the stairs, up all four flights, without saying another word. I momentarily froze, caught off guard by the admission. Then I took off, following behind him.

When he stopped in the hallway outside my quarters, I looked up at him. "What are we doing here?"

He looked down at me as though I were an idiot. "We are not doing anything here. You are returning to your room."

I stared at Zagan. His eyes were blue. And I wanted to make some comment about it, about how we were both getting better and how I had been right. But I didn't know how to bring it all around in a way that would make it obvious I was revisiting his comment on my leg. So, I let it go.

I looked into my wing of the manor and back at Zagan. Then I did something that made me uncomfortable; I told him the truth.

"I'm afraid to go to sleep."

Zagan's jaw tightened. "Although highly foolish, you are also brave. You will be fine." He gestured to my suite, and I could hear the aggravation in his voice. "Now go to your room."

I tried my hardest, but I couldn't fight a small smile. Zagan's eyes narrowed and he took a step back from me. He looked apprehensive. "Do not start with the laughing again."

"You do this to yourself," I accused. "All you had to do was try and help me with something, and instead you send me to my room. How am I supposed to react?"

"I don't like it," he seethed.

My lips twitched as I watched him, and my chest felt warm. "You're adorable," I told him.

His shoulders snapped back, and his eyes widened. It was as if he'd just heard the most horrific sentence of his life. He seemed to be at a loss for words for a moment. And he stood there looking at me like I was twenty times more psychotic then he'd ever been.

Instead of leaving though, Zagan snatched the journal from my hand and stormed into my suite. I followed behind him. And I truly felt bad. I did. But he was too ridiculous.

He marched all the way into my bedroom and pointed to the bed. "Get in," he snapped at me.

Trying my best to give him a break and be agreeable, I hopped into the bed and sat against the wall. Zagan ticked his finger to the side. "The things," he said.

I pulled the duvet away and tossed the pillow aside. Zagan eyed the empty spot on the bed as if summoning all his strength and then sat, swinging his feet up. He crossed his arms and legs, making sure to stay on the very edge of the mattress. Then he looked over at me. "You are to stay on your side," he warned. "And no laughing."

Fighting a smile, I bit my lip and nodded. He glanced down at me and eyed the snug tee and curve hugging leggings. "Cover yourself," he added.

Rolling my eyes, I pulled the duvet up around me. "Shall I place a bag upon my head as well?" I asked.

He paused, considering the idea.

"I was being sarcastic," I told him. "I am not putting a bag on my head."

He studied my hair, my face…as if they offended him. "Maybe a hat then," he offered.

I knew he wasn't serious by his dry tone, so I didn't bother with a response.

He tore his gaze from me to examine the journal he held. He kept flipping it over, looking at the front and back, without opening it.

We sat like that for a few minutes. And while I knew he would prefer not to say anything at all, I couldn't' stop myself from talking to him.

"I've been trying to go through the books in the master chamber," I told him.

"I know," he said.

"Well if you know then how about lending a hand?" I was exasperated. What was he so busy with that he couldn't help?

"You were the one who made the mess," I mumbled under my breath.

I glanced over and found his eyes on me; they were narrow and intense.

"What?" I asked, brushing my hand through my hair. "Why are you looking at me like that?"

He didn't say anything. He just gave his head a slow shake and dropped the journal onto the bed, crossing his arms over his chest once again.

I followed suit and tucked my own arms around my waist. "Anyway," I huffed, "You could at least help me get that huge shelving system back in place."

Zagan didn't reply. He simply took in a deep breath which caused his shoulders to rise.

I hesitated with what I wanted to say next, not wanting to offend him. Finally, I tried to extend an offer. "You know, if you help me in there, I could review some vocabulary with you. If you want."

Zagan continued to sit and stare into the fire. Still he said nothing, and I didn't try to push him to.

I yawned with a little sigh escaping my lips, and Zagan flinched. I leaned towards him with the intention of placing my hand on his arm to steady him. But my hair brushed against his skin, and he bolted up in the bed. His entire torso was stretched as far away from me as possible.

His voice was low and quiet and full of tension. "Go to sleep." It was a desperate command.

I could feel how he struggled, and I had known I shouldn't move closer to him. But he wasn't the only one suffering.

Just having him near me, the sound of his voice, the way he smelled, his size, it was all driving me crazy. And what was more, I liked being with him. I liked hearing what he had to say and seeing his reactions to me.

And I just wanted to touch him and press my body into his. I wanted to feel his big hands on me. I wanted to put my fingers in his hair. I wanted to keep talking with him, but I wanted it to be while I was wrapped around him with my lips at his ear.

Yet I also wanted to give him what he needed. I didn't want to drive him away. I was convinced I would get him to see things my way eventually, but I would give him the time he needed to get there.

I had no idea what The Contessa had done to him over the years. But I knew I did not want him to feel like I was coercing him into anything. Especially when there was this force driving us together that neither of us had any control over.

So I let out a shaky breath, and I snuggled down into my pillow. I even pulled the duvet all the way up to my neck. When I was settled, Zagan finally leaned back against the wall once more.

I blinked my eyes a few times, feeling them become heavy, and my skin became warm with a sleepy realization; this was becoming my favorite place to be. In my bed, in my room, in the empty Dark Manor with the fire burning low and Zagan sitting next to me.

I looked up at Zagan, and although I knew he would resent it, I told him how I felt. My voice was soft and honest. "I like being with you," I told him.

He squeezed his eyes shut and tightened his arms. He looked like he was in pain. After he'd composed himself, he opened his eyes to look down at me. Shaking his head, his voice was just as quiet as mine had been. "You shouldn't."

I looked up at him and he looked down at me, each silently trying to convince the other. Then Zagan unwrapped his arms to bring his hand close to my pillow. With his index finger, he rubbed a single strand of my hair that lay there, in one slow swipe, before tucking his finger back into his fist and resting it on his lap.

I couldn't help but fall asleep with an ache in my chest.

# CHAPTER 21

THERE WAS A PRESCENCE. I could feel it.

I sat up in bed. It was still dark. The fire had died down. And Zagan was asleep. He had nodded off while sitting against the wall with his arms crossed over his chest.

I could see movement outside the uncovered windows in my bedroom. Shifting and winking on and off, two thin beams of light sliced through the dark sky.

I knew exactly what it was.

I eased out of bed and crossed to the towering window with only the glass separating me from the night air. The little girl, in her tattered dress, was standing on the front lawn amid the weeds and bramble with her black wolf. And those two strong beams of light shone from her eyes, spilling in from the glass and pooling around me.

I looked back at Zagan, sleeping. I didn't want him to wake up. I didn't want the little girl to see him.

I swept through my quarters, out into the hall, and down the stairs. The shadows which occupied the manor were at ease. There was a peace I never would have expected to find. As I slipped through the abandoned structure, the shadows did not stir...they slumbered.

And the little girl was going to ruin it. She was going to disrupt the quiet peace. I could envision those beams of light slicing through the windows like lasers, leaving behind scorch marks wherever they landed.

The energy which emanated from her was not malicious or sinister, it was just too high of a frequency for the ancient Darkness which slept here.

Down in the foyer, I lifted the weighted latch that ran across the back of the entrance doors. They swung open with a long, low whine.

I was instantly blinded. An intense light was directed at my face, and a gust of wind whipped past, scattering leaves and dirt all around. I threw up my arm to cover my eyes and took a step back at the force of the wind. When the power of the initial gust died down, I regained my balance and lowered my arm. With my head turned to the side, I cracked my eyes open, attempting to see through the bright flare.

But there was only darkness. The light had winked off. I took another step forward and wrapped my arms around my waist. My eyes scanned the dark grounds, searching for the little girl and her wolf.

All I could see in the surrounding night was the overgrown, unkempt shrubbery, the cliff which bordered the property, and the imposing wrought iron gate with the tree tunnel beyond.

The little girl and her wolf were gone.

"What?" I called. "What do you want?"

My voice seemed to be gobbled up by the night. And the only answer I received was the wind howling through the trees as the windows of the manor rattled all along the facade.

I waited. And waited. But I knew she wasn't coming back.

Shoving my shoulders against each door, I settled them in place and set the latch. I turned around to return to my room when something on the floor caught my eye.

There amid the leaves and twigs was a crumpled piece of paper. I picked it up and smoothed it out.

Five words were printed across the center of the page:

## WELCOME TO THE NEW AGE

The flyer was scorched. It looked as though it had been held up to a flame. In the middle of the browned section of the parchment, a date and time had been revealed. And at the bottom corner of the page was a symbol—three crescent moons intertwined.

They were holding another rally.

I crushed the flyer in my hand and stomped up the stairs to return to my suite, thoroughly annoyed by that little creep and her overgrown mutt.

When I returned to my room, Zagan was gone. My ire at the little girl redoubled. I even went back to my window to look for her, wanting to spy her out on the grounds and bang my fist against the glass at her.

But with no opportunity to scold her and doubting there was any chance of convincing Zagan to come back, I climbed into bed. I was careful not to let the duvet shift onto the other side of the mattress...just in case.

And still exhausted, I went back to sleep.

***

There were things I needed to do, and I couldn't put them off any longer. The very first, was ask for help.

After taking some time to get ready for the day, I made my way out of my quarters. I was about to head downstairs. I was even prepared to be polite and knock on the plank that guarded the abandoned wing, instead of barging my way in, when I heard a deep crash reverberate through the hall.

The floorboards shook at my feet, and I sucked in a breath. Furniture was being tossed around.

I knew that meant Zagan was snapping again. And it sounded like he was in the master chamber.

I had come to hold a certain possessiveness over my wing, and it may have even begun to spread to the entire floor. Because when I pictured that room being smashed to pieces, I didn't hesitate for a moment to run down the hall and save it.

I was determined to stop Zagan before he could do any more damage. He must have just been starting an episode because the rage and Darkness had not yet spread out into the corridor. I braced myself to face the onslaught of his emotions.

The door to the chamber sat ajar, and I shoved it open so hard that the door handle lodged into the plaster behind it.

"Stop!" I insisted.

Zagan turned from the bookshelf to look at me.

My voice became quiet as I took in the scene. "Uh…Because I've been organizing in a specific way," I said with very little conviction.

The floor to ceiling bookshelf, which spanned the entire wall, was no longer in a mountainous heap on the floor. It now sat back in place. It was battered and broken in several sections, but generally intact.

Zagan was standing in front of it, clearly having just hefted the thing upright. His pants were low slung and his entire torso was on display. I stared at him for longer than what would have been considered polite.

I was going to get him some higher waisted pants. I didn't know why he'd said that clothes were painful, but if he wasn't going to wear a shirt, he at least needed higher pants. That way I wouldn't have to stare at that V of muscles that traveled down his hips. It wouldn't hide the broad width of his shoulders and chest, and it wouldn't cover the ridges of his abdomen, but it'd be a start.

Without saying anything, he began picking up books and stacking them on the shelves. The simple task alone caused every honed muscle to flex and bunch. But there was also such fluidity and precision to his movements.

Sunlight was filtering into the room from the window next to him, and I decided I disliked watching him in the bright space.

The light was doing things to his features that made my chest feel hot and tight. Swept off his face, as if he'd stabbed his fingers through it, his hair looked several shades lighter. And while anyone could see he was attractive—even in the very darkest of settings—now the chiseled angles of his jawline, the slight hollows at his cheeks, and the piercing quality of his eyes were impossible to overlook.

Simply being in the sunlight made his skin look tanner. And all of this culminated into an incredible effect; Zagan looked younger.

Without all the Darkness and shadows weighing him down, he looked like a much different version of himself.

The torment and chaos were still there somewhere inside. I could feel it. But it did not consume him at the moment.

I struggled with what to say, finally landing on, "Thanks for the help."

Zagan gave a slight nod while stacking the books.

Knowing that idle chit chat would probably irritate both of us, I jumped right in with what I wanted to say. "I need a phone. I also need to find that stone I told you about. And I need to attend a rally being held in the Shadow village."

Zagan didn't reply.

I shifted my weight and crossed my arms, hating what I had to say next. "Look, I can take care of myself. I really can. And I don't need anyone looking after me. I don't.

"But the Council of Elders has sent Archangels for me because I defied their ruling. And I haven't quite figured out the best way to deal with the—" I hesitated for a moment. Then I steeled myself, reminding myself that I would not be cowed. "The Umbra," I finished.

I let out a breath, annoyed that I had to go on. "And I don't know how to stop Maxim or others from using commands in the Dark Tongue against me."

I took a step towards Zagan and let my arms drop, swinging them in front of me. "So I need some help. And normally I would take care of these things on my own. Because I can take care of myself. But right now I need some help."

Without looking at me, without taking a break from his task, without even considering what I'd said, Zagan replied with a stern, "No."

I took a moment to stare at him. I gave him the chance to explain, to counter-offer, to…*something*. To turn around and talk to me. Just acknowledge me. And when all he did was continue to stack books, I left.

Grumbling under my breath the entire way, I marched down the hall and back to my wing. I began to gather the things I would need and packed a small bag.

I grabbed the extra pair of fighting pants I had tucked away in my closet. Luckily, I had cleaned my jacket and boots the previous day. Now I changed into them and strapped my short swords to my back. Then I braided my hair.

I had asked Zagan for help because it was the smart thing to do, not because it was my only option.

If the Archangels were coming for me, I'd be sure not to access my Light. And if I absolutely had to, then I'd deal with those that came. I'd make sure to travel by day, bypassing the Umbra, and do my best to tuck myself away at nightfall. And I would just have to flat out avoid Maxim.

I could take care of myself. I didn't need to beg or plead with Zagan. There was no need to humiliate myself.

I left my quarters, angry, but prepared.

I made it down the main stairway. I crossed through the grand foyer. Light filtered in from the windows and refracted as it passed through the chandeliers. The moment I reached for the latch on the front door, he grabbed my arm.

Spinning me around, he stared down at me. "Where are you going?" he snapped.

I dropped the bag I was carrying, and it made a *thunk*. "I told you." Although my voice was calm, it was difficult to keep the anger from it. "There are things I have to do. I laid them out for you and even asked for your help. You refused." I eyed his hand on my arm. "So you had better rethink what you're doing right now."

"You cannot leave," he said.

I rose onto my toes and moved my chest into his. Tilting my chin up and narrowing my eyes, I whispered, "Just watch me."

He leaned his face into mine, and black veins began to branch through his irises. His voice was a sinister promise. "I will never let you."

I raised a brow. "Never?" I repeated.

His eye twitched. I could feel the frustration rise in him. "You will leave," he clarified. "When I say."

I set my lips against the side of his jaw as I let out a quiet laugh and murmured, "You're adorable."

I could feel his already rigid body stiffen against me. As I pulled my face back from his, I let my lips brush against the corner of his mouth.

I left them there for just a moment, wanting to let him be in control. I could feel the tension radiating through him and the frenzy that was brewing within. When I began to pull back from him more, his other hand came up to cup the back of my head, pinning me where I was.

Torturously slow, he turned his head, inch by inch, until his lips covered mine. And when he kissed me, it was deliberate and thorough.

He finally broke off the kiss, and I looked up at him. I could see how he struggled with every ounce of his strength to hold back. And I swear, I almost climbed up him. But the instant I tried to, he placed his hands on the tops of my shoulders and held me in place.

"My god, woman! If it will keep you from pressing your body into mine, I will take you wherever you want to go!" His words were a desperate, dark, rush.

I let out an intimate sigh and sank back against the door, looking up at him. "I've had a change of heart," I said. "I think I'd rather stay here."

"Violet," he warned.

I let my head roll from one shoulder to the other. "Fine," I breathed. My skin was too hot, and tight, and tingly. But I straightened and glanced at Zagan's chest. "So what? You're just going like that?" Then I squinted at him. "Do you even own a pair of shoes?"

Without a word, he grabbed my hand and began pulling me through the hall. When we reached the end, he growled, "Stay here." Then he descended down into the abandoned wing.

I leaned against the wall and waited. I grudgingly admitted to myself that I had to stop taking actions that were fueled from hurt and anger. It wasn't smart.

I also knew somewhere deep inside that I had left with the intention of trying to stir some kind of response from Zagan, which was brash and embarrassingly immature. And I knew it.

I could do better. I could be better.

Realizing that I probably wouldn't need to take the bag I'd packed, I made my way over to the front door. I withdrew cash and a credit card, securing them in my jacket pocket. I also retrieved the small journal I'd found in the master chamber, and the rally flyer. When I stood, Zagan was in front of me.

"Whoah." The response had just slipped out. I couldn't help it. I had not expected him to come back looking so...*badass.*

257

Over his pants were black boots that went up to his calf. And he wore a black jacket made from tough material that was zipped up. I particularly liked how the back of the collar was higher. It looked good on him. Finally, strapped to his back was his sword.

"You look like you're ready for the apocalypse," I said.

His gaze traveled from my boots, to my leather clad legs, over my buckled jacket, and up to the swords handles visible at my shoulders—making his point without saying a word.

I shrugged. Then I looked at how the muscles in his jaw flexed. "Are you going to be okay in all that?"

"I'll manage," he replied.

I tilted my head to the side, wanting to soften my next question. "Why do the clothes bother you?"

Standing in front of me, so big and obviously powerful, he met my eye. "I did not have any for many years."

Feeling very cold, I pursed my lips and nodded, acknowledging his answer.

Obviously not wanting to delve any further, Zagan's shoulders rose on an inhale before he let out a breath. "Violet, there has to be somewhere else you can go. Where you'll be safe. This—" he eyed the door behind me, a figurative look at all that was out there. "This isn't for you."

I felt my spine straighten and my shoulders roll back. "This is all I have," I told him.

Unhappy about it, Zagan shook his head. Then he stepped up to me. "Where do you need to go?"

I stared at him, feeling a little empty, feeling the connection that I'd been fighting so desperately to ignore—for his sake—begin to vibrate. Being with him like this wasn't going to be easy.

But it seemed the more I was getting used to these new facets of my reality, the more familiar and manageable they were becoming. I eyed the light spilling across the chandelier above us as it refracted through the crystals, the glass bending the rays.

Sometimes something delicate and fragile could do something incredible.

Resolved. Determined. Strong. I looked at Zagan…and I told him where to take me.

# CHAPTER 22

**D**ID YOU RAT ME OUT?"

Belcalis stood with her eyes wide. She had opened her mouth when we first entered her trailer, and she had yet to shut it. She stared at Zagan.

She shook her head without taking her eyes off him. "N...n...no."

I looked between the two of them.

"It's okay," I reassured Belcalis. I was caught off guard by how fearful she seemed of Zagan. Admittedly I didn't know her all that well, but I'd come to see her as unflappable.

"I promise. Everything's cool," I told her, placing my hand on her arm. I tilted my head towards Zagan. "He has nothing to do with this. He's just helping me run a few errands."

She snapped her gaze to me. And even though she tsked before she began speaking, there was no denying her desperate tone. "Look, I had to, alright? I'm a good citizen. I got my papers in order. I only sell legal shit. I follow the rules, en...en...You know, if the authorities tell me to do somethin', I'm gonna do it."

She grabbed my hand. "I didn't want to! *I. Did. Not. Want. To.*" She smacked her dining table with each word. "But what choice did I have?"

I focused on her. "It's okay. Really. I understand. Just tell me what happened."

Belcalis let go of me to ease herself down at her little table. She picked up a piece of paper and began fanning herself.

"You know," she began. "I told you they were here looking for you. The authorities. And I called 'em and told 'em you'd been here. But I tried to give you a head start and I didn't tell 'em where you were going."

She smacked the paper down on the table. "Why you don't have him," she tilted her head towards Zagan, "tell them to leave you alone. And you can all leave me out of it."

"You know who he is?" I asked.

Belcalis scrunched her face as if I'd asked a stupid question. "Of course. I was here when they held the demonstration."

"What demonstration?"

Belcalis looked down at her lap and pursed her lips, clearly refusing to answer.

I looked over at Zagan. "What demonstration?" I repeated.

Zagan stared at me, not answering.

I rolled my shoulders, annoyed that I was not going to receive an answer. "Anyway," I said, "if you have to tell someone that I was here today, that's fine. Do what you need to. What I really want is a translation spell."

Belcalis's shoulders slumped and she looked at the table, shaking her head. I had a strong suspicion she was wishing I'd find another witch to start visiting. Then she glanced at Zagan, and I could see she was not going to say anything with him there.

262

She stood from the table and turned to her wall of supplies. "What do you mean, a 'translation spell?'"

"There are some books I want to read," I told her. I pulled the small journal from my pocket and flipped through it. "They're in the Dark Tongue, and I don't speak the language."

Belcalis stared at me for a moment, appearing thoroughly annoyed. Instead of saying anything, though, she opened a drawer and rummaged around in it. Bits of paper, plastic forks, headphones, rubber bands, and other random objects flew out the sides. Finally, she pulled out a pair of reading glasses with a thick black frame.

Reaching for one of the many jars on her stacks of shelves, she selected a container that seemed to be full of some type of creature's eyes. After dropping a couple in a mortar, she added various other indistinguishable ingredients. Grabbing a pestle, she ground the components together.

Then using a brush, she swiped the mixture over the lenses of the eye glasses. Lastly, she held her palms above the spectacles and recited an incantation. Wiping the glasses off with a rag, she handed them to me.

She still said nothing, but she eyed the door to her camper, obviously wanting me to leave.

"Thank you," I told her. "Just one more thing. Do you know where I can get a satellite phone?"

Belcalis's eyes widened and she threw her hands up, waving them around. "We're in the middle of nowhere! You can't get shit like that here. You're gonna have to go to the city for that."

I nodded, expecting as much. I still thought I'd ask.

It wasn't a problem to go into London and find one, it was just an extra hassle. And something I didn't have time for on this particular night.

I pulled the rally flyer out of my pocket and unfolded it, placing it on the workspace counter. "What's going on with this?"

Belcalis bolted backward and her gaze flew to Zagan. "I do not have anything to do with this. I swear." Then she began whispering something unintelligible over her shoulder while keeping her eyes on Zagan.

I had a feeling she'd grown so accustomed to communicating with her ghost granny that she wasn't even aware she was doing it.

"Belcalis, he's not involved with the Shadow Court. He's not a part of it. It's okay."

Belcalis stopped whispering and looked at me. She placed her hand on her waist and popped her hip to the side. Loudly and slowly she repeated, "I was here for the demonstration."

"What demonstration?!" I countered. I darted my gaze between the two of them. Neither explained.

"Fine," I said tapping my finger on the flyer. "Who is leading the revolt?"

"I don't know nothing about any of it," Belcalis insisted. "I'm not involved."

"I know," I reassured her. "But this is a small village. People must talk. There has to be something you've heard."

I crossed my arms, determined not to get worked up over the speaker. "I was at one of the rallies," I told Belcalis. "There was someone who seemed to be leading the group. Have you heard anything about him?"

"I don't know nothing," she repeated. "All I know is that people call him the *Black Knight*. And that's it. That's all I know. And they all are hoping he'll be the new leader. But not me. No, I don't want any change. And that he'll end the Shadow Court taxation and stop the mercenary recruitments. But that's it. That's all I've heard. I don't know nothing about any of it."

When there was no outburst of displeasure from Zagan, I could see Belcalis begin to relax a little. "I just want to sell my magics and mind my own fucking business," she murmured.

Feeling responsible for the situation I'd put her in, I gathered my flyer and took a step back, wanting to give her some peace. "I'm sorry," I told her. "We're in the middle of some things we know nothing about. I'm looking for information wherever I can get it."

Taking another step back I told Belcalis, "We won't bother you anymore."

She turned again to her counter of magic supplies.

"Here," she said. "I'll give you a truth tincture, on the house. You can use it on someone who actually knows something." Then she spoke over her shoulder in a low voice. "I'm not gonna charge them because I want them to get out! And do you know who that is over there?!" she snapped, tossing her head in Zagan's direction.

I stood next to Belcalis, at her work station, while Zagan remained on the far side of the trailer. She began spreading powders out on the counter.

"That's not necessary," I told her. "Thank you for the offer, though."

She tapped the counter with her finger and I noticed words were spelled out with the powder.

*Do you need help?*

I looked at Belcalis and shook my head in earnest. She swept her hand over the powder, pinching it up in her fingers before dropping it. It scattered into letters again.

*Are you hurt?*

I shook my head again.

*Get away from him! Danger!*

I held my hand out over the powder and looked at Belcalis. She gave an imperceptible nod, and I picked it up. I could feel it hum between my fingers. I thought about what I wanted to say and let it fall from my hand.

*He is helping me. Safe.*

Belcalis narrowed her eyes at the words. Then she shifted back ever so slightly and tried to glance at Zagan from the corner of her eye. She didn't look like she believed me, but she picked up the powder.

*Where do you find these men? An app?*

She picked up the powder again.

*Give me the name.*

I rolled my eyes.

She spoke loudly at first. "I don't associate with unscrupulous individuals." Then she lowered her voice and leaned into me. "But there's a guy. Possum. He hangs in the abandoned part of town. And he has access to electronics—for a price."

She handed me a little vial, which I assumed was the truth tincture. I placed a few bills on the counter, feeling the need to compensate her for both items she'd prepared. Then I turned for the door.

Before exiting the little camper, I faced Belcalis. "Do you know anything about the *Heart of Darkness*?"

The light flickered, and a gust of wind rattled the little trailer. Belcalis's eyes turned cloudy as a white film coated them. Her voice dropped several octaves and the camper shook.

In a voice not her own, Belcalis said, "It's coming closer."

Then she collapsed, and the camper shook again. At that moment, an invisible force began to push against me.

266

The powder from the counter spilled onto the floor, and in front of my feet were two words.

## GET OUT

I glanced at Belcalis, wanting to help her. But the force pushing against me shoved harder and I stumbled back. I was certain it was Belcalis's grandmother. I could only assume she knew what was best just then.

Zagan had already caught me and pushed me behind him. "Let's go," I said. "Her grandmother wants us out."

I opened the camper door, and we stepped away just as the sun was dipping to meet the horizon. I knew the sleeping village was about to wake for the night. I didn't want to stick around for anyone to see us. I looked up at Zagan. "Do you know the abandoned part of town?"

He nodded. And just as we'd arrived, we departed the little main street in a wisp of shadows.

*** 

Zagan and I walked down the dirt road through the deserted section of the Shadow village, seemingly the only souls in sight. I had no idea how we were supposed to find Possum. But I kept my eyes out for any sign of a seedy electronics stand.

"Are you going to tell me what the demonstration was?" I asked.

Zagan walked next to me without replying. I waited, and I kept glancing at him, expecting an answer. He seemed to be envisioning something, and I could feel how uncomfortable it made him. Finally, he turned his head to look down at me.

"She never told me anything," he said. "I blindly followed whatever direction she gave. Early on, I learned I did not want to make her angry. Life was unpleasant when she was angry."

Zagan looked forward when he spoke next, showing no emotion. "After being sequestered at the manor for years, she brought me to Court one day. She showed the people there the mark on my chest. They did things. And once they were satisfied it was genuine, she told them she spoke for me.

"Then the demonstrations began. She wanted everyone to know what would happen to those who defied her word. And she had me do things...unpleasant things.

"She toted me around, holding these demonstrations at Court as well as the outlying villages."

I could see confusion contort Zagan's face. "I did whatever she wanted. Always. It wasn't until the night when I saw she had you that something snapped inside."

I waited, and when he didn't go on, I kicked at the dirt. Finally I asked, "What did she have you do?"

He shook his head, refusing to answer.

"What about the mark?" I asked. "You didn't have it when we were children."

He closed his eyes, and I could tell he didn't like talking about any of this. Yet, he answered. "It began to appear gradually. It was imperceptible at first. As time went on it became darker and more noticeable."

He glanced down at my jacket. His jaw tightened and his eyes narrowed. I knew he was thinking about the silvery outline that had appeared on my own chest after we'd been together. I was willing to guess more than anything else, that was why he refused to touch me again.

I purposefully yanked on a buckle there, wanting him to stop focusing on it. "It's gone, you know," I grumbled at him. "It wasn't a big deal."

He didn't need to say anything. His opposing view was clear in the way he looked at me.

"Anyway," I said glancing around. "How are we supposed to find anyone here? This place is lifeless."

"It's on the other side of the hill, ahead," Zagan said.

I stopped walking and turned to him. "What?"

He stopped as well, facing me. "It's on the other side of the hill, ahead," he repeated.

I smashed my lips together. "I heard what you said. How do you know that?"

"I have procured certain items from this establishment in the past."

I shoved my hands on my hips. "You," I stated, my voice dripping with disbelief. "You've acquired electronics from Possum before."

He nodded.

"Why didn't you say something?"

"You didn't ask."

"I thought you never left the manor," I told him.

His wide shoulders rolled back in his jacket. "Most of the time, I don't. However, at some point when I realized I could *wisp*, as you call it, I ventured out on a few occasions. I was usually alone at the manor. No one was around to care one way or the other. And before the recent demonstrations, no one knew who I was."

"The Contessa didn't keep you locked up or under constant guard or something?" I asked. And the moment the words were out

I knew they were insensitive. I wished I had phrased them differently.

Zagan answered my question, though. His voice was quiet and emotionless, but nevertheless, he answered.

"She didn't need to."

I took a moment to let the weight of his words sink in. I felt a chill at the power she had wielded over him.

Zagan turned and began walking again. I caught up to his side and slid my hand into his. He jumped back from me and stared at his palm as if a snake had tried to bite him.

I held out my hand and looked at him. "It's just a hand, guy."

He stared at me in that way that I was getting used to—like I was crazy. And he looked at my hand in disgust. I waited. Finally, he said, "I have never done that before."

"What?" I asked. "Hold someone's hand?"

He nodded.

"Umm." I cocked my head and looked up in mock concentration. "I'm pretty sure you did, not too long ago."

"That is not the same," he snapped. "That does not count."

I straightened, and I rested my hands at my sides, letting go of any teasing tone. "Actually, it does, Zagan. You've held my hand before and you can do it again…if you want to."

I began making my way down the dirt road once more, passing between sagging, dilapidated buildings covered with graffiti, while night swiftly fell. I was alone as I walked. No one at my side. But I knew Zagan hadn't bailed on me. I could feel him a few paces behind.

I descended the hill he'd pointed out, and I knew it'd been too much for him. In my defense though, trying to touch him, to be near him, was an impulse and not a conscious decision. I couldn't help it.

I just wanted to be close to him.

I reached the bottom and I was about to turn back to Zagan and ask him where we had to go. But before I could, he stepped past me.

"It's this way," he said.

And I followed him into, what was apparently, one of his neighborhood haunts.

# CHAPTER 23

I COULD SEE HOW Possum had gotten his name. The guy certainly had a marsupial look to him. His face seemed to come out in a long narrow point. Plus, he had small deep-set eyes.

Apparently, Possum was embracing his namesake as he'd slicked back his dark hair in a stubby ponytail, placing all focus on his features. Sitting on a battered steel desk, he eyed Zagan and bobbed his chin in greeting as we walked in. He didn't seem to care much about our arrival. He continued chewing a toothpick and twirling a serrated tactical knife as he watched us approach.

His gaze didn't linger on Zagan, and he didn't seem fearful. After seeing Belcalis's reaction, I was willing to bet Possum had missed out on the *demonstration*.

He did, however, ogle me—starting at my feet and working his way up. Zagan stopped in his tracks. And he did take my hand in his then. Crushing it. Adding to my discomfort, I could feel the air around us plummet in temperature.

I sent a pulse of bright energy through my hand, wanting to jar him from whatever rage he was about to descend into.

I snapped my fingers at Possum and pointed to my face after dropping Zagan's hand. "Eyes up here, buddy." I tilted my head in Zagan's direction. "You're about to get yourself murdered. He hasn't completed his anger management training yet."

Then I looked around the gutted building. It was a freezing, sagging, rusted tin can of a place. Aside from the corroded metal desk which Possum was perched upon, there was a ripped couch off to the side.

Someone who was rail thin with shaggy hair was hunched over on the miserable excuse for a sofa. He didn't even try to hide the fact that he was injecting something into his veins.

When no one spoke, I looked at Possum. "You got a sat-phone?"

Possum bobbed his head. He looked like he was contemplating the question. "Electronics are banned in these parts," he said.

I tried to keep any expression from my face. That was something I hadn't known. "Do you have one or not?"

Possum eyed me again, but this time it was in assessment. "You don't look like any of the females from around here. Or any that travel this way to do business. You've got weapons. And you're too much of a..." he perused my face, my clothing, my figure, "a thoroughbred," he decided.

Possum removed the toothpick from his mouth and pointed it at me. "You're probably here to bust me, steal from me, or most likely a little of both. I'm just trying to figure out if I'm going to stick around to defend my stuff or haul ass out of here."

"Alright. This is a waste of time," I said. I turned to leave. "We'll go to the city."

"Now wait a minute," Possum called, jumping down from the desk. "Let's not be hasty. I've got to be cautious, love."

Zagan's chest began to vibrate with a low growl. I glanced at him and his irises branched with black.

Possum smiled, his thin lips spreading across spaced, pointed teeth. "I mean, madame," he corrected. Then he made Zagan the target of his toothpick, pointing the thing in the air, the smile disappearing. "You've always been my least favorite customer."

He began to make his way for a door behind him, casting nervous glances over his shoulder at Zagan. "Come on," he said. "Let's get this shit over with."

***

I walked out of Possum's electronic shop with my new solar powered gadget. He'd charged me three times the retail price, but I didn't care. There was a reason I'd wanted to stay in the Shadow village.

Figuring it was time to confess, I looked up at Zagan. "There's one more thing I need to do tonight," I said.

He didn't say anything, and I pulled the flyer from my pocket. "I need to attend this."

Zagan looked at the paper with disdain.

"We need to know what's going on," I told him. "This is all connected somehow. We can't stay in the dark about it."

When he continued to stare at me, I said, "You don't have to come if you don't want to. I can't force you to care. But I'm going." I shoved the flyer back in my pocket.

"I'm returning you to the manor," he said.

"What about all your people?" I pressed. "They need you. Right now, they have a deranged megalomaniac running their parliament and a lying, self-righteous charlatan attempting to lead their revolt. We have to do something. You have to do something."

Zagan squinted at me, leaning his head down to peer into my eyes. "Why do you need to save everyone, Violet?"

"I don't," I replied, caught off guard by the question.

He gave a slow nod. "You do. Why must you become involved?"

"Because those who are strong and able should help those who are not," I said.

"No," Zagan countered. "That's not it."

I shifted my gaze from him, not liking the way he was examining me. "Go back to the manor and hide out," I said. Starting down the main street I told him, "I'll see you back there when it's over." And I didn't bother to look over my shoulder.

My skin was too tight, and my chest was too small for my lungs. I felt like adjusting my hair and straightening my clothes. I felt like hiding. Guilt that I had carried and clung to for a long time stirred in the pit of my stomach. I shoved it back into submission, refusing to acknowledge it.

I didn't have to save everyone. Just to prove it, I put an extra swing in my hips as I walked. That would show how many fucks I didn't give.

A dark angry wall appeared in front of me and I walked straight into it. When I looked up, Zagan's eyes were black.

"I do not enjoy following behind you like a pet," he said, barely getting the words through his teeth.

I rolled my head to one side, feeling like I couldn't do anything right. It took me a moment to push my pride aside, but I did. Then I released a breath.

"Right," I agreed. "I wouldn't like that either. I'm... sorry."

"And you need to acquire looser clothing," Zagan said. "And walk differently."

I absorbed his demands and nodded. "Consider it done," I told him. I absolutely was not doing either of those things, but sometimes you just need to tell people what they want to hear.

"Anything else?" I asked him.

He closed his eyes and squeezed his fists. "It is difficult to be around you. To spend time with you. You are...It is...*difficult*."

I placed the tip of my index finger on his chin and tapped it there as I spoke. "It doesn't have to be."

And before he could snap at me or get even more riled up, I eased a step back from him. "So are you coming with me or what?"

He shook his head, clearly vexed. "Yes," he hissed.

"Great," I said. "There's just one tiny little thing I need you to do first."

I could tell by the way his eyes widened that he was taken aback by my impudence. I felt a small thrill at the fact that I could have such an effect on him. I knew if it'd been anyone else, he would have never tolerated it.

"You can't go like that," I said gesturing to his clothing. "If people recognize you, all hell will break loose. You need a hood. In fact it'd be better if I had one too."

Zagan's eye twitched. He picked me up—with a tad of an angry jolt—and set me down in the battered doorway to Possum's shop.

Looking around the dark, abandoned street, he let his senses roam. When he didn't find any threat, he gave me a menacing glare. "Don't move," he barked, just before disappearing.

Within a mere half of a minute, Zagan returned with two black cloaks. He shoved one into my chest and held the other out in front of himself. He eyed the thing with revulsion.

I threw the robe on over my short swords and drew the hood. When I glanced at Zagan, he was still staring at the garment in his hands.

"Here, I'll help you," I said. I did my best to ease the heavy material across his shoulders and the hilt of his weapon.

He didn't flinch or balk, but his face was tight. "You're doing great," I told him as I fastened the clasp at his neck.

"You are drowning me in fabric," he replied.

I tsked, and I ran my hands under the cloak, across the top of his chest. "Think of it as a little hidey-hole. You get to take cover in plain sight. Now lean down, I'm going to pull up the cowl."

Glowering at me like I was his own personal devil, he did. I looked up at him as I pulled the hood up and over. Then I held the sides of the hood and leaned my face closer to his. "See," I whispered.

"Do you want me to accompany you or not?" he ground through clenched teeth.

"I do," I confirmed, deciding to try and balance the tension with opposition. He was so rigid and serious. I made my words light as air.

"Then I will require the ability to walk. If you keep this up, it will be impossible. Now remove yourself from my *hidey-hole*."

I bit my lip on an exhale, finding the term I had used utterly ridiculous coming from him. He'd done it on purpose—trying to ridicule my spin on the cloak—but instead of aggravating me, he'd made me fonder of him.

278

I removed my hands from his cloak and held them up in surrender, taking a step back.

"You do this on purpose," Zagan growled. "If you insist on continuing, I will be forced to take drastic measures. Consider this your final warning."

"Hey, this isn't my fault, okay? I have no control over," I waved my hand between us, "this."

"You are not trying hard enough," Zagan chastised. "*Try. Harder.*"

I shrugged one shoulder. "Maybe I don't want to. Why should I?"

Zagan stepped into me, making me feel tiny with his presence. It wasn't just his size, although he clearly dominated me physically. It was all that he was, all the space that he required. It was difficult to comprehend how so much power and energy could be stuffed into one person.

I felt him—his presence—expand around me. Dark. Cold. Deep. He shoved his hand through the loose hair of my braid at the back of my neck. "Because if you do not fight this, you will regret it."

He held my eye, making a promise, vowing the truth of his words. And then he withdrew his hand, closing his rigid fingers inch by inch, one at a time.

Taking several steps back from me and scanning farther down the street, Zagan borrowed a line from Possum. And I didn't blame him for it. Sometimes other people are better able to express our feelings.

"Let's get this shit over with."

Then he began down the abandoned road, slicing through the darkness of night and disappearing into the very shadows.

***

There were more people. The movement was growing.

I took in the valley from the top of the hill. Hundreds of people surrounded the makeshift stage and several tents had been erected. The bonfire lit the night.

We made our way down into the rally, staying to the periphery, avoiding the light from the fire. All around us, people spoke of the Black Knight. And I seethed at the vainglorious title.

I found we didn't have to wait long for him to arrive and for the chanting to begin. "Welcome to the new age. Welcome to the new age," the stalwart people of the crowd recited over and over again.

The speaker took to the stage, watching the crowd, letting the incantation grow and consume the night.

I glanced at Zagan, and I was glad he was able to finally see this. It's one thing to hermit away somewhere and let the world burn down around you. It's another to actually experience it. His face did not betray his thoughts, but I could see he was taking in the entire scene, not missing a single detail.

Finally, the speaker, the Black Knight, raised his hands. Just as before he wore a large cowl which covered his face. And still I could not make out any defining features.

The crowd quieted and stilled. Their leader spoke. "My brothers and sisters, let us honor our mother, the moon."

Men all around the bonfire emptied buckets of water, dousing the flames until it was reduced to smoldering embers. Then the speaker turned his back to the crowd and began his chant in the Dark Tongue.

Energy began to spread and hum through the valley, vibrating in the air around us, filling the night with a certain weight. And as the

280

words and voices of the Shadow people grew, a silvery light broke from the horizon.

They called upon the moon to rise, and she appeared. Larger and closer than one would think possible.

I saw Zagan's hand rise from the corner of my eye, and I glanced at him. He had his palm over his chest, and I could see a confused ache across his face. He was experiencing something he hadn't known or expected.

I hoped it was something freeing, something that could help him rise from the dark place he kept himself.

The light which glimmered across the crowd was cool and muted. And while there wasn't a spark to it, there was a magical energy, a humble power. It was much more mysterious and seductive than that of the sun, but undeniable all the same.

Once the moon had finished rising, the chanting stopped. And after a sacred silence, the Black Knight lowered his arms and turned to face the crowd. "Welcome to the new age," he began, his voice echoing across the valley. His people chanted the mantra back, clapping and cheering.

Once silence had settled across the crowd, the speaker began again. "My brothers and sisters, the time draws nigh when we will stand up and fight for our freedom. We have grown. We are strong. And the many will challenge the few.

"We have reached a new age where we will no longer be pawns to the Courts. Our people will no longer be sacrificed for the games of those in power.

"And we have achieved our first victory!" Behind him someone was being shoved onto the stage. Her hands were bound, and a gag was tied around her mouth. Two men pushed her forward.

It took a moment for my mind to process and accept what I was seeing before me. The truth of what was happening on stage was too misaligned with my perception of the world for me to understand reality. My worlds were colliding and shattering.

The speaker's voice echoed in my ears. "We have captured the Lady of Light!" And the crowd erupted in a cacophony of whistles and shouts.

My blood boiled, and the powers within me stirred, threatening to explode. Slews of lightning scorched the earth all around the makeshift stage. And I knew my eyes glowed.

The crowd gasped and hushed, but no one was paying attention to me. They all believed the onslaught of energy had come from Adriel. She tensed at the charged air, and her eyes scanned the crowd.

She had known it was me.

But the effects of my outburst did not last long because a dense shadow crept across the face of the moon, and a dark evil began to spread through the valley. I could feel the malevolence saturate the air. The cold. The hunger.

*The Umbra.*

My head jerked to the side and I scanned our surroundings. They were emerging from the darkness all around us, dozens of them. Tall gaunt figures in black robes with grey ashen skin and emaciated faces. Their animal like eyes reflecting in the night.

The only reason I avoided Zagan's grasp was because I had expected it. I ducked away from him, and he stared at me, vibrating with rage. He took a step towards me, raising his hand to lunge for me again. I knew he was going to wisp me back to the manor.

"You need to help these people," I told him as I backed away. Confusion and murmuring began to ripple through the crowd. "I

282

have to get my mother," I said, taking another step back. "You'll be able to find me when it's time." I pinned him with one last look. "You always do."

I threw off my cloak and turned to run for the stage.

And that was when the screams began.

# CHAPTER 24

I DIDN'T KNOW IF THE Shadow people were aware of the Umbra. Maxim had said the Shadow King imprisoned them long ago. I had no idea when they'd been freed, or who was informed of their presence.

I wondered if The Contessa was nearby. She must have been the one who set them upon the Shadow Village. On the other hand, it could have been Maxim for all I knew. He'd had spies at the rally before. And he was the one who told me about the Umbra. Maybe Maxim commanded them under The Contessa's orders.

Yet as I sprinted for the stage, trying to shove my way through the crowd, none of that mattered. I had to get to my mother. I hoped Zagan was able to do something. I didn't know what, exactly, the Umbra would do to these people, but I had a feeling many lives were in danger.

And while I hated that Zagan would be faced with them—hated what it would do to him—I believed he was capable enough to battle those ancient, evil beings without irreversible harm to himself.

I was closing in on the stage, making my way through the crowd, when I saw someone escorting Adriel away. I didn't see the speaker, the Black Knight, any longer, and I figured he was off cowering somewhere or fleeing.

Picking up speed, I leapt onto the stage. I ran across the simple structure and tackled the cloaked henchman who was trying to drag Adriel away. Crashing into his back, I clung to his shoulders. We rolled together across the stage.

My back slammed against the platform as the weight of him settled on me. In one continuous motion, I withdrew a sword, swung it out in front of him, and sliced his neck.

I immediately used my free hand to push his body off of me, and as I did, I saw a boot shove against his hip. Without hesitating, I scrambled out from under him.

Looking down, I could see his face. It was Rheneas, Maxim's right-hand man. I hadn't really had a relationship with him, but still, I felt a twinge of regret.

I hadn't taken his head. And while my sword had cut deeply, he was immortal. He would recover. For now, he lay there, unconscious.

I did think about finishing him off. Picking away at The Contessa and her minions whenever the opportunity arose would be best. But I didn't have the heart to do it.

Knowing I couldn't waste time, I grabbed a dagger strapped to my leg with the intention of freeing my mother's bonds. Only when I reached behind her, I discovered she was shackled with the same type of spelled manacles I had been imprisoned with.

I looked down. At least her feet were untethered. She'd be able to run.

I yanked the gag from her mouth. "I can't get you free," I told her. "We need to get you somewhere safe."

I looked around, taking in the surroundings for an exit strategy. And as I did, time suddenly froze. The sounds of terror ringing through the night…became silent.

Inside my heart, I heard the beginnings of a ghostly song. A lone soprano singing notes without words. At least, not words I could decipher. And I knew then, as I'd known before, it was not a song for the ears but one for the soul.

Just a moment later, a second voice joined in.

*Banshees.*

They stood in the valley, far beyond the Umbra, side by side. Two beautiful women in emerald dresses. Their thin gowns floated around their slim bodies just as their hair drifted around their faces.

And while their mouths did not open with song, I knew the otherworldly notes came from them, as galaxies whorled in their eyes.

I was not in awe of them. I did not deem them a beautiful apparition. Because their presence was an ominous sign.

I'd read about Banshees long ago. They were harbingers of death. When a truly noble warrior was about to leave this world, they would sing for him.

It was to honor him. To acknowledge the valor of his deeds. And once a warrior had been venerated, there was no turning back. Death was imminent.

A Banshee's song was said to be a rare laud. It was said to ease a warrior into repose, taking away any fear and regret, providing him with a sense of peace and humble acceptance.

And I suddenly felt sick. *I had sent Zagan out there.*

While the Banshees' song was the only sound I could hear, I took in the sight in front of me as time inched forward, ten times slower than it should be.

Carnage. Terror. Horror.

Little pieces of me blackened and withered inside. I did not know how much more I could take. But I knew then, one day, I would end up broken.

Because it was all too much.

A sea of innocent people—tortured and killed before my very eyes.

The Umbra were releasing that black inky brume from their lips. And as it funneled and sifted towards the crowd, people were stumbling and falling to their knees, blood welling from their eyes and pouring from their noses and mouths. Then the Umbra would sweep in using their mere fingers to severe heads.

No one could get close to the Umbra to stop them. No one could get past the caustic smoke. No one...except for two.

One was maddened. The other honed and controlled.

One had already shed his cloak and was now about to rip free the jacket he wore in his frenzied rage—the fallen Umbra dismembered in a violent mania before him.

The other made lethal, precise attacks with incredible economy of movement, all while his dark cloak swept around him, his cowl drawn.

They would slay the Dark evil one by one, the Shadow Prince and the Black Knight, but not before lives were lost.

In a rush, as if I had traveled from a great distance, I slammed back into my body. The Banshees were gone, as if they'd never been. Time sped forward in a blur, catching up to where it should be. A wall of sound crashed over me: screams, cries, bellows. And I was disoriented.

"Violet! This way!" Adriel shouted.

I snapped my head in her direction. I stared at her.

"Come!" she insisted, trying to get me to follow her off the stage.

"I... I can't," I told her. "I have to help. I..." I turned to look out at the Umbra. "I think I can fight them."

And I didn't know with absolute certainty if that was true, but I believed the burning smoke which the Umbra spewed would not debilitate me as it had before. I believed the Darkness I now carried could somehow protect me.

Adriel's eyes widened. "Think about what you're saying!"

"They are innocent people!" I shouted at her. "There are children!"

With thinned lips, she looked around. Her distress was clear. I could see how torn she was.

Finally, she looked at me. "You have to free me. I can stop this."

"I can't. The manacles are spelled with dark magic."

Adriel's face grew stern. "You have to free me!" The determination in her voice made despair wash over me.

"I can't!" I cried.

Her voice dropped lower than I'd ever heard. Each word was a searing ember in the darkness. She burned me with her gaze. "Violet Archer, you are a warrior. You are a chosen one. And you are my daughter. When you put limitations on your strength without even trying, you will always fail. You must try. And if you do not have enough strength, then you find more!"

Two tears slipped down my face. And I saw a faint shimmer of Light fall from my cheeks.

I could feel my chin quiver and I bit my lip. I threw my shoulders back. I inhaled. I felt my body shake as my lungs released. Then I stepped up to my mother, and she turned her back to me.

I took hold of the manacles, and I instantly felt the Darkness coating them. They were so cold to the touch that they scorched my hands.

I closed my eyes. I blocked out the screams filling the night, the astringent stench in the air, and the black fumes billowing from the earth.

I found the deep wellspring of Light somewhere within. I found where the glimmers of Light trickled through the cracks of my foundation. I let it seep up, filling into a bright, glassy pool of sheer radiance.

Power charged and crackled. While I kept my eyes closed, I could feel energy spark in the air around me, arcing in growing currents.

And I pulled. Slowly. Gradually. I let it build and build and build some more. And I focused the growing intensity on the binds.

At the same time, I squeezed—gently, and then with expanding force. I felt my strength increase degree by degree, more than I'd ever realized I was capable of, more than I had ever attempted to summon in one single moment.

And then I hit a threshold. I put everything I had into that moment. Everything I was, and it was not enough. I could not do it.

My hands began to shake. I wasn't going to be able to maintain the pressure.

"Harder!" My mother yelled back at me. "You have more to give!"

She was wrong. There was no more. And I was about to fail.

Except.

Somewhere in the night was a spark. And I felt it ignite, fueling my own power, adding to the energy. With a roar, I pulled on all there was. On all I was. And at the same time I felt Adriel's Light burst into the metal from within.

The manacles cracked under my palms. And I sagged to the stage.

Almost instantly, the sky filled with Light. It was not the cool, silvery light of the moon. It was the searing, blinding brilliance of daylight.

My mother stood with one palm outstretched to the sky and her other fisted at her heart. Her head was bowed as she murmured words.

And all around, the Umbra, at least those which had yet been destroyed by the two who fought, exploded into bursts of soot.

The moment they did, Adriel collapsed. And the Light which she had called forth, extinguished with her.

The night plunged back into darkness. And as remnants of exhaust billowed from the earth, there was a moment of silence. Then the sounds of devastation set in.

I saw the cloaked figure, who had fought the Umbra, turn from across the clearing and look at me.

The Black Knight.

With a wisp of shadows, he was suddenly in front of me.

I had already staggered to my feet and drawn my swords.

He tossed his soiled weapon at my feet, surrendering. And from under his cowl, he stared at me.

"Take off your hood." My words were slow and quiet. Lethal. Because while I had just drained my Light, the Darkness stirred within, offering power.

The Black Knight reached up to grasp the sides of his cowl. Towering in front of me, spattered with the foul tar of the Umbra, and unarmed, he pulled back his hood.

I lunged for his larynx, faster than I'd ever moved before. Still, it was not fast enough. He side-stepped my attack. I spun around with my swords flying, determined to silence him.

Maxim's sophisticated voice was agitated. "I wish to talk to you. I will bring you no harm."

I let out a shrill screech and lunged for him again.

With the barest hint of motion, he moved just enough to avoid my strike. "Détente," he insisted.

But before I could tell him to go to hell, Zagan was standing between us. With no cloak or jacket to cover him, his upper body was covered with the same black sludge. While I faced his back, I was certain his gaze swam with an unhinged rage.

And he and Maxim stood eye to eye.

I tried to lean to the side and look around Zagan's back. "You're dead now!" I called to Maxim. Then I added, "Nobody puts baby in a corner!"

I don't know why I said the line. Maybe it was a pressure value. Some kind of release before I exploded from all the adrenaline and devastation. A way to cope with the intense weight this night carried. A way to cope with the hurt I felt.

I sheathed my swords, not having the strength to hold them a moment longer. And I ran over to Adriel where she lay.

She was breathing, but still unconscious. I tried to rouse her, and her eyelids fluttered.

"Mom." I held her shoulders. "You need to wake up. I need to get you out of here."

"She is not leaving," Maxim interrupted. "Neither of you are."

"Enjoy hell," I spat at him, knowing his life was about to end.

I glanced at Zagan, expecting him to do something. But he just stood there, staring at Maxim.

Several men approached the stage, looking up at Maxim. Before they could say anything, Maxim directed orders at them. "Those who are unharmed must help the injured. Use the northwest tent as a recovery center. Take the women and children to the abandoned mill. Then begin to escort them home. Assure everyone there will be no further attacks this night. We will collect the dead last."

The men turned to disperse through the chaos of the valley and carry out their orders.

Maxim looked at Zagan. "We must speak." He inclined his head towards me. "Bring her to the southern tent." Then he took two powerful strides towards me. "I will take your mother."

Although I lacked the strength to, I stood and drew my swords. "Over my dead body," I told him.

Maxim glanced at Rheneas, lying a few feet away from us, temporarily dead on the stage. He took in the pool of blood and the wound to his neck. Then he turned back to me.

"You are too hasty. You lash out in aggression before you fully understand a situation. It is most likely your greatest flaw. Stop throwing knives and wielding swords. Listen. Cease harming those who wish to help you."

"Help me?" I seethed. "I trusted you and you betrayed me. You made me believe you were a friend and then you attacked me. You chained me. You took away my right to speak! To move!" My words had begun to waver.

"You left me no choice," Maxim countered. "You disappeared without a trace. Then you returned with Darkness pumping through your veins, and you sent a dagger straight through my heart."

Maxim glanced at Rheneas. "Had I been anyone else, it would have incapacitated me. And knowing your penchant for fighting first and asking questions later, who knows if you would have tried to put a permanent end to my life that night."

"It's not like you identified yourself," I defended. "You paralyzed me. Bound me. Dragged me away."

Maxim's jaw was tight when he spoke next. "I was a tad displeased."

"A tad displeased?! You reduced me to nothing!"

Maxim closed his eyes and gave his head a slow tilt to the side, cracking his neck before staring at me again. The acrimony in his tone lessened. "We both have a chance to right our wrongs now. Will you take it? I am inviting you to talk with me, freely and of your own volition."

I opened my mouth to snap back at Maxim, but he cut me off. "The same goes for your mother, a détente."

I stared at Maxim. I didn't feel I could let go of my wrath, it was too heavy in my chest. And I didn't know if I could trust him. It was not only my own life on the line, but Zagan's and Adriel's as well.

Bracing myself to sense the veracity of his words, I asked Maxim one question. "Are you working for The Contessa?"

Maxim looked me dead in the eye. "Violet, I am doing everything in my power to stop her."

# CHAPTER 25

I GRABBED ADRIEL FROM Maxim and helped her onto a bench. She was weak and barely conscious. The instant I had my hands on her I didn't know what had possessed me to believe Maxim. He could have easily wisped away with her.

But he'd been true to his word.

And that was the thing about Maxim. I believed he was one of those rare people in the world whose word was his bond. He was someone who meant what he said. However, as I now knew, he was also someone who would go to any lengths he deemed necessary when faced with opposition.

While Adriel sagged on the bench in the canvas tent, Zagan, Maxim, and I stood around a small table.

A lantern sat on the center of the table, and in it, black flames with a red center undulated. I narrowed my eyes on the unholy fire, fighting the urge to throw the lantern from the tent.

I wanted to extinguish it and cast my own fire in its place, but I didn't have the power to.

Before I could take my eyes away, though, the flames transformed, turning bright and yellow. Unfurling from within, they shifted to a warm blaze.

I looked up at Zagan. His eyes were on me; he'd been watching. And I knew the small change had been his doing.

He held his sword, still gripped in his clenched hand, down at his side. The scabbard was probably broken and forgotten wherever the remains of his jacket lay. His eyes were black and there was no denying the glint of madness within. His hair was windswept. The planes and ridges of his arms and torso were sprayed with the blood of the Umbra.

Every few moments he would shudder—his muscles bulging against his skin.

And I was not the only one who stared at him. In their own way, both Maxim and Adriel took him in.

I did not think he noticed as he shook, fighting his demons. Then he closed his eyes.

In the dark valley, in the dark tent, the small lantern cast a dim glow on all four of our faces—my mother on the bench to my right, Zagan to my left, and Maxim across from me.

When no one spoke, I leaned forward, planting my hands on the table. But the instant I did, I regretted the motion. I straightened and dug the items cutting into my waist out of my jacket pocket.

I threw the melted sat-phone onto the table along with the small leather journal and translation glasses. While the phone was destroyed, the journal and glasses were luckily still intact.

I settled my hands on the table a second time and stared at Maxim. Then I glanced at his chest, embarrassed for him. I could respect someone who believed he was standing up for his people, but I found the fact that he'd tattooed the king's symbol over his own chest...*pathetic*.

"So, *The Black Knight*," I intoned.

He didn't flinch at my words. He held my eye. "A moniker my people have given me."

"Are you actually the Master-at-Arms for the Shadow Court?"

"Yes."

"Does the Court know you are leading the charge against them?"

"No."

"Do your people know you are a high-ranking member of the Shadow Court?"

"No."

"How are you able to wisp?"

"Some can," he said without explanation.

"Why do you spread lies about the Radiant Court? About my mother? Why drag us into your rhetoric?"

"I speak only the truth."

I scoffed. "I was here. I heard the things you said. Blaming us for the deaths of your people when it has been the Shadows infiltrating our peaceful streets and murdering innocent Radiants throughout the years."

The muscles in Maxim's eyelids twitched. "I would like to tell you about our people." While he made a point to hold my gaze, he eventually glanced at Adriel and Zagan as well.

Maxim gestured to the tent flap behind me. He stood tall and his voice was strong as he spoke. "Many of our people live simple lives as farmers, carpenters, innkeepers, teachers, housewives...simple people with simple lives.

"But a good many are mercenaries. They are soldiers of fortune who have no options available to them other than fighting for pay—

297

struggling to provide for themselves and their families. And being Shadows, these people are very good at passing through the night to carry out their orders. They derive strength and power from the darkness of night and hold no patriotic sense of obligation to any one faction, including their very own Shadow Court.

"And why would they? They were abandoned long ago by those of the aristocracy, cast to the periphery of society only to be taxed and their children recruited as servants of the select upper-class.

"For these reasons the Shadow people have been militants for hire, employed by various immortal factions. While their services have been obtained by a diverse list of groups and individuals over the years, the longest running patron of the Shadow mercenaries has been your very own Council of Elders."

Adriel's head bobbed and she drew in a breath, but instead of an outburst, she began coughing. I crouched down beside her and placed my hand on her back.

Then I glanced up, about to let Maxim know just how ludicrous his claim was, when I noticed Zagan watching Adriel. There was something in his eyes. He didn't seem to care about Maxim's words. His focus was on Adriel. And I could see something long forgotten—something that had laid dormant, never to awaken—coming back to him.

When Adriel settled, I straightened and shook my head at Maxim. "Maxim," I tried to speak softly. I tried to keep any mockery or cynicism from my tone; I really did want to find some common ground. "The Council of Elders has an army of Archangels at their disposal. They don't need to hire mercenaries. Who on earth would they be targeting?"

Maxim spoke one word in response. I knew he was mistaken. I knew he had come across faulty information at some point. Because I could feel the truth in his voice. He believed what he was saying.

"Prisms."

My mother's hands came up shaking as she placed her fingers at her temples. Her eyes closed. I knew she was in very poor condition based on her silence. In any other instance she would have taken command of the room.

I exhaled. I had to try and explain how wrong he was.

Before I could respond, though, my mother looked up, and her weak voice floated through the dark tent. "It's impossible. You must understand…In the beginning, the Council of Elders wove a spell into the fabric of our world, knowing we were incomplete. Knowing that without a Dark half, we were susceptible to the very thing we lacked—the Darkness.

"The power of the spell took form with the Prisms. The Light and energy which the Council commands was gifted upon two individuals, a male and a female. And through the union of their contrasting energies, the strength of our race was intended to be secured.

"The Council would never try to harm the Prisms. They are our hope. Our salvation."

Adriel's head rolled and her shoulders slumped. She seemed to plead for Maxim to understand. "There is no attack upon our people by the Council of Elders. The attacks are driven solely by the Shadows."

Maxim shook his head. "The story you tell is true, to a degree. But you lack a vital piece of information. Information you have willfully been ignorant to after refusing our requests for talks of peace, time and time again.

"After your Council of Elders breathed Light into the first two Prisms, your Oracle had a message for them. She had divined a prophecy from the Fates.

"The Council of Elders would one day be destroyed by a Prism made whole. One fated Prism would unleash a power which far surpassed your Council. A power that would vanquish them all.

"By toying with the elemental forces, they had written the ending to their own destiny. And learning this, they set forth to annihilate those who would rise to carry the Light. The Council swore to prevent the Prisms from ever coupling. They could never allow one to become whole."

I drew a breath, about to interject. But Maxim raised his brows and continued. "And before you argue for their army of Archangels, think upon this; if they kept only one Prism every thousand years, they could continue to grow their army of might and Light without harm to themselves. As long as the bond was never solidified, the Council could continue to exist without fear and grow a powerful army to do their bidding."

I held up my hand. "Not long ago, my unit apprehended one of your mercenaries. And he confessed that it was the Shadow Prince who led them. In essence—The Contessa."

Again, Maxim shook his head. "Violet, do you think your Council would reveal their identity to the Shadow people? The Council has gone through great pains to hire these services anonymously. Part of the arrangement is that these mercenary groups truly believe they are employed by the Shadow Court.

"Can you imagine if the Archangels found out that your very Council had been murdering those fated to them? That your very Council was condemning them to half a life?

"This is your Council's deepest sin. Their most heinous crime. They share it with no one."

I sank onto the bench next to my mother. I was beginning to lose the ability to hold myself up. I didn't dwell on my own state for long, though, because just then Zagan gave another violent shudder.

I looked up at him. I had to get him out of there. He was trying his damndest to cage all he had unleashed while fighting the Umbra. And on top of that, I could feel how Adriel's presence was creating cracks in the foundation he had in place, the one he'd buried his childhood under.

It was all too much.

Knowing that time was short, I focused on Maxim. "Look, Maxim, I believe that *you* believe this is all true, but how can you be sure of any of it?"

"I have detailed records."

"How do you know they're not forged? You just said this is a secret kept by the Council. How would anyone know?"

Maxim's already rigid posture somehow stiffened even more. "My records are from one of the Originals...of the Dark half. One of the Originals who departed Aleece. He was the exiled brethren to your Council of Elders."

Maxim paused, and I knew he wanted the implication of his words to sink in. "My records are from the Dark Manor."

The fire in the lantern dwindled and Maxim nodded towards the small book on the table in front of me. "Just as with the journal you carry, the records I possess are penned by the Shadow King himself."

At his words, a gust of wind whipped through the tent entrance, and the diminishing flames in the lantern died.

Lies…they float. They're flimsy. They slip and slither all around you. Untethered with nothing to ground them. And you continually have to try and snatch them from the air to hold them in place.

But the truth…the truth is weighted. The truth sinks. It settles at the lowest point. And becomes immovable.

In the dark valley, in the dark tent, the heavy weight of truth threatened to crush us all. I could feel the pressure of it bearing down on me, not just there in the shrouded tent, but in the very skies for miles and miles all around.

The truth which had been silently sitting and waiting for eons, buried long ago, was finally being uncovered. And this was just the beginning.

Whether I was willing to admit it to myself in that moment or not, I knew the truth of my circumstances.

I was a Prism. I had connected with another. I had solidified the bond.

The Council of Elders wanted me dead. And while that wasn't news to me. I now knew it was not because I had defied a ruling. I now knew it was because of what they believed I might do.

And I wasn't the only one. Zagan. Elijah. Myself. Any one of us could mean the destruction of the Council.

The Council of Elders, the Light half of the Originals, those who ruled the Archangels, wanted us dead.

And they already had one of us.

In spite of everything, I suddenly grew gravely concerned for Elijah.

# CHAPTER 26

THE TENT WAS QUIET AND DARK. The winds whipped against the canvas, rattling the fabric. Adriel slumped next to me on the little wood bench, and Zagan released a jagged exhale.

The lantern remained unlit. Maxim did not bother trying to stoke the flame back to life, knowing his Dark fire was unwelcome. And neither Adriel, Zagan, nor I were in a position to cast the paltry energy needed for a spark of Light.

Outside, a far-off voice shouted directions. It seemed some of Maxim's men were beginning to collect their fallen.

I gathered my items from the table and scooped my arm around Adriel's back, helping her stand. "We are not through here," I told Maxim. "But for the moment, we are leaving."

Maxim inclined his head and I could barely see him. Although my vision was adequate in the dark, Maxim seemed to blend in seamlessly with the shadows, becoming one himself. "The Lady of

304

Light is still my prisoner," he stated. "She may be granted sojourn at the Dark Manor, as long as she remains within its walls."

I felt a cold rush pump through my veins. My spine straightened, and the Darkness twisted around me. Maxim was not the only one who still held power.

Adriel stiffened in my arms as we, too, slipped into the very shadows of the tent, and a wispy quality threaded my voice. "Her chains were broken. She is not yours."

At my words, Zagan let out a low moan and his head bowed.

I tried to reel in the Darkness and lock it away. I knew it coiled in the tent around us, making Zagan's struggle all the more difficult. Before I could, however, Maxim looked at Zagan and uttered a few words in the Dark Tongue and Zagan...*eased*.

Seeing his torment lessen, I whipped my head in Maxim's direction. We stared at each other for a moment. Assessing. Reading. Each trying to size up the other.

Then the tent dissolved away, and the four of us were standing in the foyer of the Dark Manor. Maxim continued to hold my eye. He had transitioned us effortlessly.

I realized something then; while he was not the only one with power, he was the one who held all the cards. He had since the start. And there were many more he had yet to reveal.

"You can expect me tomorrow night," he said. And just like that he was gone, leaving those of us who were broken to collect our fractured pieces.

\*\*\*

I helped Adriel into one of the guest beds in my suite, ensuring the windows were unobstructed by curtains. I wanted the daylight to filter through as soon as the sun rose. And by the time I turned back, she was already asleep.

I had left Zagan down in the foyer, and I returned to check on him. As I'd expected he was no longer there. And while I knew he didn't want me down in the abandoned wing, I wasn't about to stay out.

I couldn't. I needed to be near him. I needed to touch him. I needed him to know that he was not alone.

Because when I'd seen the Banshees, I'd thought it was the end.

And with all I had learned, I knew there was a good chance the end was near. With all that we were facing, it was almost inevitable—the Council, The Contessa, the Umbra…

But I was not going to lie down and die. I was going to fight, on all fronts. And that included the battle I was in with Zagan.

I just couldn't let him disappear in that deep, dark pit of his. I knew he thought that was where he belonged. But I also knew he was wrong.

I made my way to the end of the foyer and descended the subterranean stairs. Walking through the dank, decrepit hall, I steeled myself for the chill of shadows I'd pass through. I had no Light to cast and all I could do was let the ghosts of sorrow and grief slip over me, wrapping icy fingers around my neck.

Down towards the end of the hall, I could hear the sound of running water. A door was open. And after making my way to it, I entered a small room. There was no light, no fire, but I could see a very primitive system had been rigged into the crumbling stone wall.

Zagan was unclothed and he stood under the running faucet with his back to me. His forehead and arms were braced against the stone as the water poured down his shoulders.

I could see his head shake against the wall. I knew it was in aggravation over my presence. But he did not turn to chase me away or tell me how unwelcome I was.

Silently, I undid the tie in my hair. I slipped off my jacket and swords. I removed my boots and pants, leaving my panties in place. I didn't care to keep them on, but I hoped the small scrap of fabric would serve as a type of reassurance for Zagan.

I walked up to him, and I could feel freezing drops from the spray of water. My skin instantly tightened, but I didn't hesitate. Under his raised arm, I slid between Zagan and the wall, resting my hands next to my hips against the stone.

As I looked up at him, I could see his face and chest were clean. His eyes were closed.

And while the bond compelled me to be there, compelled me to ease and comfort him, I can tell you with all certainty that I was there by my own volition. Bond or not, I wanted to be there with him.

I knew there was a power in our connection. I knew that we could benefit from being together by the forces which drove us. But I understood something much greater in that moment.

I understood that there was another kind of power at play. One that was not cast upon us by those who would manipulate our fate. I had my own power—the same as anyone. And I could feel it swell when it came to Zagan. I had a feeling it was something elemental. Something as old as time. Something that anyone who had ever cared about another could understand.

I placed my hands on Zagan's flexed abdomen and I let them glide up to his chest. His arms tensed on either side of my head, but he did not remove them from the wall. Drops of icy water fell from his chin and nose, but still his eyes remained shut.

I tried to ignore the little sparks of power I felt. Because while they were warm and soothing, I wanted to focus on what I felt from *him*. I focused on how his skin felt. I paid attention to the bone and muscle. I focused on every tick and grimace on his face. I didn't care about experiencing the power between us. I wanted to experience him. Just him.

His eyes opened then, the black streaked with crystal blue. I looked at him. And while I said nothing, I begged him to just be there with me. Wordlessly, I tried to convince him to stay.

I wanted to make him forget anything else. And an idea came to me.

I knew what he thought of himself. I realized there was something I could do that would not make him feel as though he sullied me.

Keeping my eyes on him. Feeling my skin tight as my chest rose and fell, I took one hand back. And I slipped it inside the tiny scrap of fabric I still wore.

Zagan's eyes narrowed and his Adam's apple bobbed. "Violet," he groaned. But he didn't pull away from me.

I felt my lips curl. I smiled at him in an unfamiliar way. I realized it was in a way I had never smiled at anyone before. It wasn't even right to call it a smile. It was a slant, with one side of my lips tilting. He was the only one who had elicited such a look from me. He'd be the only one who ever would.

I began to flex my fingers and I bit down on my bottom lip before they parted on a sigh. Zagan's nostrils flared as his big body tensed around me. He was a solid cage of muscle, which I knew I couldn't escape from in that moment.

The obvious power of his strength and size covered me without touching me, and I let out a moan at the building pressure at my core. I had thought I would tease and taunt him. And instead, I was finding his very presence was sending me close the edge with just a few strokes of my hand.

I rolled my head back and licked my lips. "Kiss me," I breathed.

Every inch of Zagan's body was rigid. His teeth didn't even part when he spoke. "No," he growled.

I pulled my one hand up and removed the other from Zagan's chest. I pressed both hands against the stone wall behind me, just at my hips. I panted as I stared at Zagan, my thighs shaking.

Zagan's hands fisted on either side of my head, grinding into the stone. His face lowered, mere inches from mine. "Finish," he hissed.

I shook under him, all my weight pressed against the wall. My voice wavered, barely audible. *"Kiss. Me."*

With a groan, Zagan pressed his lips against my own. I grasped the back of his head, slipping my fingers into his wet hair. My other hand rose to capture his arm. I pulled it down, gliding my fingers over his bicep and past his forearm to his wrist where I squeezed.

I placed his hand on my waist. He hesitated, about to pull back. But I kissed him deeper, and after a moment's pause, he slipped his big hand down against my slick skin, right where I needed him, and I moaned into his mouth.

I couldn't breathe and I didn't think I ever wanted to again.

The growing wave of sensation washing over me was about to crest. I broke my lips free, and my breath quickened. I rocked my hips at his touch, letting out a cry.

Suddenly Zagan pulled his hand away. My eyelids, which had grown heavy and fallen half shut, flew open. My skin vibrated. And I was about to shatter into a thousand little pieces from disappointment.

Zagan seemed to grow in size, requiring more space, demanding more air. Every muscle in his body was tense and the chords in his neck popped against his skin. His chest billowed with each breath.

He was a predator, intent on his prey. I knew then what it felt like to look into the eyes of the beast before it devoured you— promising a small death.

His hands whipped out, faster than I could track, and yanked my arms above my head. He caged my wrists in his grip.

The freezing water that trickled off him dripped across my chest. Droplets ran in rivulets down my breasts, leaving goosebumps in their wake, falling down my abdomen and drenching the small scrap of fabric between my legs.

Despite the frigid air and chilling water, I was warm under my skin. The excitement of being with him was more than enough to make my blood pump.

Giving my wrists a squeeze, Zagan spoke. "You want me to touch you?" His voice was gritty. I squirmed at hearing him speak, rubbing my thighs together.

"Answer me, Violet."

"Yes," I sighed.

"You shouldn't," he said.

I tried to arch my back against the wall. "We can do something else, if you want."

A deep growl vibrated in his chest.

A low, quiet laugh bubbled in my own. I loved the way I could affect him.

While his grip remained clamped around my wrists, he brought his free hand up to lightly grasp my neck. He lowered his head so that his lips were at my ear. "You make me do things I do not want to do. You make me want to give you whatever you ask for."

His hand trailed down my chest, over one breast, and traced a path to my waist. "Witchery," he murmured.

When his fingers reached the top of my waistband, he paused. "Tell me what you want me to do."

"Touch me," I whispered.

He slid his hand between the fabric and my skin, stroking right where I needed.

My eyes slid shut and my head rolled to the side, my cheek resting on the wet stone. Zagan removed his hand to grasp my chin in his fingers. He turned my head. "Look at me, Violet."

I opened my eyes and was met with Zagan's electric blue gaze as it crackled with Light. "What do you want me to do?"

My head tried to loll to the side, but Zagan held my chin in place. I surrendered. My shoulders went limp. "I want you to make me come," I whispered with a tinge of agony.

Pinned against the wall, completely under his control, Zagan slipped his hand against my skin one last time and finally released me. I was no longer whole. I did become thousands of fractured little pieces then. He had broken me, and I would never be put back completely.

I sank against the wall, my legs unable to support my weight. Zagan caught me, wrapping his arms around my waist, and picked me up. He rolled against the wall so that we were no longer under the running water but off to the side. His back rested against the stone and my legs had instinctually curled around his hips.

I snaked my arms around his neck. Letting out a breath, I looked down at him. He had been in total control just a moment before, but now the muscle in his jaw ticked, his features were tight, and I knew he waged a war within. Biology was demanding one thing of him then, and he was refusing to give in.

311

I cupped his face in my hands and gave him a soft kiss that he did not return. "I'll go," I promised. "Put me down, and I'll go." I gave him an encouraging nod.

With his entire body rigid, he released me, shaking with the effort as I slid down him. But when my feet touched the ground, I didn't turn and walk away. Instead, I continued to slide down until I was on my knees and I let my breasts rub over his erection.

His hands clenched at his sides and he threw his head back, letting out a groan of agony. "Violet!" He yelled my name on an angry burst of air.

I ran my face along his shaft, trailing a line with my tongue from base to tip. He stared down at me with a mix of rage and fascination.

I knew he was going to tell me to leave, and I'd have to walk away from him.

His voice was guttural. Unintelligible. "Do it again."

I had been wrong.

I did what he demanded. And this time when I reached the tip of his shaft, I opened my lips and covered the head of him with my mouth. I placed my hands on the side of each of his thighs and drew him in deeper. Then with a wet suck I pulled my lips back, freeing him.

I looked up at him and he stared at me. He was so angry. But there was no turning back.

"*Again.*"

I traced another line with my tongue and drew him in, between my lips as deep as I could. But this time I used my hands as well. He was so large and hard that I had to work both hands along his shaft.

I could feel my cheeks hollow as I looked up at him, and he shook his head at me. I knew he felt as though I needed saving from

312

him. And I knew he was too far gone to be the one to save me. Just to prove how wrong he was I closed my eyes and made an "umm" sound around him.

There was a pause. His breathing stopped. His body stilled. I looked up at him again. His eyes had widened. Then with a groan of capitulation he fisted my hair with his hands, and he began guiding me back and forth over him.

I didn't try to taunt him or tease him. I knew he wasn't in a place for that. I tried to give him exactly what he needed, with happy little sighs. And when he finally erupted with a roar that shook the ceiling, I made sure to take everything he had to give, reluctant to release him.

He leaned against the wall, completely spent, with his head thrown back and his hands still in my damp hair. I leaned my head to the side and kissed his thigh. Then I ran my hands up the sides of his legs and over his hips and abdomen as I stood. I continued to graze my hands up over his chest and shoulders to push myself up on my toes and loop my arms around his neck.

I could feel Light and energy well in my chest. But it wasn't enough. I needed to be with him. And he was still holding so much back.

As I wiggled my body against his, I could feel that he needed more too. He was already hard and bruising against me. His hands enveloped my hips and he stilled my little motions.

Finally, his head tilted forward, and he looked down at me, his voice stern. "Violet! No!" he snapped.

I laughed, and the sound filled the dark, sad hole in the ground with a note of buoyancy.

Zagan's eyes narrowed. "Go to your room," he growled.

"Actually, I'm going to stay here. With you," I told him. Then I closed the few inches of distance between us and gave him a big smack on the lips, as if it were the most natural thing in the world. "But I promise I won't try anything else." Keeping my arms looped around him, I turned my face to yawn into his shoulder. Then I looked back up at him trying to make my eyes large and round—an innocent little angel. "I just want to sleep."

"Your promise means nothing," he seethed.

I sighed and pulled back from him, letting my heels hit the floor and my hands rest on his chest with a little tap. "That's true," I admitted. "But the only way you will get me to leave is with a fight. And I won't make it easy on you." I shrugged, giving him my best 'whatcha gonna do' face. Then I shimmied out of my panties, turned, and walked out the door without looking back.

# CHAPTER 27

~Violet's Playlist: Creep, Radiohead~

ZAGAN CAME STORMING in after me. He looked at me sitting on his bed and was clearly speechless. He stared at me and then the dark empty room. Me again. Back to the room. Finally, he said, "You can't stay here."

"Sure I can," I replied. To prove my point, I scooted back on the bed and curled up on the fitted sheet.

Zagan looked around the depressing space, at a loss. Then he took a step towards me. "I am taking you to your room."

"I want to be alone with you," I told him. My suite was large, and I had the entire wing for my quarters, but I possessed a very strong suspicion Zagan wouldn't stay up on the fifth floor with someone else nearby.

More than that, though, was the fact that there was just too much happening up those stairs and out that front door. Down in the abandoned wing with Zagan, buried away…none of it could reach me.

I was realizing how much I needed the Dark Manor. It was a place to retreat. A break. Without it, it would all be too much. And I was also realizing that the man who lived within its walls was essential to it.

While surrounded by death and Darkness and the constant threat of the end looming near, Zagan made me feel *lighter*.

But just then, I was also cold. I wrapped my arms around myself. "My god, it's freezing in here."

Flummoxed, Zagan took one last look around the room, and finding no answers to be had, he stomped out the door.

I sighed, knowing I had to leave. I didn't want to force myself on him, and I didn't want to drive him away. I'd thought I could give a playful, sassy nudge in the right direction. But I wasn't willing to torture him or completely abandon any self-respect I possessed.

I tensed my arms, about to push myself up from the bed when a pile of items was dumped on top of me. I was buried in a heap of fluffiness. Once I made my way out from the avalanche, I looked up at Zagan.

"Your *things*," he rumbled.

I stuffed one of the pillows under my head and pulled the comforter around myself. There were clothes which had been delivered with the bedding. I kicked them off the mattress. Then I settled myself on one side of the bed. Looking up at Zagan, I noticed he had put on a pair of pants.

"Help yourself to a pillow," I yawned. And while I pretended to not care what he did, I held my breath waiting to see if he would leave.

With a heavy exhale, he rubbed his pectoral, seeming to contemplate his next move. He didn't budge for quite some time. Then shaking his head and massaging his chest the whole way, he trudged around the bed to the opposite side.

Swinging his legs up, he sat with his back against the wall. "At least put your clothes on," he said as he looked down at me.

I was buried under a huge blanket. I didn't see the urgency in the matter. I turned onto my side to face him. "I will," I said. "Later."

I adjusted the pillow under my head. "Now if you don't mind, I'd like to get some sleep. In case you didn't know, I've got a few things I need to sort out, like fate of the world type stuff. And I can't spend the entire night entertaining you."

He gave me a look that said he was not amused. Then he crossed his arms and leaned his head back, shutting his eyes. He was at ease, more so than any other time he'd sat next to me. Whatever Maxim had said to him had helped. And I was also convinced that finding a bit of physical release—and fostering the connection we shared— had subdued the worst of his tension as well.

My chest felt warm. I realized how much I loved being able to do something that made him feel good, something that drove him crazy. And I was determined to continue my efforts in persuading him that we should not be fighting the attraction we had to one another.

There was silence between us for a while. Every few minutes I would glance at him, though, debating whether to crawl up on his chest or not.

He let out an irritated huff, probably feeling my gaze, and his eyes snapped open. "Why do you persist, Violet? Time and time again, I have tried to push you away. Why do you not give up?"

I sat, shifting the comforter around my shoulders, holding it closed at my chest. I tucked my hair behind my ear, and I met his eye. I took a moment to think about what I wanted to say. And when I spoke, my voice was raw.

"You came for me, Zagan. Every time I've needed you, even when I didn't realize it, you've come for me. I don't know if you remember that night, when everything fell apart, up on the cliff. But you said you always would."

I paused, my eyes staring at the mark on his chest, searching for my next words. "That was a moment of truth. Whether you want to admit it to yourself or not. Despite your best efforts, you continue to come for me time and time again. And I'm beginning to believe you always will, even if you haven't accepted it yet."

I looked up in the room at the place where light and shadow once danced through the air, wanting to see that again. Then I met his eye. "I'm not going to stop coming for you, either."

With a shrug, I gave Zagan a huge smile, feeling the need to chase away the heavy weight of my words. Afraid they might crush him. Afraid they might crush us both.

I leaned my hand down on the bed next to him and inched closer. "Plus, I like you." I raised a brow. "And let's be honest. You're fucking hot."

Zagan's eyes narrowed. "You ridicule me." There wasn't hurt or offense in his voice. It was just a statement of fact.

"I don't," I said simply, meeting his fact with a fact, letting him see the honesty on my face. Then I shook my head. My voice was quiet in the dark. "You know, right now your song is *Creep*." I shifted closer and curled up next to him. "It's time for a new anthem, Zagan."

319

He was stiff and kept his arms crossed, but he didn't shift away. After several long moments, he finally said, "I do not know what that means."

"You don't. But you do."

After another long pause, he asked, "And what anthem would you suggest?"

"I don't know, but I've got an extensive collection on my music player upstairs. I'm sure you could find something."

"Violet, you are so certain that you will elevate me to some higher level. What you fail to understand is that in the end, I will drag you down with me. If you prefer to think of it in terms of music, then whatever this song is that you speak of, I will always be."

I yawned. "Hmm. Maybe. But you know what? I'm beginning to realize it's not so bad down here with you."

I wished I was not so exhausted and on the verge of passing out, because I wanted to pull out my little Violet scoreboard and give myself a big fat point for that doozy.

Zagan let out a jagged exhale.

I patted his arm. "Face it, handsome. You're not going to win any arguments with me tonight."

"And besides," I said interrupting myself and circling back to my comment about music, "come to think of it, that song is pretty good for the girl. So, I think I can live with it." Then I shifted even closer to him. "Now sit next to me while I fall asleep."

Muttering something about my audacity and making him do things he didn't want to do…Zagan stayed where he was.

Without realizing it, I hummed a few bars of a sad song as it played in mind.

Because I liked things that were dark and deep.

I always had.

***

I was alone. When I finally opened my eyes, I was alone. However, I wasn't disappointed. I knew Zagan had slept next to me throughout the day. And I rubbed my cheek against my shoulder at the thought of it.

Hopping out of his bed, I rummaged through the pile of clothes on the floor, laughing when I saw the baseball cap. And while I didn't opt to wear it, I did slip on the black leggings and short-waisted sweatshirt.

Leaving my *things* where they were on the mattress, I went to collect my items from the previous night which were still discarded in the make-shift shower. Before I left Zagan's room, though, I glanced back.

I knew it wasn't actually brighter. I knew it was my eyes having adjusted to the darkness down there. And I knew it wasn't actually warmer. I knew it was my body adjusting to the temperature. But it was impossible not to see things differently.

After collecting my discarded jacket and clothing from the other room, I was about to make my way up to the fifth floor. Before I did, though, I checked my jacket pockets. Finding the glasses from Belcalis, I slipped them on, wanting to test them out.

As I walked down the hall, I also pulled free the leather journal. Flipping open the cover, I glanced at the first page, before stopping in my tracks.

I could read the words penned there. The words—according to Maxim—which had been written by the Shadow King himself.

I was just outside Zagan's room. I darted in and dropped my handful of clothes on the floor, before stumbling to the edge of his bed, all without taking my eyes off the journal.

I sat, down in the cold, dark, abandoned wing of the manor, and a chill crept up my spine. I couldn't tear my eyes from the pages.

Within the covers of the Shadow King's journal, I found a story which I never would have expected. A story that validated Maxim's account and made me believe in him. There, in what was once the heart of the Shadow Court, I found the story of the first two Prisms.

*\*\**

*Our brethren have acted. They have followed through with their contrivance, and the mighty fools will find success in their deceit. Henceforth, they will control and manipulate their people for their personal benefaction.*

*The girl, Aurelia, barely escaped with her life. Dragging herself away, bleeding and dying, she called my name. There was such agony, the likes of which I could not understand, that I felt the vibrations of the call and had no choice but to answer.*

*Our brothers and sisters of the Light are now intent on destroying their chosen. They do not realize they have set in motion a force which cannot be stopped. The power of it will ripple through time.*

*But they will soon learn.*

*Cortho, the boy, is believed dead at the hands of my people. The Council, as they are calling themselves, has concealed their involvement. And now they wish to pit us against them as their enemy.*

*So be it.*

*I will not sway the destiny of my people. If they chose to engage in this war, their women and children will weep the tears of their sins.*

*The girl has fled, seeking asylum. I pity her as she is not long of this world. She was gravely injured during the attack against her—her Light extinguished.*

*The most extraordinary facet of her circumstance is the fact that her Light was expelled of her own will. When Aurelia found Cortho's dying body, she released her Light in an act so selfless, so powerful, and so desperate, that she gave all of herself unto him.*

*Now the Darkness has entered her soul, and it is swiftly killing her. Yet, before the Darkness may claim her, I believe she will die of a broken heart.*

*Aurelia did not know she had been chosen by the Council. She only knew that she was half a soul, and when she found the boy, she was made whole.*

*I could see him when I searched her mind. Cortho was valiant and honorable. Yet a young man, he had been a fine choice for a chosen. He had held Aurelia's very heart and discovered the stars in her eyes.*

*When I questioned Aurelia on how she knew her own Council was responsible for the attack upon her, she revealed she had caught a glimpse of a white robed member, directing the assassination against Cortho before disappearing. A mistake I am certain my Light brethren will not make again.*

*This too I have confirmed in her memories. There was no denying the Council member had outed himself. Divine light shimmered from his robes, and I recognized him as kin.*

*Now Aurelia awaits her final breath. I can see she wants nothing more than to join her beloved Cortho on the other side. While Aurelia is a strong young woman, she is no match for the Shadow assassins deployed against her. I found it difficult to believe she had been able to escape. But she spoke of a little girl, an archer, who had impaled the hearts of her foes with arrows of Light.*

*She will take her final breath any day now and join her beloved on the other side. Of this I am certain. I have offered to return her to her home. She claims she has no family to return to and she fears the Council will only finish the attempt against her. She is, of course, correct.*

*My final question for her was why she chose to petition my favor. It had been my own people whose hands had carried out the grievances against her. It would not seem prudent to seek protection from their very king.*

*Her answer made my blood run cold. Her answer makes me ever more curious as to the ways of love and the lengths individuals will go in its name.*

*With the blood of her broken heart pouring from her lips and her final breaths upon her, she seeks punishment for those who killed her one true love. She pleads for me to smite my brothers and sisters of the Light—the Council.*

*I told her it is not for me to pass judgement. I am a guiding force and a protector of those under me. That is all.*

*Seraphina is keeping vigil over the girl for now. She is the only one of the Dark half whom I have found. However, the elements of this world have not blessed her as the moon has blessed me. And so, it is difficult for her to stay long in this realm. She must leave from time to time.*

*I have tasked Seraphina with finding the other eleven of our Dark brothers and sisters. She is concerned the attempt is an act of foolishness. But balance must be restored!*

*We became scattered and lost as we fled Aleece. We did not wish to burn our home to ash in the fiery war the Light half threatened.*

*When our world was fractured, they believed we had split into good and evil. They did not understand that the Light and Dark are neither one nor the other. But those who gravitated to the Light deemed themselves to be more holy and divine.*

*I should like to show them the face of the Umbra. Then they would understand evil.*

*It angers me still to think upon it, and I will cease to revisit the topic as it leads me astray in my thoughts. I find my records repeatedly smattered with the same prolixity. I will no longer waste my ink upon it.*

*For now, the girl remains here. I will return her body to her people once she has passed to the other side. And while this is the end for her and her beloved, an unbreakable chain is now in motion. The Light from both the girl and the boy will find its way to the next generation. There will come another and another. On and on, this Light will be passed down. And on and on, the Council will take the lives of those strong and valiant enough to carry it.*

*Until balance is restored.*

\*\*\*

I shut the journal. I placed it on the bed next to me, and I removed the glasses, setting them on the book.

I sat in the dark room and my heart broke for Aurelia. I found a kinship with her. I could understand her. Could understand her actions. Her sacrifice. And her desire for retribution.

And my blood boiled at what the Council had done to her.

They needed to be stopped. I didn't desire some dramatic demise for the Elders. I didn't wish to fulfill any prophecies regarding their ultimate destruction. I knew there had to be a way for them to see the error of their ways and to put an end to it—to find peace with each new Prism.

I was going to try my best to work with Maxim. I had to. I was still angry at what he'd done, but I needed him.

I needed help in stopping the Council, The Contessa, and the Umbra. I knew it was not going to be easy, though. I knew there would be more bloody battles to come.

The Council could be swayed—I was certain of it. The Umbra could be locked away—it had been done before. But The Contessa...

There are some people who have nothing left to lose. These are the people to fear. These are the people who are the most dangerous.

Because these are the people who have rotted on the inside. And if you're not careful, the rot will begin to eat away at you too.

# CHAPTER 28

ADRIEL WAS NOT WELL.

I looked down at her in the bed as she slept. Her skin was sallow, her hair matted around her temples, and her breathing irregular.

The last dying rays of the setting sun tried to stretch their way in through the window, but they were too feeble to reach the bed.

As I stood there, contemplating whether to wake her or not, Adriel's eyes opened. She gave a weak smile, and then began to cough.

Helping her sit, I grabbed the glass of water I had brought in and handed it to her. She took a tiny sip before coughing more and then eventually settling.

"What can I do for you?" I asked, wringing my hands.

Adriel touched her hair. After swallowing a few times, she finally said, "A bath." Her voice was reedy, and there were dark hollows under her eyes.

I nodded and went to collect some things for her and start the water. When I returned to the bed, Adriel was sitting where I'd left her with her eyes closed.

"Mom?" I asked. She opened her eyes to look at me, and I couldn't find any words.

Adriel gave a tight smile. "I will be fine, Violet," she reassured. "I just need a little time."

I nodded, not trusting my voice. Instead I held my hand out, and Adriel took it. I helped her out of the bed and into the bathroom.

Once we'd entered, she dismissed me. "I am fine, Violet," she repeated. "Thank you."

I gestured to the simple, comfortable dress I'd left out. "There are some clothes for you," I told her, before leaving.

I waited just outside the door in case she needed anything, and by the time she was dressed and ready, night had fully fallen. I had her take a seat in the anteroom of my quarters with both fires burning brightly. Then I left for the kitchen to prepare some food.

I knew she'd expended an incredible amount of energy the previous night. I'd always known she was powerful, but I hadn't known she could do something like summon the Light of day.

It was a feat which must have required untold amounts of power. But at what cost? I was unsettled, seeing her as she was.

And while I was incredibly grateful for all she had done, I wished she wasn't at the Dark Manor.

I wished she was at the Radiant Court where she would be safe. Seeing her as Maxim's prisoner was too upsetting. Seeing her in the Dark Manor…she just didn't belong here.

I didn't dwell on the thought long, though, because as I collected the tray of food to take to Adriel, I felt incredible Dark power out in the main hall. I snatched the tray up in my hands, causing the plates to rattle, and I made a beeline for the front entry—knowing full well who it was.

Lighting the chandeliers throughout the foyer in angry bursts of energy, I walked right up to Maxim. And I eyed him without saying a word. He stared down at me in that infuriatingly calm way he had about him.

I bit my cheek. While I was still in my leggings and my hair was swept up in a high pony tail, he was in an immaculate dark suit with that confident posture he possessed.

We stood in silence. I refused to speak, and Maxim was patiently waiting to be greeted or invited in or something. Yet he hadn't bothered entering through the front door. He'd just wisped his way into the manor.

I drew out the silence a little longer, clearly irritated by his presumed license. While Maxim had overseen certain aspects of the manor, I felt he had forfeited his right to come and go as he pleased when he'd imprisoned me.

Eventually I broke the silence, though. One detail from the previous night had stuck with me more than anything else. Narrowing my eyes, I tilted my head and pursed my lips. "What did you say to him last night?"

Knowing precisely what I was asking, Maxim responded in his deep, sophisticated voice without hesitation. "I told him to be at ease."

"Can you teach it to me?" I asked.

The dark slash of his brows intensified as he searched my face, and his cool, polished demeanor wavered. His voice dropped and he spoke slowly, as if making an unexpected discovery. "You *care* for him."

I didn't reply. Instead I notched my chin and set my jaw.

Maxim recovered immediately, his control returning. "No," he said, answering my question.

My grip on the serving tray tightened. "Why not?" I snapped.

"There are a multitude of reasons—for which I do not have the time nor the inclination to discuss—but the most obvious of them is the fact that you are unteachable."

I was about to reply, but I felt a wall of Dark power coil around me. There was a protective air to the energy. But there was something else as well, something raw and intimate. The air around me was saturated with *possession*. I almost dropped the tray I held at the incredible strength of it.

Maxim's eyes focused behind me. If he had any particular opinion on Zagan's presence, he didn't show it. His urbane confidence did not falter.

I glanced over my shoulder, and as I'd expected, Zagan was standing just behind me. His face was cold and hard. In his eyes I could see a note of warning as he stared at Maxim. It looked like he'd just thrown on a shirt; the black garment was open down the front. And while he wore a pair of pants, his feet were bare.

I directed my attention back to Maxim. Still, he emoted nothing and stood his ground.

When I couldn't take another second of the tension, I hefted the tray I held, and it clattered. "Have you two even officially met—?"

"Violet?"

We all turned to the stairs. Adriel had descended, unnoticed. She stood a few steps up from the bottom, holding herself at the rail. I let out a huff and shoved the tray I was clutching into Maxim's hands.

"You should have waited upstairs," I told Adriel, crossing to her and wrapping my arm around her back. I glanced up at the multiple flights and decided to instead usher her into the receiving room that was just around the corner.

With a pulse of energy, I had the fireplace roaring and the overhead chandelier twinkling. Then I sat Adriel down on one of the sofas, incredibly grateful that'd I'd asked Maxim to have the first floor cleaned, all that time ago. I couldn't imagine trying to make Adriel comfortable if the room had been covered in dust and cobwebs. As it was, the space was in an acceptable state for guests and there was no overlooking the elegant and dignified decor.

Having followed in behind us, Maxim set the tray on the coffee table. However, after examining the contents, he gave a scowl and left the room.

I noticed that Zagan had also entered, but he stood off to the corner, staying to the shadows. And I pasted a tight smile on my face, shifting where I sat, trying to find a way to sit that felt natural.

Because the whole situation was awkward as hell. I didn't know what to say. I didn't know if I should formally introduce Adriel and Zagan or just gloss over the fact that this was an unsettling reunion or...*what?*

To make matters worse, Maxim returned a few minutes later with a blanket and a cup of tea. He set the tea down on the coffee table and held the blanket out to me. I grudgingly took it and placed it over Adriel's lap, feeling like I'd been scolded.

Then Maxim glanced back at Zagan before taking a seat in one of the armchairs across from us. Giving me a once over, he said, "You are uncomfortable."

I had to fight the urge to squirm. He'd just made it worse. Of course, I was uncomfortable. Pointing it out wasn't going to help.

But just to prove him wrong, I leaned back against the sofa and crossed one leg over the other, trying my best to look casual.

I felt ridiculous.

Giving up, I set my feet on floor and leaned forward. "Look," I said, diving right into it, "I was thinking about some things, and there are holes in your story about the Council."

Instead of interrupting, Maxim raised a brow and waited for me to continue.

I glanced over at Zagan, wishing I didn't have to revisit what had happened. But things needed to be said.

"When I left here," I told Maxim, "I was confused and...*unwell*. Somehow, I ended up with the last Prism—the one who came before us—and sensing the Darkness I carried, he tried to..."

I looked down at my hands. I hadn't realized how upsetting my interaction with Elijah had been. I hadn't realized I would be so affected by it. And while I knew it wasn't my fault, I felt embarrassed about what had happened. I was ashamed to speak about it.

I spoke in a rush, wanting to get the words out and leave them behind me. "When he tried to take my life, an Archangel was sent to stop him. The Council had sent her.

"So, it doesn't make sense. If the Council wanted me dead, then why stop him? Why not let him carry through with the attack against me. Elijah would have been doing them a favor."

Adriel placed a shaking hand on my forearm, preventing me from continuing, and she looked at me with glassy eyes. "Davis sent the Archangel," she said softly.

"What?" I asked, not understanding.

Closing her eyes, Adriel said, "Your father was the one who sent Daphne." She swallowed before continuing and then opened her eyes to look at me. A solitary tear slipped down her cheek. "Violet, he was the one who sent an Archangel to find you, when you were lost. He instructed the Archangel to take you to Elijah's. And when the Oracle told him of Elijah's intention, your father was the one who sent Daphne to stop him."

I searched Adriel's face, still not understanding. "But how would he have known? How could he have commanded Archangels? Or spoken with the Oracle? He's just a volunteer in Aleece."

Adriel's hand on my arm tightened, and she looked deep into my eyes. There was so much regret on her face. "The voluntarius in Aleece...*are* the Elders."

I let my head fall forward, and I rubbed my temples. I wasn't sure how much more I could take.

"*Why?*"

Although thin, Adriel's voice was patient. "It's a way for them to compartmentalize their psyche, to exist separately from the collective. It is a way for them to maintain a sense of individuality."

"Are you telling me that my father is a member of the Council of Elders, and he wants me dead?"

"It's more complicated than that," Adriel said. "He is one of the Elders. But he is also separate from that. He is also an individual, who cares for his daughter and does not want her harmed. Unlike the other members, he wanted to try and experience a life outside of the Council. But he cannot escape who or what he is. He cannot cease to be an Elder. That is not an option for him."

"And he couldn't have given me a head's up on what was going on?!" I stood and took a few steps away, needing some space.

"He cannot speak of certain things. It is not possible for him to. There are some things that can only be spoken by the collective.

And while his insight is great, he is not omniscient. None of the council members are."

Adriel took a gasping breath, and her shoulders slumped. She seemed to collapse inward. "He did not know it was you. Not until recently when Elijah returned. I meant what I said. I never told a single individual that you were the Prism. Never wrote it down, never shared it. I did not trust the ways of this world or the lengths our enemies would go to destroy you. If I spoke the words they could be overheard or stolen on the wind. Because of who he is, I assumed your father knew. And I never spoke the words aloud.

"But I recently learned it is not the Council who chooses each Prism. It is the Angela. They are the ones who seek those most worthy and pass on the Light. They have not involved the Council from the beginning, believing it was in the Council's best interest and safety."

I paused for a moment, taking in Adriel's words. My father had been the one to find me in Aleece. He'd been the one to tuck me away in a room, and he'd been the one who encouraged Elijah to leave with me against the Council's ruling.

But most importantly, he'd been one of thirteen who had ordered the death of Prisms since the beginning of their time. My hands shook and I clasped them at my chest. Then I looked at Adriel, and I felt pain, because I realized what this all meant for her.

She had been fighting to save Prisms since she was a little girl, and she had just found out that my father had been a part of the group behind the attacks.

She was barely holding herself up, barely keeping herself from slumping over.

"Mom...I'm sorry."

She nodded without replying.

"You're not well. What can I do for you?"

"I need to return to the Radiant Court. I need to see Davis," she said.

"Is that safe?" I asked.

Adriel smiled. "He is more than a member of the Council. Being a husband and father have been the greatest joys of his eternal life. He will do everything in his power to reconcile the different facets of himself."

Maxim stood. "I will take you."

I looked at him, unable to hide the surprise I felt.

"There are matters to be settled between your Court and my people," he told Adriel. "But I will return you to your Court so that you are able to recover and enter into discussions with us. And if you are willing to protect my people against the Umbra as you did last night, all grievances against you will be absolved."

Adriel looked up at Maxim from where she sat and shook her head. "That is not something I will be able to do again."

After a moment, Maxim gave a disappointed but accepting nod. I took a step closer to him and crossed my arms over my chest. Before he had the chance to go anywhere, I asked, "Why did you come here tonight, Maxim?" I knew the anger I was feeling in that moment was towards Davis and Adriel, but I ended up directing the intensity of it at Maxim.

He crossed his arms as well, mirroring me. "I have come to ask for help. It is time for the Shadow Prince to fight for his people."

He turned to direct the full force of his gaze at Zagan. "It is time to rise to your lineage. You cannot allow she who calls herself The Contessa to rule the Darkness. It is time for you to take what is rightfully yours. You must master the night and lock away the Umbra—as our king did.

"You have inherited his responsibility. Your time has come."

Maxim looked between us. "I am offering to work with you. Both of you. If you are willing to fight The Contessa and the Umbra. While she did not reveal herself last night, she is nigh. I can feel her. For some reason she has not shown herself for some time now. But she will return.

"If you accept my alliance, there are things I can share with you. There is ancient knowledge I have uncovered, and I can provide tutelage on how to control the powers you possess."

At that, he gave me a pointed look, and I knew he was thinking of the request I'd made earlier when I'd asked him to teach me the command he had used to calm Zagan. There were also the commands which he'd used against me. And I desperately wanted to know how to block them.

"I appreciate civility," Maxim continued. "But these are desperate times. If you choose to do nothing," he glanced at Zagan, "then you are my enemy."

After the last of his words settled over us, I rubbed an eye. "We're already trying to help," I informed him. "I traveled to the Realm of Lost Souls to petition the god of death. If I can find a stone for him—one called the *Heart of Darkness*—and return it to him, then he'll tell me how to defeat The Contessa."

At my words, the fire darkened and dwindled. The flames in the hearth and chandelier turned black around the edges. A shadow passed across Maxim's face, and he leaned into me. "What did you just say?"

At his invasion into my personal space, I again felt Dark power coil around me, and I took a step back from Maxim, not wanting Zagan to get worked up. I shrugged, not understanding Maxim's agitation. "If I find a stone, I can uncover a way to stop The Contessa."

"What did you call it?" Maxim pressed.

"*The Heart of Darkness,*" I said.

Maxim took another step towards me. "Do you have it? Have you seen it? Do you know where it is?"

I shrugged. "I had it for a moment, but then I lost it."

"*Where?*" Maxim boomed as he grabbed my arms.

In a streaking blur of shadows, he went flying across the room, slamming into a bookcase. To Maxim's credit, the strike did not cause him to collapse. He managed to right himself and remain on his feet. However, Zagan stood in front of him, leaving a mere inch of space between them.

Seeing them stand toe to toe, it was unclear who possessed more power and strength. They were similar in height and build. And the amount of power that exuded from both was unfathomable. But it differed between them.

It was difficult to predict a victor if a fight were to ensue. It would be a battle of feral, deranged chaos verses honed, controlled skill.

The temperature in the room had plummeted, and the shadows along the periphery had stretched and grown, brushing the ceiling of the room and closing in all around us. Zagan spoke right in Maxim's face, his voice dark and menacing. "I vowed you would not touch her."

Maxim met Zagan's eyes with a ruthless intensity. "I do not wish her harm. I only wish to know of the stone. It is of great importance. I will apologize to her for my temporary lapse in control. But I must have that stone. It is a key which can lock away the Umbra."

The air of power Maxim possessed seemed to dissipate. It was as though he was pulling back. And while he did not appear smaller in any way, he seemed to take up less space.

Calmly and reasonably, he told Zagan, "I wish to work with you." Then he looked past Zagan to me. "Both of you."

"It's all right," I told Zagan.

I addressed Maxim's comments, weary of it all. "I don't have it. I lost it. But I can try to help—" Before I could say any more, though, shuffling sounded out in the hallway.

I paused, recognizing the sound. For as feeble and quiet as it was, the sound somehow took over the room. And everyone seemed to note the importance of it. We all turned to watch the doorway. As we listened, the shuffling was the only sound, not even the fire dared to crackle. And second by second, the shuffling grew louder.

Hunched and hooded, the Crone limped by. She stopped just outside the door, and the tattered brown hood of her robe swiveled in our direction. From the complete darkness beneath the cowl, I could feel the far-off power of her gaze as it landed on us all. She stood there, staring at us, making a point—of what, I didn't know—for much too long. Then her head swiveled forward, and she continued down the hall, hobbling and shuffling away.

The Crone had returned.

# CHAPTER 29

I SAT ON MY BED in front of the fire. I had bathed and changed. And all I could do now...was sit.

Maxim had left to escort Adriel to the Radiant Court. Before wisping her away, he had said he would return the following night to begin discussing our strategy for moving forward.

Then Zagan had stepped up to me in the empty room. He'd raised his hands as if he were going to take a hold of me, but he'd stopped himself. He'd said he needed to check on the Crone, and he'd left.

I hadn't known what else to do but run a bath. Then I'd wrapped myself up in a floor length black robe from my closet. The silk was cool and soft, and the wide kimono sleeves swept around my arms.

I looked down at my hands. I was a Prism. I had been gifted the Light of the Angela. I had been meant to connect with my other half. And because I had, the Council wanted Elijah, Zagan, and me, all dead. I now knew it was because they believed one of us would be their doom.

As I sat in my room a fire blazed in the oversized hearth, and the floor to ceiling windows stood unobstructed by drapery. I looked over at the towering glass panes. They kept the night at bay, preventing it from spilling into the room. But the night did not seem to mind. It sat and listened, patiently waiting…for something.

We stared at each other.

After it had eyed me for some time, I began to hear a quiet beating. It was faint at first, then it began to grow, steadily increasing in volume. It grew stronger the longer I sat there, filling my ears. At some point, each steady thump came with an anvil's strike. A clang that would reverberate through my mind. And flash by flash, the thoughts came.

The Council wanted me dead.

My father was one of them.

My mother had kept so much from me.

Radiants were becoming sick and infected.

The Contessa would come for me.

The Umbra were free.

I had lost the *Heart of Darkness*.

Elijah was a prisoner of the Council because of me.

And Zagan would not accept me.

Each thought came with a strike, until a final crescendo crashed over me. A deafening clang reverberated through my mind with my final thought. And once the last ping had ricocheted through my head, there was an impossible silence.

Yet in the silence, a thought took seed. This one was different from all the others. This one took hold and sprouted.

*They all toyed with me.*

Those of the heavens used me as a pawn. Those of this world treated me as a child. They all played with me.

342

My shoulders slid back. My head lifted. I was no one's pawn. I was not a child. I would show them all.

My wrath. My demons. They were great. Was I to deny the incredible power I possessed?

It began as one small drop of ink. One small black cloud in my blood. Then it swirled and stretched, dancing through my veins. Seeping in through the cracks in my foundation. Filling and offering. Surging. Pumping. Blocking out the Light. Supplying strength and retribution.

The Darkness.

And it was not *wrong*. Light and Dark are not good and evil. They are the opposite sides of the same coin. Their value—equal.

I rose in my black robe and it fluttered behind me. I could feel the veins of black branching through my eyes. I required nothing. No shoes. No weapons.

The Darkness demanded I rise. It demanded I vanquish my foes and strike down all those who would dare to stand before me.

I did not know why, but I needed to find the Umbra. And I did not need to know why. The Darkness knew.

I left the manor. I approached the gate. The Darkness spoke the necessary words for me, and the gate opened. I stepped into the tree tunnel.

I walked through the mighty oaks and they bowed to me. Their entwined branches knit together—tighter—squeezing out all light from the heavens above. The wind swept the ground at my feet, clearing the dirt of pebbles and twigs. The hem of my robe billowed around my legs, and my hair flew through the air.

I was alive. I was the night. I was power. And nothing would stop me. I was certain of it.

Until I heard my name.

Instead of continuing forward, I stopped. And I turned. I had no choice. I could feel an incredible will behind me.

Zagan stood at the open gate.

I smiled. I was beginning to understand what it meant to possess such glorious strength and power. I couldn't fathom why he would fight as he did.

Even now, I could see him struggle, trying to maintain control, to keep the Darkness leashed.

"Stop." He did not raise his voice or shout. The one word was quiet, but it carried through the cold air.

I looked at him. His shirt had been removed. And where he stood, the moonlight could still reach him. The mark on his chest seemed silvery in the light. I wanted him to step under the cover of the trees and let it blacken.

Purposefully defying him, I began walking backwards while I faced him. I knew the smile on my lips was wicked, and I was glad for it. "Come with me," I told him.

He shuddered and took one jerking step before stopping himself. He shook his head and spoke with a cold, quiet fury. "I will not let you leave," he warned. "If you force me to drag you back, you will be sorry."

I stopped walking. I stared at him. I waited. Knowing he would come for me…I turned and ran.

My feet flew over the path as the black robe billowed behind me. I was faster than I'd ever been. Shadows whispered and wailed all around me, urging me to make haste. The Dark One approached. He'd be upon me any moment. And his displeasure was great.

I was nearing the other end of the tree tunnel. I was going to make it. Perhaps he'd let me go after all. It was what he'd wanted.

344

Time and time again, he'd bid me to leave. If he truly wished to be free of me, now was his chance.

But those were foolish thoughts. And his hands came around my waist. He yanked me back with such force that we both went tumbling over the ground. I ended up on my back as he pinned me down, my hands in his punishing grip next to each of my shoulders. He gave my wrists a violent shake.

In response, I forced my hips into his, biting my bottom lip. The belt of my robe had remained tied around my waist, but the fabric along my thighs and chest had slid to the sides.

That one simple act—that one simple invitation—was his undoing.

Shadows coalesced around him and he stared at me with black eyes. The Darkness I possessed purred.

Zagan's voice was guttural as he spoke. "This is what you want? This is what you want to become? Up until this point, you have had a chance. After this, there will be no escape from me. *Ever.* I will not release you. You will never be free of me. If you try to leave, I will be a monster from your nightmares as I hunt you down."

He gave my wrists another shake. "Do you understand?!"

I almost laughed. Because he didn't realize. He didn't see. I was the one who was the monster…disguised as his helpless prey.

This whole time, I had been the one coming for him. Hunting him. Waiting for him.

And I had already known that he'd never be free of me. I had already known that I was bound to him.

I broke free from his grasp and yanked his pants open, freeing him. I could *feel* the gaping hunger he had for me. I could recognize the precise tone of it. And I knew I was the only one he would ever want.

345

He could not stop himself. It was impossible. He shoved into me. I was swollen and slippery for him, but he still had to work to enter me. With each demanding thrust, he wedged himself a little deeper. He was just too big to accommodate easily.

I clawed his arms where I grabbed a hold of him, hanging on to him with each crazed advance. He was not holding back. He was giving in to his most basic instinct without regard for the consequences.

*Finally.*

The intensity. The build. The pressure. I would only ever know such things with him. I arched my back beneath him, trying to fight the fact that I was rapidly approaching the cliff's edge.

He hadn't even worked himself halfway in. With each thrust, I could take just a little more, before he was forced to retreat and try to wedge himself deeper. And that alone had me about to reach my breaking point.

I didn't want to fall. I didn't want to explode and shatter. I wasn't ready to. I wanted more of the incredible agony.

I placed my hand on his chest, trying to push him back. At the same time, I squeezed my thighs around his hips, wanting to slow him down. I couldn't find words. I was beyond speaking. "No," I managed on a breath.

Zagan stilled and he looked down at me with his black eyes. The shadows around us flared and wailed streaking high into the tree tops. There was madness in his voice when he spoke. "No?" he growled. "No?" he repeated. "*No?!*" he roared.

He thought I wanted him to stop entirely. I hadn't had a chance to explain what I'd meant.

And I promise you, I never would have done what I did next if I had been myself. I never would have tried to tease or torment or toy

346

with him—especially knowing how crazed he was. If I had been myself, I would have known it was a cruel, wicked thing to do.

But if you ever find yourself possessed by the Darkness, you'll understand that sometimes you can't help but do cruel, wicked things.

I placed one foot on his chest, and I pushed him away. Then I rolled onto my hands and knees and began to crawl from him, making him chase me. Finding some kind of high in the knowledge that he had to give in to his impulses and hunt me down.

Within a second, he was on top of me, crushing me to the ground. He fisted my wrists behind my back and shoved the fabric of my robe up around my waist. Then he lifted his weight from me, kneeling behind me, and picked up my hips so they were propped in the air.

I could feel him shaking and fighting and snarling behind me. He warred with himself, believing I no longer accepted his advances. Yet he was too far gone to stop.

I pushed my shoulders into the ground and turned my head to the side, letting out a desperate cry. Then I pressed my hips back into him.

He couldn't fight the offering, and he squeezed himself into me. He gave me what I wanted, but not without punishment. He entered me achingly slow, giving a sharp thrust when he was fully sheathed and then paused before a deliberately unhurried retreat. Each time I was an inch away from finding my release, he would completely withdraw from me to begin the entire process over again. I didn't know how he could exercise such control and determination amid his frenzied need to claim me.

But the Darkness makes us all do wicked things.

He tormented me, long past the point when I was begging for him to release me. And once he finally did, once he finally freed the both of us, I discovered he was not nearly done with me.

At some point in the night, I found myself on top of him. And the Darkness was pleased. I sat with my knees on each side of his thighs and I let my head hang back, my chest heaving as my breathing slowed. I knew it would be impossible to come again. But with each of his hands gripping my hips, he wrenched me down onto him one final time, and rich, dark, inky waves of pleasure rippled through me.

I stilled as his big body shuddered under me. I probably would have been jostled from him had he not held me in place.

I looked at the shadows surrounding us, realizing I could no longer see the trees. I rolled my head so that my hair slid across my back—my robe having been discarded long ago. I was more powerful than I'd ever been. I reveled in the strength and energy. I would never lock the Darkness away again.

I could feel Zagan's big body rise with an exaggerated inhalation. I looked down at him. His shoulders and chest expanded. Then the shadows around us began to dissipate. And his hands which had been on my hips began to clench into fists over and over again.

Something was happening, I didn't understand what. He seemed as though he was struggling.

And then cracks of electric blue began to break through his black eyes.

I realized what he was doing too late. I tried to hold on to the Darkness. I tried to construct a wall of it in front of me. But it wasn't enough.

Zagan released the most powerful blast of Light that I'd ever experienced, straight into my chest. It flooded me, consuming me, and it obliterated the Dark.

The Darkness shrank and retreated, screaming, locking itself away in the deepest parts of me where the Light could not reach. I took a gasping breath, rushing back into myself. And I collapsed on top of him.

# CHAPTER 30

I DRIFTED SOMEWHERE for a while. It was dark. I was alone. Weightless.

And everything somehow just...*settled*.

***

When I roused, I found myself in my bed. And a stone sat next to me.

It was ruby red. It was the size of a plum. And the multitude of facets across its surface glittered in the firelight.

I sat up and stretched my arm out to take it, holding it in my palm—unexpectedly calm. I wasn't sure if I could be surprised any more.

I twisted and turned my hand, mesmerized. Incredible strength and power beat from within the stone—the *Heart of Darkness*.

Eventually tearing my gaze from the gem, I noticed that the night had not yet taken its leave. It still sat outside my windows, unwilling to depart just yet, insisting on watching a little longer.

I wrapped the bedsheet around myself, feeling vulnerable after what had happened. It was not what I had done with Zagan that made my cheeks flush, it was what I had let happen.

I was embarrassed, ashamed even, that I'd allowed the Darkness to take a hold of me as it had. If Zagan hadn't stopped me, if he hadn't summoned the strength to force his energy upon me, I don't know what I would have done.

But I think it would have been something irreversible.

I stood from the bed with the stone in one hand while my other gripped the sheet at my chest, the train of white fabric trailing behind me. I went to stand next to Zagan at the window where a pool of moonlight seemed to concentrate around him.

Looking up, I could see how the silvery rays highlighted his face. The tension there had eased. He was relaxed, and the churning storm that always seemed to be brewing inside had calmed.

There was more balance now. I didn't know the ways of it, but I suspected what he'd done outside, the energy he'd forced himself to gather, had somehow instilled more of an equilibrium between the Light and Dark.

I could feel both facets of energy within myself as well, but I didn't trust them. I knew I had to begin working with Maxim straight away. I wanted to be able to control the forces with the same level of precision and strength that Maxim did.

There was just one thing that worried me about him, that made me suspicious of him, that gave me the chills when I thought of him…

*That tattoo.*

It scared me. It made me question what type of arrogant, zealous savior complex drove him. And why he felt the need to brand the mark onto his chest.

I shifted the sheet a few inches higher on my own chest. I could feel the way my skin shimmered there, just above my heart, and I knew the faint silvery outline had returned.

Zagan noticed the slight shift and looked down at my hand. He pulled it aside to reveal my skin. After a long pause, he traced the barely visible glimmer with the tip of one finger.

I still wore the black diamond ring. I had not once taken it off. It sat on my chest as I clutched the sheet in my hand, and it too seemed to flare to life with Zagan's touch.

He looked at the ring, looked at me, and gave a somber nod.

He pitied me.

He had meant what he said. There was no going back. He was not going to try and fight what was between us any longer. I would not be free of him now, and he felt it was a tragic destiny.

I didn't know if I could ever get him to see it any other way…but that wouldn't stop me from trying.

Instead of attempting to sway him then, I looked down at the pulsating stone—*the Heart of Darkness*. "How did you get it?" I asked.

He stared out through the glass in front of us. "I picked it up that night, when you dropped it."

"You had it all along," I stated.

He nodded.

Standing in front of the floor to ceiling window, high up on the fifth floor of the manor, we both studied the night. After a while he asked, "What will you do with it?"

"I don't know," I told him. And it was the truth. I honestly didn't know what to do with it. I wasn't sure if I'd return it to the Gwarlock in exchange for the information he could give me about The Contessa or share it with Maxim in the hope that he could lock away the Umbra with it.

Instead of trying to decide then and there, I tilted my head and let it rest against Zagan's shoulder.

"I don't want this for you," he said.

"I know," I told him.

"I don't want this for you," he repeated, "but I will destroy anything that comes for you."

It was his offer of a consolation. Because I would never be free from him again. Any foe which came between us, he would annihilate. Any wall which kept him from me, he would crush. Any beast, he'd slay. And any distance, he'd traverse.

I could see his faint reflection in the glass in front of us, and I could see it all play there within his eyes. It was a story from the beginning of time.

Some entities are bound together. It is just the way of the universe. Some stars collide in a fiery crash which entwines them for eternity—a *stellar collision*.

I could see the moment of impact behind his eyes.

But I will tell you that that kind of absolution is dangerous. Because there was nothing that he would not do to protect me. And I would soon come to find how perilous that was.

I looked past his reflection at the darkness.

"Something's out there," he said.

I knew what he meant. I could feel it too. It was not a person or a thing or an entity. Not the Umbra or a little girl with shining eyes. It was a force. Something that was barreling towards us—something unstoppable. And at some point, it would reach us. There would be no avoiding it. No hiding from it.

The pressure of it pushed against the glass.

And somehow the words which I spoke next just slipped out. I couldn't control them. Couldn't stop them. They tumbled from my lips before I could catch them. And I wished I could take them back. But something was in motion which could not be stopped.

I accepted it.

I would face it.

And I would keep Zagan from it at all costs.

Standing next to him at the window, I looked out into the night and told him...

*"It's coming closer."*

*xxx*

Follow along on Facebook at

## TMHartShadowSeries

Or on Instagram at

## TMHartAuthor

For book release announcements

Made in the USA
Columbia, SC
08 May 2021

37525372R00214